The admiral leaned forward. His heavy eyebrows came down again and made him look a little like Dracula. 'You'll not be living in a room,' he snapped. 'Either overlooking the harbour or anywhere else. You're going to sea.'

It was a shock to Magnusson, who'd been looking forward to a nice cushy job. 'As captain, sir?' His voice came out as a squeak and he had to clear his throat and repeat himself.

The admiral gave a bark of laughter. 'Not damn likely,' he said. 'The Navy looks after its own far too well for that. You'll be under Commander George Seago. He's an excellent sailor, but he doesn't know those northern waters as you do and will need a little help. In addition, he doesn't speak Norwegian. Or Finnish.'

Magnusson frowned as a thought occurred to him. 'Finnish, sir? We'll be in Norwegian waters. Why Finnish?'

'Because your ship's Finnish,' the admiral rapped. 'A three-masted barque. You're going to war, my lad. In a sailing ship.' He grinned unexpectedly as he ended. 'I dare bet you didn't reckon on *that*.'

John Harris

NORTH STRIKE

Arrow Books

Arrow Books Limited

17–21 Conway Street, London W1P 6JD

An imprint of the Hutchinson Publishing Group

London Melbourne Sydney Auckland
Johannesburg and agencies
throughout the world

First published by Hutchinson 1981
Arrow edition 1982
© John Harris 1981

Made and printed in Great Britain
by The Anchor Press Ltd
Tiptree, Essex

ISBN 0 09 928090 6

Author's Note

At the time this story opens, the Second World War was in a curious sort of stalemate. Germany had conquered Poland in a matter of days, but from then on, apart from an occasional clash at sea or in the air, the war appeared to have come virtually to a standstill. The Allies had no idea how they might aid Poland; Germany was in the way, and all they could do was sit down in France behind their fortifications. The Germans seemed quite content to do the same.

Then, at the end of November 1939, Russia – who had made a non-aggression pact with Germany which had enabled them both to attack Poland in safety – invaded Finland. Well aware that she could not trust her new ally, the Soviet Union's aim was to secure strategic territory in case Germany attacked her next. At first the Finns were able to resist and even inflict defeats, a fact which gave rise in England and France to the view that Russia was no more than the old 'steam-roller' of the First World War, possessed of millions of soldiers but with no decent arms and no skill at fighting. Since the revolution of 1917, the Russians had never been popular in the West and the British, angered by the treachery of their pact with Germany, were delighted at their poor showing. Since the Germans felt the same, the lessons of the campaign were lost on them, too, and in 1942 they attacked Russia with eventually disastrous results. However, before the war in Finland ended, hundreds of young British volunteers, impeded in their own war by the indifference of the Chamberlain government which appeared to think that it would simply fizzle out, went to Finland to form a British legion to fight against the Russians. Fortunately for the day when Russia became Britain's ally, it was already becoming apparent that the Finns could not hold out and they never went into action.

The presence of sailing ships in a war as late as 1939 and 1940 was not the anachronism it might seem. In addition to smaller lines, the houses of Laeisz, of Hamburg, and Erikson, of Mariehamn, still ran great wind-driven vessels, and the last grain race from Australia actually took place in 1939. It was won just before the war began by *Moshulu*, the Erikson ship, with *Padua, Pamir, Passat, Viking* and *Olivebank* arriving soon afterwards, and *Lawhill, Archibald Russell, Pommern, Kommodore Johnsen, Killoran* and *Abraham Rydberg* following later. Two famous sailing ships, *Admiral Karpfanger* (originally *L'Avenir*) and *Herzogin Cecilie*, were lost only just before the war. Also just before the war, the author was aboard *Lawhill* and when the war was half over he saw and photographed her, together with *Mercator* and a vast six-masted schooner which had once been used as a gambling ship off the American coast during the days of Prohibition. They were all three far from their home ports at the time and they were all still working.

PART ONE

Northwards

1

'Lieutenant Magnusson, sir.'

As Murdoch Murray Magnusson stepped into the room, Admiral Sir James Cockayne lifted his head and stared at him with piercing blue eyes. He had a thin nose, bushy black eyebrows and a lean face that ended in a strong jaw which showed no signs of softness despite his age.

'Better sit down, my boy,' he said. 'Shan't be a minute. Smoke if you wish.'

As the admiral bent over the desk again, Magnusson sat, quietly and without fuss. Though he was dying for a cigarette, he didn't light one, feeling it wiser for a mere reserve lieutenant not to risk making the wrong impression on an admiral.

He could see his own face in the glass front of the bookcase behind the other officer, a strong face, he liked to think, that had served him well and won over more than a few girls in foreign ports. It was topped by blond hair that was as unexpected as his opal blue eyes, the sort of face you got from the Orkneys, the Shetlands and from Stornoway in the Hebrides, from where so many merchant sailors came – British yet not quite British.

As he waited for the admiral to finish what he was doing, he stared through the windows. London was grey with the fag-end of the year and the barrage balloons hung in a grey sky like grey fishes in a grey fish bowl. The building's entrance had been sandbagged against bomb splinters but after two months of war, when little had happened beyond the sinking of a few merchantmen and the shooting down of a few enemy planes, the general attitude was clear. No one expected any damage to be done.

The only mayhem being wrought, in fact, seemed to be at the hands of the Russians and the Finns who were suddenly at each other's throats in Finland and, since nobody was sure how to get at the unwilling Germans and most people objected to Russia's unexpected attack, British volunteers were already heading for Helsinki in the hope of working off on the Russians some of the bad temper they couldn't work off on the Germans. It was a curious sort of war.

When it had broken out, Magnusson had left the tanker he'd been in the minute she had docked in an English port and had reported immediately to the Navy. Since then he had been employed in a boom defence vessel based at Ryde in the Isle of Wight, and over the weeks, had become aware that he was growing bored and wishing to God something would happen.

Nothing had, however. The war ticked along slowly and it was clear that most people were beginning to hope – even to expect – that it would not flare up into action at all.

The admiral coughed and Magnusson started to life, aware that he was being studied.

'I expect you're wondering what you're here for,' the admiral said.

'Yes, sir, I am a bit,' Magnusson admitted cheerfully.

'Well, we'll come to that all in good time. Pull your chair nearer where you can see the charts.' The admiral opened a file on his desk and pushed forward a chart that Magnusson recognized at once as the Norwegian coastline. With its hundreds of islands, inlets and narrow waterways it looked like a complicated jigsaw puzzle which had been dropped and the parts jolted out of their places.

'Murdoch Murray Magnusson,' the admiral said, peering over his spectacles. 'Born in Lerwick in the Shetlands.'

'Yes, sir.'

The admiral stared at him for a moment, scribbled a few words on a paper in the file, then nodded.

'Lieutenant, Royal Naval Reserve. Before finding yourself in the Royal Navy you were with Lamport and Holt.'

'Yes, sir.'

'You have a good record.'

Magnusson acknowledged the admiral's comment with what he hoped was a modest smile. If being drunk in every port of the seven seas was a good record, he thought, then yes, he had a splendid record.

'And you have your master's certificate in steam.'

'It wasn't much good, sir. The depression stepped in about then. Masters were going to sea as mates and mates as bosuns. I was never more than third. I was just beginning to hope things would be better when the war started.'

The admiral frowned. 'I'm well aware of the depths to which our political masters allowed us to slip,' he said stiffly. 'It applied to the Navy as well.' He was watching Magnusson closely – a bit like a terrier at a rathole, Magnusson thought uneasily. His next words made him jump.

'You did your apprenticeship in sail, I believe?' he barked.

Magnusson's eyebrows rose. This was a ghost from the past and no mistake. Deciding while at school to go to sea to avoid study, he had taken a day ticket on the ferry from Glasgow to Belfast and signed on the four-masted barque, *Priwall.*

'Yes, sir,' he said. 'That's right. I did.'

'Enjoy it?'

Enjoy it? Magnusson hesitated. As far as he had been able to make out at the time, he had signed his life away for three years or the duration of the voyage, which meant, in effect, as long as the captain or the owners chose to keep the ship away from her home port.

Yet he supposed he must have enjoyed it. At the end of the trip out, after living in the narrow-gutted forecastle, with a dozen noisy, quarrelsome Finns, Letts, Esthonians,

Lithuanians and other assorted nationalities, with rats, cock-roaches, bed bugs, bad food and the smell of damp, the fact that he'd seen quite a bit of the world hadn't seemed just then to make up for the hardships he'd suffered; and he'd fled from the ship as though the hounds of hell were after him, even passing the rest of the crew on their way to the nearest pub. Enjoy it, he thought again. Well, he'd stuck it out, and on the trip home, had even come to the conclusion that it wasn't as bad as he'd thought, that the food was bearable, his companions pleasanter than he'd imagined, and his thwartships bunk, which in bad weather stood him upright on one tack and on his head with the blood pounding in his temples on the other, was better than no bunk at all. He had finally even opted for exams and a mate's ticket.

He glanced up to see the admiral watching him keenly. The old eyes across the desk looked like the muzzles of a double-barrelled shotgun.

'Well, boy? Well?'

Magnusson licked his lips. 'Yes, sir,' he agreed. 'I think I did enjoy it. But when I told my father I wanted to make the sea my profession, he didn't consider the enjoyment part of it. He'd been to sea in sail himself as a young man and I think he considered life a bit more real and a bit more earnest than I did. Shetlanders tend to. It must be the weather up there. He said I should do it properly and, since he'd done business with Captain Erikson, of Mariehamn – who's one of the most successful operators of sailing ships there is – '

'I know who Erikson is, boy.' The admiral sounded impatient. 'Go on.'

'Well, sir, he got me aboard one of Erikson's ships – *Lawhill* – as an apprentice.' Magnusson paused, his mind full of masts, rigging and tiers of white sails. 'She wasn't a beautiful ship, sir, but she was a splendid sailer and one of Erikson's best.'

Cockayne stared narrowly at him. 'You sound like a man who likes sailing ships.'

Magnusson shrugged. 'They won't be around much longer, sir.'

'Learn Finnish?'

'I didn't have much option, sir.'

The admiral was leaning forward, his eyes bright and interested. Magnusson had come across this excited interest before. A trip in a windjammer? How splendid! It made people think him a virile, manly character smelling of salt sea breezes. In non-seafaring communities, it got him a lot of free drinks and a lot of girls.

'Go round the Horn?' the admiral asked.

'Six times, sir. I stayed with Erikson long enough to get a third's ticket in sail.'

'Forgotten all you ever learned now, I expect.'

'Not likely, sir.' There was a hint of boastfulness in Magnusson's words. 'You never do. It's like riding a bike – '

He had been going to say ' – and going to bed with a girl. It all comes back when you get on.' But he stopped in time.

The admiral continued to show the same man-to-man interest. 'Think you could still handle a sailing ship if you had to?'

'Sure I could, sir.' Magnusson was still crowing a little. He knew he could but he didn't fancy it, all the same.

'Good.' The admiral nodded. 'Excellent. Pleased to hear it. Speak Norwegian?'

'Yes, sir. Quite well. I taught myself during the time we were doing the Scandinavian run.'

'Good,' the admiral said again. 'Then that sorts that out.'

Magnusson could hold his curiosity in check no longer. 'Sorts what out, sir?'

Cockayne ignored him. 'What do you know of Norway, boy?'

Magnusson was puzzled. 'It's long and narrow, sir, with a lot of inlets. Roads are few, railways fewer. Most of the travelling's done by coastal waterways. There's a lot of snow.'

'Go on.'

'Polar conditions in the north. West coast surprisingly warm and free of ice, though.'

'Good. Good. Splendid.' The admiral settled back in his chair. 'Now, as you're doubtless aware, with the army in France staring at the Wehrmacht and waiting for the fun to begin, the RAF and the Navy are the only services who are following their calling and fighting to the death. And so far, we've not done so damn badly.'

Magnusson waited. He wasn't arguing.

The admiral continued. 'However, we do still have problems. Your experience ever take you through the Indreled – or Inner Leads, as you probably call them – off Norway?'

'Yes, sir. Often.'

'What do you know about 'em?'

Deciding he'd been called in to give the benefit of experience, Magnusson wondered why in God's name the Admiralty hadn't found someone a bit more senior.

'Well, sir,' he said. 'You can travel by them almost all the way from north Norway to the Skagerrak without going out of Norwegian territorial waters, and for a lot of that distance with land outside of you. The islands make a good break against the weather from the North Atlantic. The winds funnel between Iceland and the north of Scotland, and they can be diabolical. We had to shelter more than once on the way to Narvik from Mariehamn.'

'Doing what?'

'Taking coal up, sir. Bringing Swedish ore back to Germany.'

'Good.' The admiral nodded. 'Well, as you know, the Norwegians are supposed to be neutral at the moment but it seems to us here at the Admiralty that they're being rather more neutral to the Germans than they are to us.' He shifted in his chair. 'Actually, you can hardly blame them with Germany on their doorstep, but they're allowing them to use Norwegian waters as a back door past our blockade. The Inner Leads provide a route from Narvik right round the southern tip of Norway to the safety of the Baltic, that we're powerless to interfere with. Repeated protests have been made without avail. Norway is not at war with Germany.'

He let what he had said sink in then he leaned forward, his elbows on the desk, his hands together, his fingers forming a spire on which he rested his chin. He sat like that for a moment, then he flung himself back in his chair and began to speak again.

'There's another thing: this iron ore you just mentioned. Swedish ore. It's among the richest in the world and Germany's imports of it are reckoned at about nine million tons. Her total imports for 1938 were twenty-two million. We've already cut off nine and a half million from various other sources by the blockade. If we could stop the ore from Sweden, we'd have practically, as you can see, cut off their supply and injured their armaments manufacture. Are you still with me?'

Magnusson smiled. 'I think I'm way ahead of you, sir.'

Cockayne frowned. 'I doubt if you are, my lad,' he said briskly. He fished out a pipe and went on slowly. 'As you doubtless know, this ore normally moves to Germany from the ore fields at Gällivare via Luleå in the Gulf of Bothnia. But Luleå freezes over in winter, so then it's sent by rail across Sweden to Narvik in Norway, which is touched by the Gulf Stream and doesn't ice up. But, as we've agreed, almost the whole of the journey from Narvik to the Skagerrak can be made in Norwegian territorial waters, which is a great advantage. We also think that blockade runners and armed raiders are using this northabout route as they leave for or return from the Atlantic, and we're coming to the view that we should stop them. But first of all we need someone up there to let us know when things are moving.'

The admiral paused and, studied his pipe before continuing. 'This war along the Russo–Finnish border – it's pretty clear that the Russians have gone into it because they're expecting a German invasion of Scandinavia. Since we are, too, it seems to me they're showing considerable political acumen.' He paused again, tapped his pipe in a large glass ashtray and began to pack it with tobacco. 'Now the Norwegian coastline, as I'm sure I don't have to tell you, would provide valuable bases for a British blockade against Germany. Or, for that matter, for a German naval offensive against British shipping. Winston wants a foothold there but the cabinet are against it.' He fished out matches, lit up, then, blowing out clouds of blue smoke, pointed with the stem of the pipe at Magnusson.

'You've been brought here because you speak Norwegian and Finnish and because you've worked on the Swedish iron ore run. You're to watch what's happening up there.'

Magnusson's smile was faintly relieved. He'd been expecting something either incredibly boring or incredibly dangerous, neither of which he particularly fancied.

'You'll be given the silhouettes of known raiders,' Cockayne went on. 'As well as blockade runners and all ships engaged in the Swedish ore trade. It will be your job to keep us informed.'

Magnusson sat up. 'Where will I be stationed, sir?'

'In Narvik, where it starts.'

'I see, sir.'

The admiral smiled, more menacingly this time. 'I dare bet you don't, my lad,' he said. 'Think you can do the job?'

Not half, Magnusson thought. Narvik wasn't exactly Blackpool or Piccadilly Circus, and the workers on the railway and the iron company's books there constituted practically the whole population of the town. And since summer came only every fourth year, the winters tended to be somewhat dark and burdensome. The mountains, the sea, the ever-changing colours, however, were breathtaking, and he liked Norwegians – especially Norwegian girls. He remembered one who believed in freedom of thought and action and was almost acrobatic in bed. He could visualize a splendid life of ease in a hotel with binoculars and a notebook.

'Of course, sir,' he said enthusiastically. 'What arrangements have been made for accommodation, et cetera?'

'Accommodation?' the admiral's eyebrows shot up.

'Well, I'll need a room somewhere overlooking the harbour and a reason for being there, I suppose.'

The admiral leaned forward. His heavy eyebrows came down again and made him look a little like Dracula. 'You'll not be living in a room,' he snapped. 'Either overlooking the harbour or anywhere else. You're going to sea.'

It was a shock to Magnusson. He'd been looking forward to a nice cushy job, and sea-going near the Arctic Circle didn't appeal one bit.

'As captain, sir?' His voice came out as a squeak and he had to clear his throat and repeat himself.

The admiral gave a bark of laughter. 'Not damn likely,' he said. 'The Navy looks after its own far too well for that. No, my lad, you'll be under Commander George Seago. But Commander Seago, while he's an excellent sailor, doesn't know those northern waters as you do and will need a little help. In addition, he doesn't speak Norwegian. *Or* Finnish!'

Magnusson frowned as a thought occurred to him. 'Finnish, sir? We'll be in Norwegian waters. Why Finnish?'

'Because your ship's Finnish,' the admiral rapped. 'A three-masted barque. You're going to war, my lad. In a sailing ship.' He grinned unexpectedly as he ended. 'I dare bet you didn't reckon on *that*.'

2

There was a long silence as Magnusson stared indignantly at the admiral. No wonder the old bastard had been so keen on finding out about his experience in sail! Forgotten all you know? Think you could still handle one? The old sod had just been setting him a bear trap to fall into, so he couldn't back out when the big question came.

The admiral was watching him, one eyebrow raised quizzically. He seemed greatly amused.

'A barque, sir?' Magnusson croaked.

'Exactly. *Oulu*. Know her?'

Magnusson's mind roved wildly over the Finnish yards he'd visited and the tall masts and slender hulls of windborne ships he'd known.

'Yes, sir,' he said bitterly. 'We once lay behind her at Mariehamn and I had a friend who was second mate.'

'Only,' the admiral said, 'this isn't *Oulu*.'

Magnusson frowned. 'Sir?'

'Actually,' the admiral admitted, '*Oulu's* in the West Indies. This one's *Jacob Undset* done up to look like *Oulu*, so you'd better start calling her by that name straightaway and get used to it. She's an old ship and she's not exactly ship-shape and Bristol fashion but we intend to work at it. When she's ready, she'll be seaworthy, but she'll still look a bit neglected, which is just what we want. She was built in 1866 by Gardners of Sunderland to serve in the China tea trade as *Dolly Grey*, but she was sold in 1913 to your friend, Gustaf Erikson, of Mariehamn. She's nine hundred tons and she's claimed to be an unlucky ship because she's been dismasted, damaged by fire, the victim of quite a few minor accidents, and more than once posted overdue. But she's always made port, though sometimes short of one or two members of her crew.'

Magnusson listened with a sour feeling of being cheated. Unlucky ship. Built in 1866. Not exactly shipshape. It got worse and worse the more he thought about it. The admiral went on, as if he were relishing the expression on his face.

'Even Erikson grew tired of her in the end,' he said, 'and after she'd collided with a tanker which swept away her starboard rail, he sold her to some bright-eyed entrepreneur in Falmouth who put gingerbread on her and rigged her as a galleon for some film about the Armada. Since then, she's been a sort of floating museum there with fish tanks in her holds for holidaymakers to visit at a bob a nob.'

Magnusson's heart was sinking. Living aboard would be about as comfortable as a leaky pigsty. The admiral was actually smiling at him now, as if he'd guessed at the thoughts of comfort and wild nights in a Norwegian hotel that had been running through his mind.

'Since most of her fittings were adapted for Finnish usage,' he said, 'the two ships could easily be confused. We have to call her *Oulu* because everybody – and that includes the Germans and the Norwegians – will know that *Oulu* is still around, while *Jacob Undset*'s been off the active list for several years. *Oulu* was built at Nystad, in Finland, in 1870 and her dimensions are roughly the same. Eight hundred and fifty tons and a hundred and eighteen feet long with single topgallant sails and royals. She was damaged in a storm in 1929 and condemned, but she was eventually refitted and sold to Danish owners and later to Erikson, who still uses her on the West Indies run. At the moment she's in Tobago and we're making sure that that's where she stays.'

The admiral paused and puffed at his pipe for a while. 'We're having to do the job this way for a variety of reasons,' he went on. 'We could put a man up there in a number of capacities, but the Germans are watching Norway like hawks and it's known that some of the Norwegians are Nazi sympathizers, so they'll be on the look-out for tricks too. Since you'll be sailing a Finnish ship – or a supposed Finnish ship – and since you'll all have Finnish papers, you'll pose as Finnish seamen, caught away from home by the war with the Russians and trying to get back to become part of it. Your cargo is rum from Jamaica and grain in sacks from America and, though it was intended for Britain, as was the genuine *Oulu*'s, you have decided it will be of more use to beleaguered Finland. To avoid being stopped by the British and forced into Falmouth, where your sailing instructions directed you, you are not going via the North Sea, through the Skagerrak and the Kattegat into the Baltic, but intend to sneak home through the Leads. It will be *your* job to convey all this to the Norwegians. In Norwegian. Preferably with a few words of Finnish to make certain they believe you're who you're meant to be.'

Magnusson interrupted. 'Won't they expect the ship's captain to do that, sir?'

'The ship's captain on such occasions will be in bed with a high fever and will be asleep.'

It might have been a better idea, Magnusson thought, to have made *him* the ship's captain, but he supposed a naval ship had to have a naval captain.

'I see, sir,' he said.

The admiral gestured. 'A great deal will depend on you, my lad,' he said briskly. 'Which is why you're being done the honour of a personal briefing, something not normally granted to a junior officer. At the right time a sighting will be reported, showing you to be in mid-Atlantic, and inevitably the Germans will pick it up. Another sighting will be arranged later to show you off the Faeroes. In fact, you will sail up the Irish Sea, through the Minches, and, keeping well out from land to avoid being spotted, you will make your landfall west of the Lofotens and put into Narvik.

There, you will be informed of what's going on by our contact, a woman called Annie Egge, who runs the Norwegian equivalent of our Missions to Seamen. She will give you – you, Magnusson, because as the linguist, she'll be dealing with you – she will give you your information. I don't know what she's like – like most middle-aged ladies who run Missions to Seamen, I suppose – all God and woollen comforts – but she *has* been feeding us reliable information for some time about German shipping, gleaned no doubt over the cups of tea and the meat and potato pie or whatever it is they serve up in Norway. Since, in the event of a German move into Norway, we shall need to know a few facts, you will keep your eyes open and take note of all Norwegian naval vessels, fortifications and movements, and all army and air force installations. You will remain there for several days under the guise of Finnish sailors making repairs after the voyage across the North Atlantic to enable you to reach Mariehamn. Commander Seago will know what to arrange. He has a certificate in sail.'

Has he, by God, Magnusson thought. At least, they had *something* in common.

The admiral seemed to sense his wandering interest and brought him back to the present sharply. 'Your job,' he snapped, 'will be to fend off suspicious people.'

'In addition to normal ship's duties, of course, sir?' Magnusson said with a trace of sarcasm.

It was entirely wasted. The admiral didn't even notice it. 'Exactly,' he said. 'In case anyone searches you, you will live as Finns.'

Magnusson had visions of Finnish cooking – salt pork, salt beef, labskaus, kabelgarn, ängelskit and the tinned meat they called Harriet Lane, after a long-forgotten young woman who'd been murdered and cut up to go in a trunk.

'That means the food will be awful, sir,' he said gloomily.

The admiral gave him a grim smile. 'You will have a receiver-transmitter in the hold,' he went on. 'Hidden behind the sacks of grain. And your aerials will be hidden among the standing rigging. You will keep a watch at 9.30 each evening, and on receipt of your call sign and the letter 'A', repeated several times, you will move south down the Leads towards Trondheim, reporting en route in code all that you've seen in Narvik. You will put into Bodø for more repairs and will do the same there. Once more you will be contacted, this time by a chap who runs a ship chandlers there. You will do the same there as at Narvik, and on receipt of the letter 'A' will once more put to sea, reporting again what you've seen. From Bodø you will put into Trondheim, Bud, Statlandet, Hovden, Bergen, Stavanger and Egersund, in each case reporting en route to your next call. The visits you make will be for water, fresh vegetables, et cetera. It's all being arranged and you will be expected to use your native wit, your knowledge of the language and local conditions to assist Commander Seago to improve on it. Your orders will make everything clear, and it goes without saying that if you're searched they must not fall into the hands either of the Germans or of the Norwegians. Think you can manage all that?'

Magnusson was doubtful. It sounded too intelligent and responsible by a long way. 'Do you, sir?'

The admiral nodded cheerfully. 'Yes, I do. After all, we don't expect bloodshed. You're there to keep your eyes open, that's all. You're bound to have a few curious Norwegians aboard, because there aren't all that many sailing ships about these days, so you'll have to use your savvy. If there's trouble, Commander Seago has instructions to drop everything and bolt. That shouldn't arise, however, because, since you're supposed to be Finns, the Norwegians won't be suspicious and neither will the masters of German ships you might meet. And because *Oulu*'s a sailing ship she'll be regarded as slow, ineffective and not very dangerous – a greatly mistaken assumption to make, as we discovered to our cost with Count von Luckner and his *Seeadler* in the last war. You'll carry a radio officer who's an expert and two telegraphists to work your radios. They will be your responsibility. Commander Seago's duties will be concerned with the ship.'

Commander Seago, Magnusson thought, was getting off bloody lightly and most of the work seemed as if it were to be done by Murdoch Murray Magnusson.

'How about crew, sir?' he asked. 'They'll need to sound like Finns, I'm thinking.'

'No problem,' the admiral said cheerfully. 'Apart from one or two specialists and one or two Royal Naval men, who will be kept well out of sight if you're boarded, they will be exactly that: Finns. We have a number of them here in English ports. With the Russians knocking their country about, they're as anxious as we are to join the fun.'

'Is the cook a Finn, sir?'

The admiral smiled. 'He is.'

'I just hope the crew don't mutiny, sir.'

The admiral stifled a smile. 'The Finns will be *your* responsibility,' he said.

Like the radios, the reports, the sightings, the handling of officials, the old bag in Narvik from the Missions to Seamen, and every other bloody thing, it seemed.

'You will translate Commander Seago's orders for the Finns, and their complaints, et cetera, to him. However, you'll have a junior RN officer to back you up. He, too, has experience of sailing ships.'

There seemed to be more of them underfoot than Magnusson had thought. He'd believed they were a dying breed.

'Like everyone else,' the admiral was saying, 'you will have a Finnish seaman's pay-book and you will see that the British naval ratings get used to the names they've been given. Since a great many of the Finns on the Australia–Falmouth run have learned to speak some English there should be no problem there, though it'll be up to you to see that the Finns are always more in evidence than the British during the fitting out and when you're in Norwegian waters. You'll have the assistance of all naval resources at Falmouth and Devonport. And I suspect you'll need them, because *Jacob Undset*, or *Oulu*, as she'll be known from now on, won't be quite what you expect. When she's ready I shall bring your orders myself and I shall inspect her – personally.'

There seemed to be something ominous behind the admiral's promise.

'I'll endeavour to make sure she's looking at her best, sir.'

'You'd better,' the admiral said darkly. 'Because I shall know exactly what to look for. *I* did my first years at sea in sail too. HMS *Martin*, brig. 1901.'

3

Commander Seago – like Magnusson in civilian clothes –
was waiting in Devonport, and to Magnusson at twenty nine
he seemed very old for the job he'd been given. Before
retiring as a passed-over commander to open a sailing
school, most of his time had been spent teaching the mys-
teries of sail to midshipmen and he had a sad reproachful
school-teacher's attitude to everything, so that he looked
like a dog waiting for someone to pat him. However, he
also had that strange indefinable mystique of the Royal
Navy, the mixture of arrogance and the belief that they
were among God's chosen few that clung to them all, from
the admiral down to the pinkest-cheeked cadet from
Dartmouth.

It made Magnusson feel vaguely vulgar, a feeling that was
not diminished by the arrival of his junior, Rodney St Clair
Campbell, Regular Navy and only recently promoted from
sub to lieutenant. The son of a much-decorated captain who
was a contemporary of Seago's, despite his youth he had
done sailing ship training, was an expert navigator and had
been recommended for a decoration for saving life during
the *Royal Oak* disaster at Scapa Flow in October. What was
more, he stood in line for a title, was heir to a large estate
in Yorkshire, and belonged to a family which ran an Anglo–
Danish firm in Hull which had been importing Scandinavian
foodstuffs for generations. He even had Danish relations
and, as a boy, before opting for the Navy, had spent half
his holidays in sailing ships off the islands round Copenhag-

en so that, like the rest of his family, he spoke the northern languages as well as Magnusson himself. Scandinavian gloom seemed to be well developed in him, too, and his stony-faced naval manner made him look like a puppet operated from somewhere in Whitehall.

'Merchant Navy, I see,' he said condescendingly, eyeing Magnusson's reserve braid.

'Yes,' Magnusson agreed cheerfully. 'We're the chaps who kept the ships at sea while you lot polished brasses and held reviews for the royal family.'

He had meant it as a joke, but Campbell's face didn't slip, and Magnusson eyed him, wary and uncertain, like a dog expecting a fight. While he accepted the need to choose men with a knowledge of sail and the northern languages, he had a feeling that the Navy might have shown more intelligence in their selection. On top of Seago's sad, chilly, lost manner, Campbell's aloof contempt for anyone who hadn't been to Dartmouth gave him the feeling that the professionals were ganging up on him.

With Seago still in Devonport seeing the senior naval officer there, it was Magnusson's privilege to be the first to travel on to Falmouth to see the newly-christened *Oulu*.

He was staring down the river. Not far away were the spars and rigging of a square-rigged sailing ship. She had been a great ugly brute of a four-masted barque, with a flat square stern, and under the grey skies, she looked black. There was no sign of life about her, and she lay silently in the water, sagging in the middle, with the tide flowing back and forth across her deck. Her hull was festooned with weeds, like the remains of the ropes that had once held her to the shore but were no longer needed because she had long since become welded to the mud of the estuary.

'Is that her?' he said.

The grey-haired lieutenant-commander from the Falmouth dockyard sniffed. He was a veteran of the first war called Snaith and he had all the Navy's icy ability to put his contempt into his sniff. He gestured in the opposite direction. 'Not that,' he said. '*That.*'

As Magnusson turned, what he saw didn't seem a lot better than the first ship. There was a string of washing across the poop attached to the iron chimney of her cabin, and on her bow and stern sheets of shaped plywood, painted like gilt-work, formed curved artificial buttresses and rails, the colour on them faded and old. She seemed dead; just not quite so decayed as the other.

She was riding high out of the water, sails unbent, yards askew, odds and ends of gear left about. The river around her was dirty but the grace of her line and her original seaworthiness shone out of her, and there was about her still an irresistible air of readiness to do battle with the winds.

'What sort of condition's she in?' he asked.

'She's getting all her old cordage and sails replaced,' Snaith said. 'And work has already been done on her bottom.'

'Sounds like a Wren being pawed by a stoker.'

Snaith frowned at the levity. 'All the rubbish that was put aboard her for the film company will be removed,' he said. 'Her fish-tanks will follow. She has a short poop and an open main-deck and she's steered from aft. She draws twenty-one feet when fully loaded.'

Magnusson followed Snaith down the jetty. At close quarters the ship looked even more of a wreck than at a distance, but it was obvious work had been started on her because piles of rust and chipped paint lay about the deck and there was no moss on her planks. She'd been caught just in time.

An old man appeared on deck, emptied a pail of washing-up water into the river, spat after it, and turned away.

'Hey, there!'

At Snaith's shout, the old man turned.

'We're coming aboard.'

'It's your ship, mate.'

The vessel didn't improve with further inspection, and it was hard to believe the reeking ill-lit forecastle had ever contained human life. There were the remains of clothing, boots and newspapers, and the smell was that of a very old and decrepit dog basket.

'Looks like someone's brought a cartload of planks and portholes and bits of rope, and thrown them all down in a heap in the river,' Magnusson said.

Snaith sniffed again. 'She's in better condition than she looks,' he said. 'Her timbers are sound and we'll have her ship-shape in no time. She's been closed up for months, but when we open some doors and portholes and get the hatches off the smell will disappear. To keep a ship tied up all this time's sheer murder. A ship's for sailing, not for collecting stinking mud from a river bed.'

Magnusson glanced quickly at him but he was perfectly serious.

'How many crew are we having?' he asked.

Snaith shrugged. 'Well, I don't know what you're up to,' he said. 'It's none of my business. But we've got seventeen or eighteen laid on. Biggest part of 'em Finns or Balts or something. That should be quite enough. After all she's not colossal.'

'You a sailing ship man?' Magnusson asked.

Snaith smiled. It was the first time he'd let his face slip. '*William Holder*'s half-deck in 1909,' he said. 'I decided the Navy would be a lot easier.'

Seago and Campbell were bad enough, but to Magnusson the arrival of the communications officer was like thumbscrews after the rack. He had been expecting a newly-qualified youngster straight from radio school, full of knowledge and brisk as a kipper; instead he got Sub-Lieutenant Willie John MacDonald, RNR.

Willie John came from Portree in Skye and had first gone to sea as a second operator in the Merchant Navy twelve years before. It was in that capacity that Magnusson had

met him in Bahia – as drunk as a coot and tearing a night
club apart, much to the annoyance of the local police – and
the occasion had been hectic enough for him to remain
firmly etched in Magnusson's memory. He was thirty,
looked sixty, and had only four interests in life: drinking,
radios, women and making mischief. His heavy face had all
the appeal of an elderly bloodhound's, his kit was a disgrace,
and he was bedraggled, unshaven and stank of whisky. His
reputation ran through the entire Merchant Navy. There
was only one consolation: drunk or sober, he was a good
operator, was experienced with sail and, like all Skye men,
knew the sea and in an emergency could act as a spare deck
officer.

As Magnusson knew from the past, however, his capacity
for mischief was vast, though he seemed a likely relief from
the 'life-is-real-life-is-earnest' attitude of Campbell. He was
the Merchant Navy at its worst and it seemed to Magnusson
that the Naval Appointments Board had sent him to *Oulu*
simply because they couldn't fit him in anywhere else.

As he dragged his kit from the taxi which had brought
him and dumped it on the jetty alongside *Oulu*, he fished
a whisky bottle from his pocket and offered it to Campbell
with a wink that screwed his battered face up like a worn
concertina.

'A *wee deoch an' doruis*?' he suggested.

'No, thanks,' Campbell said coldly.

''Tis *uisge beatha!* Whisky, mon! The water of life!' Willie
John looked shocked. 'The best it iss, too.'

'I'd rather not.'

'Suit yersel'.' Willie John took a quick swig himself.
'*Slainte mhor*, boy, anyway.' An eyebrow cocked and he
looked up at Campbell from a bleary grey eye alive with
humour and cunning. When he spoke again, his accent was
noticeably thicker and he began to talk with the light, high-
pitched tone of the Western Isles. 'Are y' all richt, poy?' he
asked. 'Pecause ye sount ass if ye had a potato in yer gob.'
He offered a grimy paw. 'Ma name's MacDonalt. Willie

John MacDonalt fra' Skye.'

As Campbell somewhat reluctantly introduced himself, Willie John's eyes gleamed and his shaggy eyebrows worked like a set of railway signals operated by a man with St Vitus' Dance. 'Ye're no' one of them treacherous Campbells who murdered ma ancestors, the MacDonalts of Glencoe, are ye?' he asked.

Campbell looked startled. 'I come from Yorkshire,' he said quickly as if he thought Willie John were about to attack him. 'And the massacre at Glencoe was over two hundred years ago.'

'No matter, poy, 'tis will remempered. Especially by the likes o' masel'. I'm also related to the MacDonalt of the Isles.'

As MacDonald disappeared, breathing whisky fumes and dragging his appalling kit, Campbell stared after him disgustedly. 'If he *is* related to the MacDonald of the Isles,' he said coldly, 'it's a pity he doesn't behave as if he were.'

The sun was out the following day. The Cornish slate roofs shone brightly and the air was fresh after the rain. The old watchman had disappeared from *Oulu* and there were four very obvious naval ratings in civilian dungarees sweeping the decks. They had formed three tidy piles and had the hatches open. Even the forecastle had been cleaned and, though the dog-basket smell still lingered, it was clearing rapidly.

'Only wants a bit of 'oly-stoning, sir,' one of the sailors said to Magnusson, 'and she'll do for a fleet review. I'm Leading Seaman Myers, sir.'

As Magnusson introduced Willie John, the sailor flinched visibly. Though he was stone cold sober, Willie John still managed to look drunk, his eyes sunken, the lines on his face deeply etched by his years of debauchery. Recovering, Myers introduced the other three men. 'I don't recommend living aboard yet, sir,' he ended. 'We're all right in the forecastle. There's plenty of room and it's been occupied, but the cabins is a bit damp still.'

During the afternoon, shipwrights, riggers, caulkers and sailmakers appeared. They were all elderly men who had been employed by the boatyards. Between the wars, they had been occupied in building and rigging yachts for week-end sailors or had opened 'gifte shoppes' for holidaymakers; but with its usual efficiency, the Navy had dug them out and recruited them for their skill and knowledge.

There was a metal-worker who knew about rigging a ship, who'd come from a foundry at Devoran, far up the river where it was little more than a stream and meandered among fields. He'd been making lanterns for sale to tourists. There were also two old men, a shipwright and a rigger, who had been bribed to come out of retirement because they had worked on ships like *Oulu* in their youth and were pleased to do so again.

'They don't build ships like these nowadays,' the ship-wright said.

'An' a bluidy good job it iss, too,' Willie John murmured.

The old ship had not had so many feet across her deck since the queues of holidaymakers had lined up to goggle at the tanks of fish, and she seemed to heave and lift with the tide as though she were aware of what was happening.

'This 'ere planking's so 'ard, me dear,' the shipwright said, 'there ain't a worm in 'er anywheres. What she wants is a good zinc sheath round her now that'll keep her clean.'

'Where can we get one fitted?' Commander Snaith asked.

'I know a master caulker lives up to Bossiney'd do it for a price sir.'

'What sort of price?'

'Navy price.' The old man grinned. 'Government's payin', ain't she? 'E'd probably do it for fun otherwise. He's been retired for six months and 'e's bitin' 'is thumbs for somethin' to do. 'E's me brother-in-law.'

Two days later *Oulu*, née *Jacob Undset*, was towed to a builder's yard downriver. Several of her crew were aboard her now, but all wearing civilian clothes and showing no sign of naval discipline.

The Navy had provided the tug and, to disguise their interest in what was going on, had put out a story through the *Western Morning News* to the effect that they were lending a hand to help the Finns reach home. An elderly newspaper reporter, clearly in Snaith's confidence, had been allowed aboard and had produced a guarded article that didn't even mention her name and a photographer had taken a picture from a dinghy.

'Makes her look almost as though she'd float, poy,' Willie John observed, glancing at Magnusson. ''Tis a nice picture of you, too. Makes ye look very Errol Flynn.'

Campbell's attitude was one of stiff rectitude. Despite the fact that they were supposed to be merchant seamen – and Finnish merchant seamen at that – he chose to stalk about the ship as if he were Nelson watching the Battle of the Nile. He rarely smiled, his stiff humourless face rigid with self-righteousness, echoing Seago's thoughts to the point when he seemed to be trying to think them for him.

Seago's manner, while still that of a beaten spaniel, managed yet to be one of solemn hopefulness. 'Most of my experience,' he said as they gathered in his room at the Green Bank Hotel, 'was in *Swallow*, which is a brig, but sailing's the same in principle, whatever the ship, and it seems there'll be no need to try anything clever or silly. I shall take big tacks rather than try to sail fine into wind, and take the canvas off if it comes to a blow. We aren't taking part in the grain race and we aren't a tea clipper trying to be first home from India. We've only to get to Norway in one piece, sail down the Leads in short stretches and when the job's done, sail home again. The hard work'll be getting the ship ready for sea.'

Magnusson was pleased to hear it.

Seago produced a pink file tied with red ribbon. '*Oulu*,' he said, 'née *Jacob Undset*. Dimensions, rigging plan, deck plan, and surveyor's report. In addition, we have the log hook of the real *Oulu* and what manifests and documents they were able to dig up. You'd better study them.'

He leaned forward. 'By the time we set off home,' he said, 'we ought to have collected enough valuable information to stand us in good stead in the event of the Germans going into Norway. With our job done, therefore, we shall appear to head for the Skagerrak, the Kattegat, the Baltic and Mariehamn, but instead, we shall head west for Rosyth, and hope to be escorted home.' He looked at the shabby shape of Willie John who was slouched in his chair with his cap still on. 'In ports, our reply to the identification letter transmitted to us, will be only O – for *Oulu*. Understood?'

Willie John seemed to be asleep and Seago raised his voice. 'Understood?' he repeated.

Willie John stirred himself at last. 'It iss listenin' I am,' he said. 'An' I'm after addin' that I do not like this job.'

Seago seemed faintly dismayed by the unexpected disclosure. In his world what the Navy wished went without question. 'Why not?' he asked.

'Because o' yon hold where we ha'e the radios just.' Willie John's lined face twisted with disgust. 'She hass the rats and other beasties down there, hass she not?'

Seago was still more often in Devonport than in Falmouth and with most of the work about the ship falling on Magnusson's shoulders, he found it surprisingly heavy. As somebody he could appeal to for assistance, he had long since written off Willie John, who wouldn't have lasted five minutes on a ship with any vestige of naval discipline. Willie John would attend to communications and, apart from emergencies, from him that would be the lot. Campbell was always willing, of course, and knew his job, but it was clear there was little rapport between himself and the other members of the wardroom.

'Do ye no' ever smile an' gi'e y'r face a joy-rite, boy?' Willie John asked, staring at him as if he'd just appeared from under a stone.

'My father,' Campbell said coldly, 'didn't get his rank – or his decorations – walking about the quarter-deck with an inane grin on his face.'

'I pet,' Willie John said darkly as Campbell vanished, 'that yon father o' his wass about ass popular with the crew ass a loat o' mad dogs.'

It was obvious it was not going to be easy, especially with Seago a stiff humourless Norfolk man as dour as his own flat countryside and Willie John regarding *King's Regulations and Admiralty Instructions* merely as a thick volume with which you could prop up the leg of a broken table. For him at least the venture had the aspects of a lark and, with the clannish freemasonry of a fellow Scot, he took great delight in discussing the other two in their presence in the Gaelic that only Magnusson understood.

'Perhaps they're dead,' he suggested. 'They're pretty good at embalming these days.'

As often as not, Lieutenant-Commander Snaith, like the rest of them dressed for the occasion in civilian clothes, was on board to discuss what was to be done. He was usually accompanied by a Wren writer called Dowsonby-Smith, whose family owned an enormous house at Perranarworthal and used her private means to support herself in a flat in Western Terrace. She was engaged to the son of the owner of one of the shipyards along the river who was now, unfortunately, in the Navy and stationed in Thurso, which was as far as you could get from Falmouth in the main mass of the British Isles without falling off the edge. Magnusson and Willie John both already had their eyes on her, and the mating sounds made Snaith wince.

'Ye ha'e no need tae worry about yon Snaith, boy,' Willie John said gaily. 'He goes with Seago. One wass trainin' vegetables tae stand in rows when war broke out, and the other wass runnin' a trainin' school for little girls.'

It was a callous lie, because Snaith was a good engineer with a sound knowledge of sailing ships and, whatever his faults, Seago appeared to know his job.

They had moored the ship as far from prying eyes as they could but, despite the cold weather and the fact that there was a war on, visitors from Exeter and Truro down for the day still managed to find their way among the old ropes and blackened timbers on to a patch of waste land to watch. By this time, on the understanding that there was no point in living aboard ship until necessary, Magnusson and Willie John were sharing a flat in the old part of the town. Conscious of a guilty feeling at excluding Campbell, they had offered him the spare bedroom but he had declined with the comment that his place was aboard ship.

'I'd rather be where I can be on hand to watch developments,' he said.

The flat was a tiny affair of low ceilings and minute bedrooms. It could hardly be called comfortable but they'd already started trying to live up to their roles as poverty-stricken Finnish ship's officers and they were lucky to get it because Falmouth was full of people who had evacuated themselves hurriedly from London at the beginning of the war when they'd expected plane-loads of bombs to drop on them.

With a pub just round the corner it was never easy to keep Willie John entirely sober, however, and it was as he sang his way to bed one night that the owner, a small, pink-faced widow called Vera Tredinnick, thundered on the panels.

> 'Pin a rose tae y'r permanent wave,
> The Navy's at the door!'

He was singing as he wrenched at the knob. 'Well if it iss not herself. Come in beauty like the night! Come away in, *cearc fhraoich*, an' put y'r feet up.'

'I'm not used to this sort of thing,' Mrs Tredinnick informed Magnusson sharply. 'And I can get a much higher price than you pay if I want.'

'Who from?' Willie John was standing at an angle, propping himself up with his head against the sloping ceiling. 'Dwarfs?'

To keep up the picture of distressed seamen, they hired bicycles from a shop which let them out to holidaymakers during the summer. The frames were so crooked they seemed to have been run over.

'Made for the Swiss, boy,' Willie John said gaily. 'One leg iss shorter than the other for walkin' on mountains.'

The dishevelled appearance of the ship began to change surprisingly as rust was chipped and paintwork was scraped and the old men gradually made sense of the rigging. They were bent and grey but they were enthusiastic and capable of an extraordinary amount of hard work. Ballast was carted aboard, and a grizzled chief petty officer by the name of Marques had appeared. Since *Oulu* was to be a naval ship – at least below decks – she had to have someone to run the discipline, and Marques was master-at-arms. The ratings all seemed good sound men and at one time or another they had all done time in sailing ships, either in boys' training for the Navy or in fishing boats, and all knew the difference between a hoist and a downhaul and how to handle sails. Every one of them had been carefully selected and they had all given an undertaking that what they were up to was to be kept secret.

Then, suddenly, with the weather a West Country wetness, full of greyness and damp mist, the war sprang abruptly to life when three British cruisers ran into the German pocket battleship, *Admiral Graf Spee*, which had been on a raiding foray into the Atlantic, off the river Plate. Outweighted and outgunned, their superior tactics forced the German ship into the neutral port of Montevideo where, far less damaged than her smaller opponents, she was scuttled. It brought a gleam of excitement to what had become a very dull war and the only thing that bothered the Admiralty was what had become of the prisoners that *Graf Spee* was known to have taken from the nine British ships she had sunk. Several British officers who had been aboard the pocket battleship throughout the battle had been released in Montevideo but the bulk of the crews were known to be aboard the German freighter, *Altmark*, which had kept *Graf Spee* supplied, and *Altmark* seemed to have vanished without trace.

If nothing else, it made something to read in the newspapers other than the reports written by elderly journalists who filled their columns with references to 'pincer movements', 'strategic retreats' and other rubbish disguised as expertise. You could hardly say the war as a whole had wakened up, but at least something had happened and, in the inertia that seemed to have lain over it ever since Warsaw fell, that was something.

'Makes the saddle sores easier to bear,' Willie John observed.

By the time they applied the last lick of paint to *Oulu* and the old man from Bossiney applied the last tarred whipping, the lockers were full of twine, sheet metal, paint, tallow, tar and the hundred and one other things a sailing ship needed, and the masts carried sails made from weathered canvas begged or bought all over England. Stores had appeared alongside and the hold was already half-full of crates and sacks.

Finnish, West Indian and American money appeared and the neutral Finnish flag was painted on the ship's sides. Then, during the hours of darkness, arms were brought on board and stored away, and Willie John, who had vanished to Devonport, arrived back with two telegraphists, a radio receiver and a transmitter, and the crates were hoisted aboard and lowered out of sight, also after dark while there were no bystanders to watch.

'I didnæ realize it involved work,' Willie John complained. 'Ma sex life's become a disaster area just. I reckon I'm in the last eight o' the world celibacy championship, due tae meet the Pope in the quarter finals.'

For the look of the thing, a small pink pig, christened Vera after the small pink landlady, was placed in a coop on the after deck, and finally they were adopted by a ginger cat which wandered on board, went to sleep in the captain's cabin and resolutely refused to leave.

'We'll call 'im Nelson if that's all right with you, sir,' Leading Seaman Myers said. 'All ships need a cat, sir, to keep down the rats.'

'Better rate him a leadin' seaman,' Willie John suggested. 'In case any more come aboard an' need someone tae keep 'em under control.'

They were ready to leave when the Finns arrived.

The stink of cockroaches and damp was now heavily overlaid by the smell of the new canvas and stockholm tar. Everything on the poop had been scraped preparatory for re-painting and varnishing, and the wheezy anchor winch stank of new oil. The stores had come aboard – bread, biscuit, salt and preserved meat, potatoes, dried vegetables, flour, coffee, sugar, everything the ship needed, with acres of extra canvas and miles of extra rope and wire.

They were so ready, they'd all gone into town to celebrate with Snaith and Wren Dowsonby-Smith. When they returned to *Oulu*, there were several strangers aboard. One of them, as prepossessing as Caliban with a stubbly red beard and pale eyes, looked about eight feet tall and was built like a Percheron. He was doing gymnastics on the boatskids. Another was clinging to the rigging and a third, watched by dock-workers and what seemed to be half the population of the surrounding area, to say nothing of the crew of a police car, was balanced on top of the mainmast. They arrived just in time to see him stand on one leg, one foot in the air and begin to flap his arms and crow like a cockerel.

'Good God,' Snaith said. 'He'll fall!'

The man doing gymnastics on the boatside turned. '*Nez*,' he said. 'Dat bawsted not fall. He drunk.'

Seago, his face white and frozen in an expression of disgust and anger, was still staring upwards when one of the policemen approached him.

'This your ship, sir?'

'Yes.'

'Then you'd better sort out that customer up there. He'll break his neck. What you do is none of our business, of course, sir, but he's causing an obstruction and we were sent along because traffic can't get through. You'd better get him down.'

Seago stared up the mast. The man on the top was flapping his arms and crowing again. They could hear him quite plainly. The crowd gave an uncertain titter, not sure whether to laugh or hold its breath.

'Who is he, anyway?' Magnusson asked.

The man swinging on the boatskids stopped what he was doing and turned to him.

'He Nils Astermann,' he said. 'I Ek Yervy.' He indicated the man on the rigging who, with bulging muscles, seemed to be holding his legs and body at right angles to the rigging simply by the strength of his arms. 'He Nestor Worinen.'

'What the hell are you doing aboard this ship, anyway?' Campbell demanded. 'What are you, a blasted circus act or something?'

Snaith's pale cold face was smiling for the first time. 'The Finnish members of your crew,' he said, 'appear to have arrived.'

Yervy grinned, came to attention and saluted. 'Seamen, captain,' he said. 'Ve Finns. Ve like Finland. Ve not like Russians. Ve vant to go home.'

Seago was staring at the man on top of the mast who was pretending now to be about to dive into the sea.

'That's a hundred and ten feet,' he said. 'And there's a lot of driftwood in the water.'

'He no dive,' Yervy said placidly. 'He seely focker but he also good seaman. He no dive.'

'Bluidy good job, too,' Willie John grinned. ' 'Tis a messy job he'd make for the ambulance people if he hit a bit of floatin' timber.'

Snaith leaned towards Magnusson. 'I think you're going to have to handle these chaps as if you're walking on eggshells,' he murmured. 'They aren't Navy. They're civilian volunteers.'

Yervy nodded. 'Sure t'ing. Ve sail your ship fine.' His smile stretched from ear to ear and, despite his size, his voice was gentle.

'Now,' he said. 'Because I am gentleman, I love the lady.'

He clutched Wren Dowsonby-Smith in a bearlike grip and kissed her. As he released her, pink-faced and with her cap over one ear, Worinen leapt from the rigging and Yervy literally tossed her into his arms for a repeat performance.

As she staggered free, she saw Astermann swarming down the rigging like a monkey and took refuge behind Snaith.

'That's enough of that,' she panted, pushing her hat straight. 'I don't make a habit of this,' she said to Snaith, 'and I think it'll cost you a large gin and lime, sir.'

4

Last-minute arrangements were made and last-minute stores were brought aboard. They were still wearing civilian clothes, and to all intents and purposes *Oulu* was a Finnish ship crewed by Finnish sailors about to leave for Finland. The press had not missed Astermann's performance at the top of the mast but nothing was given away.

Marques had kept his men well under control and Snaith had been careful to send plenty of beer aboard so that the ship's company didn't have to use the dockside pubs where something might have been let slip. There had been no leave and they had been allowed ashore only after undertaking to remain sober and guard their tongues.

It had been a trying period, however, and it came as a surprise to find it was time to anchor in Falmouth Roads ready to leave when the word was given. Willie John was shocked. For the last few days he'd been seen around with the landlady of a bed-and-breakfast down the road. She was called Chrissie, wore her hair so frizzed you could have pulled corks with it, and had patently false false-teeth that showed pink vulcanite gums every time she opened her mouth.

'They look as if they were rifled off a corpse,' Campbell said disgustedly.

'They probably were, poy,' Willie John admitted gloomily. 'But 'tis no' a matter o' great importance in bed, iss it?'

Though Willie John's Chrissie was far from the type who might have been invited to cocktails in a wardroom, Magnusson had not discouraged the liaison because, if nothing else, it kept Willie John out of the pubs and doing his drinking in Chrissie's front parlour.

'Going to marry her when we get back?' he asked.

Willie John's ravaged old-man's face split into a grin. 'Not likely, poy. There's somethin' a bit too final for me about marritch.'

Campbell frowned his life-is-real-life-is-earnest frown. 'Not since the war started,' he said.

Ensign at the peak, the Erikson flag at the main truck and the Blue Peter at the fore, the ship moved slowly into the river. The tug was moving ahead and the hawser was passed, only a stern line holding the ship to the quay.

As the Blue Peter came fluttering down, they moved slowly out past Pendennis Castle and Pendennis Point to where they could see Zoze Point and Rosemullion Head and the entrance to the Helford River.

'Let go!'

The carpenter swung at the pin holding the chain stopper round the anchor and down it went with a splash, the rattle of cable, and a cloud of rust. As the tug left and they began to breathe the southerly breeze coming up past the Lizard, they all felt better. They had long since grown tired of being alongside. Coal dust, from a tip next door, had settled half an inch thick all over the decks, coated ropes and wires with a pasty mess in the drizzling mist, and filtered into cabins and on to bunks and blankets and covered decks that were littered with all the rubbish the dockworkers had left.

Campbell had had the force pump erected and got the crew on to washing the decks at once. The Finns were good workers but the past few days had shown their poverty-stricken state. Some had no oilskins, some no sea-boots, some neither, and when Seago had allowed them money to purchase what they had needed, to his horror they had merely spent it on booze. Only a few had decent gear, and even that was patched and repatched, and blue with cold and shivering in their thin dungarees, they padded about the deck, scrubbing with coir brooms at the water gushing from the canvas hoses.

To a man they seemed to possess minds like sewers and suffered from a sort of Scandinavian melancholia. All except Yervy, who came from Åland, called himself a 'Baltic sea Jew', and claimed allegiance neither to Finland nor to Sweden. Because both languages were taught in the schools there, so that Ålanders were proficient in neither, he preferred to speak in a curious sailorman's English and acted as bosun, interpreter and mediator for the rest of the crew.

At dawn next day, they began dragging the sails out of the sail locker. They were piled one on top of another like rolled carpets, the largest eighty feet across and twenty-five feet deep; looking for them by the light of a torch was like loading enormous bags of fertilizer in a darkened barn. The main royal went up first. A gantline rove through a block at the masthead was bent on to the middle of the sail and it was hoisted skywards and left hanging, the main topgallant following immediately afterwards. Men ran along the deck, holding ropes, and everybody was brought into the action, even the telegraphists, the cook and Willie John, looking like something the cat had dragged aboard. The royals and topgallants were rolled on their yards and secured with gaskets, and every available hand started bending on the great foresail.

All they had to do now was wait for final instructions, and Seago had arranged to see the SNO, Falmouth, for his orders. He seemed at times to be a little out of his depth, and the arrival of the Finns had highlighted the problems likely to be faced with men used to no discipline except the fists of mates and masters of sailing ships. With the exception of Yervy, they were all young, most of them looking no more than seventeen, but they were all tough, all a bit wild and all in the habit of using the foulest of foul epithets both in English and Finnish.

Because of the difficulties, Seago was only too glad to leave all arrangements ashore and aboard to Magnusson, who could at least lard his English with Finnish oaths. It suited Magnusson fine, because Seago had the old-time naval officer's inability to let his hair down, and the main-deck of a 118-foot barque was hardly the quarter-deck of a battle-cruiser.

On the excuse that he had last-minute arrangements to make, he begged passage aboard the launch taking Seago ashore, because Wren Dowsonby-Smith had let it be known that she would be laying on food and drink; and Willie John – his collar grubby, his shoes scuffed, his uniform spotted with night after night of drinking, but determined like any good sailor to say good-bye to his woman – had also wangled a passage. Seago was none to keen but, with Campbell aboard, Marques trained in sail, the sea flat calm and the weather forecast good, his objections didn't hold water.

'There iss always Ek Yervy tae help,' Willie John pointed out cheerfully.

Unfortunately, Ek Yervy decided to go as well, and along with Astermann and Worinen, who had always been the noisiest of the foreign element in the ship's company, tumbled aboard the launch just as she was leaving the ship's side.

'They should stay aboard,' Campbell said bitterly over the side to Magnusson, his thin face taut with disapproval. 'We'll lose 'em. Tomorrow, we'll wake up and find we're three short.'

After a fortnight of them, Magnusson couldn't have cared less.

Seago was clearly annoyed but the launch's owner didn't wait to argue and they were soon several boat's length from *Oulu*'s side. As they stepped ashore, Yervy insisted on buying drinks all round. In his stiff manner, Seago begged off. He looked angry and irritated and curiously grey-faced and strained.

'You all right, sir?' Magnusson asked.

'Feel a bit off,' Seago said tautly. 'Probably got a cold coming on.'

Yervy gave the other two no chance to escape but swept them up with his fellow Finns into the first pub they saw, a small smoke-pickled place with ships in bottles and ancient swordfish snouts. The Finns went at it as if they'd been dying of thirst in the desert for a month.

'What are we celepratin', poy?' Willie John asked.

'*Själfständighetsdagen*,' Yervy said.

'What iss that?'

'Freedom-from-Russia Day. Those Russians is all *forbannad* focking *boggerts*, and Russia is vun big *skithus*.'

They begged off at the fourth drink, Magnusson in a state of apprehension at the way the Finns were still sinking them.

'Make sure you turn up for the launch,' he said. 'Seago'll be narked if you're late.'

'Seago seely focker,' Yervy said cheerfully. 'He can *kyss din arshålet*.'

They arranged to meet outside the pub in time to catch the launch and separated. Wren Dowsonby-Smith had prepared a splendid meal.

'If you ever decide to be unfaithful to your fiancé,' Magnusson said, 'can I have first refusal?'

She was in an expansive mood. 'Why attractive men have to waste their time going to sea I can't imagine,' she said as she buttoned her blouse.

Come to that, Magnusson thought, neither could he. Going to sea meant unwashed clothes, the smell of newly greased oilskins, cockroaches, the amorous squeaking of rats, bugs like ravening wolves behind the saloon wainscoting, calendars black with pencil marks to tick off the days, and wrecks like Willie John MacDonald. It meant moping waterside streets, dockside alleys, pornographic wit, pubs of heart-breaking squalor; and ill-designed, cranky vessels, meanly found and beggarly with short rations.

'I expect it's the call of the sea,' she said.

Not on your life, Magnusson thought. The call of the sea was a journalist's cliché. Most sailors stayed at sea because they were cut off from land by their first voyage which made them different creatures from landlubbers.

All the same – he grinned at her – going to sea also meant a wild infinity of water, flying fish, dolphins, whales and the whining of mouth-organs on warm nights in the tropics. It meant Copenhagen with its tall waterfront houses; Buenos Aires on the yellow Plata and *vino del país* in umbrella-ed cafés. It meant Bahia, like a decayed aristocrat; and Freetown, with the Bunce River mangroves and the pot-bellied kids on the Portuguese Steps. It meant Perim, Penang, Malacca, Yokohama, Java, the Philippines, Soerabaya, Panama and a thousand other places that shone in his mind like beacons and would still be there when he was an old man. He suspected it was the same with Willie John and even with Campbell, and guessed that Seago, Snaith and Admiral Cockayne thought of it that way, too, at times.

She said good-bye in floods of tears, but he suspected she wouldn't miss him all that much in the end, and he set off down the hill towards the waterside. Willie John, smelling of whisky and wearing the dazed look of a cod on a slab, was waiting for him outside the pub.

'She wept a wee bitty,' he announced gloomily.

As it happened, it wasn't the Finns who failed to turn up but Seago. They had a last drink with no sign of Yervy and the others, but as they came out they bumped into them on the pavement, Astermann with a large pumpkin in his arms.

'He like pumpkin,' Yervy said. 'He cook for crew.'

They waited for Seago, arguing in a mixture of English, French, German, Norwegian, Finnish, Esthonian, Latvian and Lithuanian. There was still no sign of him an hour later when the Finns, all of whom had bottles in their pockets, were becoming noisy and had started to teach Willie John a song in Finnish that made Magnusson blush at the shattering vulgarity of the words.

With the launch owner growing plaintive and angry by turns, it seemed to be time to get the Finns back aboard *Oulu* before the police shoved them all in clink.

'Seago'll be able to get back aboard,' Willie John said,

deep in drunken gloom. 'He iss Navy, boy, iss he not? Real Navy.'

In the end they decided to risk Seago's wrath and set off to the small boat basin. Though the Finns were now embarrassingly drunk, at least they were showing no signs of bolting. At the top of the steps, Astermann missed his footing and went head over heels to the bottom. The pumpkin rolled after him and plunked neatly into the water alongside the jetty and, while they were picking up its owner, drifted out of sight beneath the piles.

Convinced he'd been attacked and his precious pumpkin stolen from him, Astermann began to spar a few brisk rounds with himself to show what he intended to do to the thief, given the chance. In the end, Yervy tired of his performance and hit him over the head with a fist like a maul so that he collapsed on to the timbers of the jetty. Almost indifferently, Yervy scooped him into the launch and they cast off.

The moon was up and the tide was just beginning to make as they set out for *Oulu*, and the smell coming off the sea was strong, damp and exciting with the scent of adventure. Willie John was singing softly to himself:

'Spare, oh, spare, ma baby's chair, the chair I love sae well.
You can sell ma grandfather's fiddle but spare me the chair
 wi' the hole in the middle. . .'

The flat calm sea and the moon made Magnusson itch to be off. Then, halfway out to the ship, Astermann recovered consciousness and, still convinced he'd allowed himself to be attacked and have his pumpkin stolen, began in fury to bang his head on the engine cover.

'He'll fracture his skull,' Willie John said.

'*Nez*.' Yervy squeezed his knee with a huge hand. 'He drunk. If he fall off topmast he still all right.'

Astermann was again lying in a huddle at the bottom of the boat by the time they reached the ship. As they bumped alongside, a few heads appeared over the taffrail. One of them belonged to Campbell.

'Is he drunk?' he asked coldly.

'No, boy,' Willie John said. 'He was run over by a train. There was a lot of 'em aboot in Falmouth the night.'

Yervy clambered to the deck with an ease that spoke of years of practice, and a line rattled down to the launch. Neither he nor Worinen spoke, and Worinen lashed the rope round the unconscious man's ankle. As Yervy hauled him up, all flapping arms and dangling legs, his head hit the side of the ship with a solid *thunk*, then it hit the rail and, as they dragged him over the rail and on to the deck, it thudded once more against the planking.

By the time Magnusson had clambered to the deck, Yervy was dragging Astermann by his feet towards the forecastle, his head appearing to clang against every ringbolt they passed. Sliding back the hatchway, with a yank of his great arm Yervy flung him into the black patch of shadow. There was a distinct pause before they heard him hit the deck below.

'Ye've killed him, I expect,' Willie John said.

Much to Magnusson's surprise, Astermann was on deck the following morning when they roused the watch. He had eyes like knot-holes, a bruise on his forehead, a cut on his cheek and a patch of dried blood in his hair, but apart from a scowl that spoke of a heavy headache, he seemed none the worse for his treatment.

There was still no sign of Seago, and Magnusson began to grow worried. Then at midday a naval launch came alongside, and he was startled to see that the figure in the bridge coat sitting by the engine was not Seago but Admiral Cockayne.

'I'm afraid Commander Seago's not aboard, sir,' he announced as Cockayne heaved himself over the side.

'I know,' Cockayne said, his face grim.

For a moment, Magnusson wondered wildly if Seago had deserted and was being chased along the south coast by the

Regulating Branch, to be dragged back in chains like some drunken matelot.

'We'll go below,' Cockayne said, and headed for the saloon as if he'd known the way all his life.

Campbell was correcting charts on the saloon table. His shoes off, Willie John was reading *Men Only*, and opening and shutting his jaws as if his tongue was clove to the roof of his mouth and refused to come adrift. They leapt to their feet, Willie John trying to stuff his feet into his shoes as he did so.

'Sit down,' Cockayne barked.'All of you! Things have changed a bit. Commander Seago had a heart attack in the SNO's office last night. They've shoved him in hospital. It looks as though it'll be up to you, Magnusson.'

Magnusson gave him a nervous glance, rather like a colt shying away from a backfiring motorcar.

'Me, sir?'

Suddenly, he suspected that it had been Cockayne's intention all along that he should run the show. He'd never shown a lot of enthusiasm for Seago, as if he'd suspected he was a bit past it and that in the end they'd have to fall back on the younger man.

'Me, sir?' he said again.

Cockayne glared. With his grey whiskers, he looked like something out of the last century, because the saloon was an Edwardian mixture of red plush, brass and banquettes. 'Yes, dammit,' he snapped. 'You!'

Magnusson wanted to protest that he was only a reservist and not a real naval man, that he wasn't even very efficient at his job, that he was terrified of responsibility, a bit idle, and far too young to die. He managed to hold his tongue.

'Think you can do it?'

To his horror, Magnusson found himself saying he thought he could. He was surprised at the confidence in his voice.

'Good! You've got Campbell, who's Regular Navy.' Cockayne made it sound as if Magnusson's training had been done on nothing more arduous than the Serpentine and he needed someone to keep an eye on him.

'Two of you should be enough,' he went on and Magnusson frowned. Watch and watch about, he was thinking, with him responsible for everything. It was going to be bloody awful.

'You'll also have Marques and this chap, Yervy, to help,' Cockayne was saying now. 'Marques understands navigation and Campbell's an expert. Yervy'll give sailing advice if you need it.'

If he wasn't drunk, wanting a fight, or just disinclined, Magnusson thought.

'We'd call it off if we could,' Cockayne said. 'Or at least find somebody else. But there aren't that many sailing masters about.'

'Commander Snaith's one,' Magnusson suggested desperately.

'Commander Snaith has other responsibilities.' Cockayne cut him short. 'Besides, we haven't time to find a relief for *him*. Things are happening.'

He tapped the chart Campbell produced and stared at it, frowning, while he packed his pipe. Then he struck a match, blew out smoke and gestured.

'Despite the fact,' he began, 'that there's no sign of life in France and that the Prime Minister and several of our more purblind newspapers are still firmly of the belief that the Germans have lost their nerve and won't fight, a few intelligent people at the Admiralty have guessed that they're only biding their time, and they're wondering where the blow's going to fall. We suspect it'll be Norway in the spring, and arrangements are in hand to prevent them by going in first. We've also decided to make the running by denying the use of Norwegian territorial waters to vessels carrying contraband of war to Germany, and plans are being made to lay mines in the Leads to push shipping into the open sea.'

He tapped the chart again. 'When the time comes, we

shall inform the Norwegian government of our intentions, and I imagine they'll be hopping mad. For your information, the mines'll be here and here in Vestfjord. We expect the Germans will react strongly and a plan's been prepared to deal with any attempt to seize Norwegian ports in retaliation. Stavanger, Bergen, Trondheim and Narvik are all to be occupied as soon as any such intention becomes clear.' He looked at Magnusson. 'There's another thing,' he added. 'Narvik's a strange port. Come to that, all neutral ports are bloody strange these days, with both British and German ships in them, their crews eyeball-to-eyeball, each watching the other like mad. But Narvik's a bit different. There, all the advantages seem to be with the Germans because we suspect the military commandant has Nazi sympathies. And there's the fact that the Germans can get to the Baltic through the Leads whereas *our* ships have to cross the North Sea, where too damn many of them are being torpedoed.'

Magnusson waited and Cockayne went on angrily. 'Somebody in Narvik's been passing information by radio,' he said.

It occurred to Magnusson that, since they were proposing to do exactly the same thing, there was little ground for complaint.

'There are a lot of German ships in there,' Cockayne went on, 'and it could be any of them. But we suspect a ship called *Cuxhaven*, which has been lying there for some time. Since she's been there the sinkings have increased.' He glanced at Willie John, who managed with a struggle to look sober and intelligent. 'You will listen out for her and if she *is* the one, you're to follow her when she leaves and signal her position. The Navy will then attend to her.'

'Sir.' Magnusson frowned. 'How do we follow *anything* in a sailing ship? We're rather at the mercy of the wind.'

'So's *Cuxhaven*,' Cockayne said grimly. 'She's a four-masted barque and, since she was a training ship for a while, we know she's fitted with radio. We suspect she's in contact with submarines. We want her.'

'I see, sir,' Magnusson gave a nervous smile. 'There'll be rather a lot of sailing ships in that neck of the woods when we arrive.'

'More than you think,' Cockayne snapped. 'The Polish training ship, *Kosciuszko*'s up there, too. You probably know her. Built by Blohm and Voss. Full-rigged with an auxiliary and a radio like most sail-trainers. They were at the end of a round-the-world voyage and had to put in with storm damage just before the Germans went into their country. They've been there ever since. I'm glad I'm not a Pole.'

He puffed at his pipe for a while before continuing. 'The Egge woman will brief you,' he said. 'We have a feeling – and so does she – that her usefulness is coming to an end, because the Germans are growing suspicious. One last thing, if there's any sign of the Germans going into Norway, you'll come home. At once.' Cockayne allowed himself a grim smile. 'And you'd better make sure you do,' he added, 'because ten to one the Norwegians will have cottoned on by then to what's happening and *they'll* be looking for you, too.'

He rose and headed for the gangway. On deck, he paused with one leg over the side. 'Oh, by the way – ' he tossed the final titbit across as if it were a lump of sugar to a well-trained poodle ' – you've been upped to lieutenant-commander. You can put your half-stripe up. It's to give you some muscle over those other two clots you've got aboard.'

5

They watched Cockayne's launch leave. The admiral didn't look back.

'Think we can do it?' Campbell asked. It was the first indication he'd given that he had any doubts.

Magnusson shrugged. 'Shouldn't think so for a minute,' he said. 'But I suppose we've got to try. We can always bolt for Sweden if it doesn't come off. It wouldn't be too bad spending the war in comfort in a neutral country.'

Campbell gave him a cold look, as if what he'd said was blasphemy, but Willie John seemed to consider it a good idea.

'I've heard that Swedish girls are no' bad.' He grinned at Campbell. 'There iss nothin' tae worry apout, boy. At least, not tae a MacDonald. I cannae speak for a a bluidy Campbell, o' course, who're a lily-livered lot by all accounts.'

As he disappeared, shabby, shaggy and unwholesome, Campbell stared after him disgustedly. 'The bloody man doesn't even speak King's English,' he said.

'So long as they can write it,' Magnusson said, 'radio operators don't have to.'

'Well, all that bloody rot about the Campbells and the MacDonalds!'

'For God's sake, man,' Magnusson said, 'he doesn't give a damn about the Campbells and the MacDonalds, and if you just once stopped taking him seriously and smiled, he'd have no excuse for it. He does it to irritate you.'

'Why, for God's sake?'

'Because you irritate *him*.'

'Then I think he should be bloody well put in his place!'

Magnusson turned angrily, losing his patience. There was only one way to deal with people like Campbell and that was to be more naval than they were. 'Nobody's asking you what you think, Mister,' he snapped. 'And since you want to know, I'll tell you why you irritate him. Because you irritate *me*, too! So I'll thank you to think about it and not argue. I'm running this ship and I'll have neither discord nor disagreement.' He stared after the disappearing launch and drew a deep breath. The sky was a pale saffron with long banks of grey cloud lying across it like sword strokes. 'And now,' he said sharply, 'we'd better get on with it! Rouse everybody out.'

As Campbell began to shout orders, staysails and jibs crawled, fluttering, up between the masts and from the jib-boom, to be steadied by their sheets. The spanker was hauled out and the ship began to heel over to the weight of the wind in them.

'Loose the topsails!'

As the gaskets were thrown off the rolled sails, they fell in folds. The lower topsails were sheeted home and the upper topsails hoisted.

'Foresail!'

With the foresail and mainsail set, the naked spars became clothed.

'Topgallants and royals!'

As they grabbed for the thick halyards, Magnusson gave the order – '*Tramp på däck*' – and they all stamped along the deck to begin a fifteen-minute chore of muscle-cracking heaving. Under a dark cloud of canvas, the ship, with every stitch set to a beam wind and leaning well over, stood down-Channel, her side lights showing the direction of her ghostly progress. As the hands began to flake down the braces for running and to straighten the tangle of ropes that lay about the decks, *Oulu* surged forward, lifting her bow to the waves and moving before the soft southerly wind.

'Better shove the Finnish flag up,' Magnusson said, and the white flag with its square pale blue cross broke out at the stern.

'Keep it there,' Magnusson ordered. 'And let's have another one at the masthead, so there can be no mistake. We shall be sailing with lights at night like any other neutral.'

Everybody was at work in the hold, trimming and securing the sacks of grain to prevent them shifting – *Herzogin Cecilie* had once been laid over at an angle of seventy degrees with her hatch coamings under water because of shifting cargo – and there was a great deal of complaining from the Finns who hastened to point out that they weren't 'focking farmers'.

As they rounded the Lizard in the dusk and left the lee of the land, the wind freshened and changed direction, and the slots of grey cloud that lay across the pale night sky grew thicker, banded together and became a broken mass carried swiftly overhead. The ship, moving along now with the wind four points on the quarter, was leaning over until the water gurgled in through the scupper holes and set the deck awash. Aloft, everything was cracking, the canvas standing out as if carved from ebony, and the sea was getting up, the wave crests curling at the barque and breaking against her weather side to lash spray into the rigging.

They passed several ships, destroyers moving swiftly about their business, a large tanker slipping along the coast in the safety of darkness, and one or two small coasters, from one of which as it slipped past within yards of them an angry voice came, 'Your bloody port light's screened by your foresail, you stupid bastards!'

The moon lifted over the horizon, laying a narrow glittering reflection towards the ship as they headed northwards round Land's End towards the Irish Sea, but the sky had changed and the wind had backed again and was now beginning to push black cliffs of cumulus before it, knocking up a stiff sea against the tide that made the passage lumpy and ugly. They were still close enough to the shore to see the line of the land against the water, dark, lightless and empty.

They had picked up the weather forecast with its advice of increasing wind, and there were a few misgivings in Magnusson's mind as he stood on the poop; not of his ability to sail the ship but of what awaited them. He knew how much his skill was worth, all the same, and preferred to play safe with the putting on or taking off of canvas until he had the feel of the ship. As the sky darkened, he was aware of loneliness and nervousness.

The ship seemed to be rolling rather more than she ought to be and he wondered if they were sufficiently weighted. Wandering forward to make sure everything was in its right place he felt a few stinging needles of rain in the wind. The barometer was falling, he noticed, but the moon was still there and he could see its cold reflection on the spars above them.

As the first big Atlantic rollers lifted the ship, a slash of spray came over the bows and rattled on the deck. Climbing into the hold, Magnusson listened. He could no longer hear the howl of the wind, but caught the swish and gurgle of the bilge water; it sounded as though the ship were sinking. The place was alive with creaks and groans where the timbers chafed as she rolled, and he noticed it was beginning to grow cold.

It was the wind that woke Magnusson to the realization that his bunk was at such an angle he had been holding on unconsciously in his sleep with feet and elbows, to avoid rolling out. As his eyes opened, he heard the roar of the growing gale and the clatter of the sea along the hull.

Leaping out of the bunk and dragging on his clothes, he went on deck. The wind had backed now to north-westerly and the ship was carrying too much canvas, staggering along hard over, beating into a high sea, with all round her a sky which gave every sign of a stormy twenty-four hours ahead.

Yervy was on the wheel, with Campbell beside him staring at the sails, an uneasy expression on his face in the half light.

'*Koms vest vind*,' Yervy pointed out. 'An' dis ship too heavy.'

Magnusson glanced at the barometer. 'Storm on the way,' he agreed.

'Unless, of course,' Campbell said coldly, 'something crawled in there and died. It might well have, aboard this ship.'

Oulu was lurching badly, whipping back at the end of each roll with a jerk that jarred the masts and made the rigging twang.

'Come round,' Magnusson ordered. 'It's either that or end up dismasted or broached to. Let her run before the wind till daylight.'

'There's going to be a great deal of tooth-sucking from Cockayne if we turn up off Falmouth again tomorrow,' Campbell observed bitterly, as if he considered it a personal defeat.

Yervy let the wheel spin and immediately the list grew less dangerous and the whipping rolls less violent, but the ship was still plunging into the sea in a way that took the bowsprit deep every time. By daylight they were running with as little canvas as possible but if the weather was going to continue it would be better to snug her down as far as possible. They furled the spanker and, with the Finns performing miracles of strength and gymnastics, managed to close-reef the mainsail, furl the foresail and upper topsail, and haul down the inner jib. By the time they had finished, the wind had dropped and there was a hint of sunshine through the rushing clouds.

As they reached the Hebrides the wind came again, hitting the ship in a flurry of blinding rain, and before they had made everything ready to put her about she had swooped round and was heading at full speed in the wrong direction. With the wind still in the east, they beat to windward through the second night in a smoking sea that threw up clouds of spray on which the starboard navigation light shone in clusters of green diamonds, then the fore royal blew out and Magnusson kicked himself for trying to be too clever.

'One thing, boy,' Willie John said, staring upwards at his aerials, his hangdog face wet with spray. 'Goin' tae sea this way ye get plenty o' fresh air.'

The following day the sea was still rising and the ship was running heavily. Overhead, the sun struggled through the masses of torn cloud. The responsibility was like a leaden cloak on Magnusson's shoulders but, curiously, he found he was enjoying himself, and he guessed it was being at sea in sail again. When ships like *Oulu* went – and there weren't so many of them left now – there would be no more and that would be the end. He had a feeling that the war would see them off and was happy to be in at the death.

The barometer was still dropping and they prepared for the bad weather that was clearly on its way. Fiddles were on the saloon table and the hawsepipes had been stopped with blocks of wood; lifelines were rigged, and wire safety nets set up to prevent anybody being washed overboard; while the sacks of grain in the hold were held in place with railway sleepers lashed with chains and secured with wooden wedges driven home with sledge-hammers. More timbers were laid across the hatch covers and lashed down to ring-bolts in the hatch coaming. Until the weather slackened there would be no using the big transmitter-receiver Willie John had installed in the hold.

As they passed between the Faeroes and the Shetlands the wind blew harder and they had to fight to bring the ship on course. She drove headlong before the wind at a spanking pace, rolling until her lee rail scooped up great avalanches of green sea. As she thundered along with the sun sparkling on the heaving water, towering waves flung themselves at her, but always she lifted and let them pass harmlessly beneath, and with each escape, Magnusson's expression grew more confident.

The evening sunshine made the scene breathtaking, tremendous waves, flecked by rainbows as the spray caught the light, striking the ship in shuddering blows to pour over the bulwark and soak the watch. The galley was washed out, and plates and bottles were broken. As she heeled over, they walked with wide legs, their ears full of the gurgle of water in the scuppers, the roaring of sails and the wailing of the rigging, all coming together in a satanic orchestration as they slid through the sea, stripped and gaunt as a skeleton.

There had been far less problems than Magnusson had anticipated and no unexpected accidents except a split thumb belonging to one of the Finns.

'You practised in surgery, boy?' Willie John asked as Magnusson bound it up.

'Read it up,' Magnusson said. 'The captain of *Lawhill* dumped a medical book on my lap and told me to get on with it. It seemed to work out.'

Willie John indicated the Finn. 'He'll probably die o' lockjaw.'

Magnusson shook his head. 'Shouldn't think so,' he said. 'When one of the apprentices in *Priwall* went down with appendicitis, he was operated on by the chief mate with the same knife he used to scrape teak and cut rope. The kid was still writing to me right up to the beginning of the war.'

As they sighted the Lofotens, the blustery wind fell and, as they reached the islands and were approaching the coast of Norway itself, it slackened almost to nothing. The sun disappeared, the temperature dropped dramatically and there were patches of fog and mist that made *Oulu* look ghostly as it swirled about her spars and masts.

They were nearing the Arctic Circle now. Flurries of sleet and snow kept arriving, and it was bitterly cold. Nobody seemed to have any dry clothing, and the forecastle was foetid with the odour of steaming jerseys and the rank smell of unwashed men. Everybody hung about the mess-room or the saloon, drinking coffee and fighting the inertia that came with tiredness.

The BBC news gave nothing away. 'All quiet in France' became like a litany repeated again and again, and the dance music that followed made Magnusson feel homesick for Wren Dowsonby-Smith.

'Should be there tomorrow.' Campbell's words, clipped and phlegmatic, broke in on his thoughts. He jabbed at the chart. 'That's where we'll make our landfall. The island of Væröy.'

'Unless, o' course, 'tis a fly speck on the chart,' Willie John observed cheerfully. 'In which case, poy, we'll probably run aground off Flakstadöy.'

Campbell went red. 'I don't mistake fly specks for pencil marks!' he snarled. 'Why don't you mind your own bloody business?'

'Shut up, both of you,' Magnusson snapped, wishing for the first time that *Oulu* was an honest-to-God naval ship and he could bring them both up before the captain. 'This is no bloody place to be fighting with each other! We've got enough with the Germans. And while we're at it, we'd better have the arms broken out. And now that the wind's dropped and we're in the lee of the land, let's have the hatches opened up so that the telegraphists can get in there.' He turned to Willie John. 'Better keep a sharp radio watch from now on. I've got a feeling in my bones something's going to happen.'

Edging their way slowly eastwards just off the north Norwegian coast, it was difficult to fix their position exactly. Somehow the mist seemed to awe everybody and they spoke in whispers, as though moved by the silence. Through the damp they caught the smell of the land and the curious indefinable scent of approaching snow.

'Tell the look-outs to keep their eyes open,' Magnusson ordered, and he had hardly spoken when the man in the bows sang out.

'Ship dead ahead sir. Looks like a small destroyer.'

As the other vessel emerged from the fog they identified it as a Norwegian torpedo-boat.

'Flashing K, boy,' Willie John said. ''Tis tellin' us tae stop they are.'

As the wind was spilled from the sails, *Oulu* slowed down gradually until she was lying silently in the lifting sea.

'Warn all hands,' Magnusson told Campbell. 'They're to remember for Christ's sake that we're Finnish. Nobody but the Finns, myself or yourself in conversation. And go round the ship to check there's no sign of naval uniform or equipment.'

As the Norwegian ship stopped opposite them, a boat was lowered and began to head towards them. The Norwegian officer who climbed aboard was a lieutenant-commander, a tall, red-haired pale-eyed man wearing a suspicious look.

Magnusson introduced himself. 'First mate,' he said.

'Where's your captain?'

'He died. We buried him in the States. Burst appendix – ' Magnusson shrugged '– and akvavit. I have the ship.'

'You speak Norwegian?' the Norwegian asked.

'A little,' Magnusson said hesitantly. 'Not much. We're Finns.'

'What's your business?'

'We're heading for Narvik.'

'Why?'

Magnusson trotted out the story Cockayne had provided. 'We were for Falmouth with a cargo of grain. It was for English mills but we thought it'd be of more use to Finland. We're taking it to Mariehamn and they can sort it out there. We have gale damage to repair, then we propose to go south through the Leads to the Skaggerak and home.'

'I'll need to see your papers.' The Norwegian gestured. 'We have to be careful. The British and the Germans are up to all sorts of tricks and we don't want to get involved in their war.'

In the saloon, he sat down at the table and began to

examine the ship's books. Quietly, Magnusson placed a glass of whisky alongside him.

'Bought in New York,' he said.

Outside the cabin, he could hear Yervy, Worinen and Astermann chattering away and he guessed that Campbell had stationed them there to give the appearance of genuineness.

'I'll leave you to it,' he suggested, but the Norwegian looked up.

'No need,' he said. 'Everything seems in order. Watch yourself in Vestfjord. There's a lot of traffic there and this sort of weather isn't the thing to be caught in, with a ship that manoeuvres as indifferently as a sailing ship.'

6

They lay in the entrance to Vestfjord in the darkness, on a clear frosty night with the aurora hanging in the sky like a brilliant curtain whose folds gently wavered and danced. The gap in the land was well lit but Magnusson elected to wait until daylight, and the ship became silent in a quiet sea except for the occasional shout from one of the Finns on the forecastle head. '*Klara lanternor*! Lights are bright!'

At first light next morning they moved into the fjord and, taking on the pilot, ran the blue-crossed white flag of Finland up to the gaff. It was bitterly cold and the ropes of the running gear had become half-frozen and jammed in the blocks so that it required an almost superhuman effort to move them. As the sun came out the ship lay directly across its path and seemed on fire, her sails agleam and golden. In contrast, her dark hull seemed shabby, the rust streaks like the honourable scars of a long voyage.

As they moved down the fjord, the mountainous coast of Norway unfolded in magnificent vistas of spotless white. The snow came even to the water's edge and, against a background of the sort of scenery that would have done justice to a Christmas card, great flocks of eider duck rose from the water.

The pilot was inclined to leave everything to Magnusson. He wasn't a sailing ship man and could only indicate the channel, but the fjord was still about ten miles wide, fringed by rocky, sparsely populated islands. As it began to narrow into Ofotfjord, which was only half as wide, huddles of small fishing villages, mere groups of twenty to fifty wooden houses clustered around a church, appeared along the edges of the subsidiary fjords.

Near the village of Djupvik, two converted Norwegian trawlers, *Michael Sars* and *Kelt*, on outpost duty, signalled them to stop. A launch was already heading towards them and, as the Norwegian naval officer appeared over the side, Magnusson introduced himself once more with the story of the captain's death in the States.

There was no difficulty. The Norwegian Navy had obviously picked up the sightings put out by Cockayne, and the Norwegian officer was not only helpful but sympathetic.

'The war is going well for Finland at the moment,' he said. 'They are still throwing back the Russians with heavy losses.'

'But they have bombed Helsinki,' Magnusson pointed out.

The Norwegian shrugged. 'The Mannerheim Line holds,' he said, 'and your president has appealed to the world for assistance. It's said that Britain wants to send a token force.'

'And both Norway and Sweden have refused to allow it passage,' Magnusson said.

The Norwegian officer shrugged again. Handing back the papers and manifests, he saluted. 'What use is a token force anyway?' he said. 'The Russians have too many men.'

The entrance to the fjord had contained ice but the passage was clear now all the way up to the port which they approached slowly with the wind, close to the northern shore until they were directly opposite the town, a circle of houses and buildings along the waterside under the steep wooded slopes of the hills. There was a concrete pier where the ore ships loaded, and an electrified railway line which brought the ore from Gällivare in Sweden. At this point the fjord split up into four long fingers thrusting into a mountainous coast.

'Makes land communication difficult,' the pilot said. 'You have to go all the way round. But we have ferries and that makes it easier. Do you need dockyard facilities?'

'*Nez*,' Magnusson said. 'We do what we want without that. We have no money to pay, anyway.'

'I see. They'll place you at the entrance to Herjangsfjord, I expect. You'll find plenty of water. You'll be right opposite the town, out of the way of the ferries but within reach of the launches. I'll radio the harbourmaster's office to keep a look-out for your signals.'

There were ships of all nationalities lying off the Ore Pier, and Magnusson saw British and German vessels close beside each other. As they edged slowly down the fjord, they were met by a harbour official in a launch who directed them to the entrance to Herjangsfjord about a mile from where the iron ore railway curved round from Narvik, and they dropped anchor alongside a modern four-masted steel barque flying a German flag.

Just beyond the German was another sailing vessel, a full-rigged ship over two hundred feet long, painted white with a sweeping bowsprit covered with scrollwork round her figurehead. But she was bald-headed, her topmasts missing, her yards a-cockbill, her running rigging neglected. At her stern she carried the emblazoned white and red flag of Poland.

There were a few birds about as they took in the headsails and they rose in a cloud as the Finns went up the standing rigging. Campbell was on the forecastle head waiting for the order to let go the anchor.

'*Ned med rodret!*'

As Yervy put the helm down, the foretopmast staysail halyard was cast off its pin and the down-haul manned, the men rushing along the deck as it shrilled down the stay. *Oulu* came up, the main topsails aback, and gradually drifted astern.

'*Låt gå babords ankaret!* Let go the port anchor!'

Campbell hit the pin securing the chain stop and there was a tremendous roar as the anchor crashed into the water and the cable roared out of the chain lockers. As the ship swung, Yervy stared at the land.

'Vestfjord is de arsehole of de vorld,' he said flatly. 'And Narvik is right up it.'

From where they lay they could see heavy ore trains moving slowly through the centre of the town, and the buildings of the business district spreading towards the mountains. Most of the houses were small two-storey affairs, though there were bigger ones in the better residential district along the low forested ridge on the edge of the peninsula. The air smelled cold and tangy with salt and an odour of seaweed mixed with tar, and it was filled with the cries of seagulls wheeling and diving for fish.

'Do we go ashore here, boy?' Willie John asked.

'No,' Magnusson said.

'Fock notting to see anyway,' Yervy added.

As the pilot launch came alongside and the pilot prepared to board it, Magnusson indicated the barque.

'What's the German ship?'

'*Cuxhaven*. She was built at Wessermunde as the *Hildegaarde Hahn* in 1926. She was a nitrate carrier but then she became a training ship and was renamed *Cuxhaven*. She's a nitrate carrier again now.'

The German ship was clearly very modern, her four masts and the flying bridge running aft to her poop making her eminently suitable for training ship work.

'Big,' Magnusson said, studying her through his binoculars. 'Over three hundred feet long, I'd say, and over three thousand tons.' He indicated the Polish ship just beyond. 'And her?'

The Norwegian shrugged. '*Kosciuszko*. She came in here on 28 August, last year. She ran into a gale off the Faroes and was carried north. She lost three of her cadets overboard and was dismasted. She was trying to make repairs to get home to Gdynia, but then, of course, the Germans went into Poland and she's been here ever since.'

Magnusson said nothing but his eyes narrowed as he remembered what Cockayne had told him about the Polish ship and *Cuxhaven*. He had seen a few Polish sailors from escaped warships in Portsmouth, rootless men with tragic faces and hard eyes, determined to die for their country because honour was all they had left after their defeat. 'What are they going to do?' he asked.

The Norwegian's shoulders moved. 'What can they do? There's no Polish Consul any more and they can get no help. The Germans say she's theirs now but the Poles swear they'll never let them have her. They can only take her by force.'

The men aboard the other ships were as interested in *Oulu* as *Oulu* was in them and they could see themselves being studied through binoculars.

'Yon German job hass got a lot o' radio aerials aboard her,' Willie John pointed out.

'She's also got a very large crew,' Campbell said, studying the crowded decks. 'It's a wonder they don't elbow each other overboard.'

As they waited, the harbourmaster's launch arrived. The harbourmaster was a reserve naval officer called Vinje who seemed suspicious and, under the thin excuse of being interested, demanded to see the ship. His eyes were everywhere and Magnusson suspected he was looking for radio aerials.

He insisted on visiting the hold but there was nothing to be seen there and he stood for a while in the gloom, sniffing, so that Magnusson wondered wildly if he could *smell* Willie John's sets. Did they give off the scent of hot bakelite when they were used and the valves heated up?

The Norwegian prodded one or two of the bags of grain and ran his hand over the cases of rum, but he said nothing and climbed back to the deck.

He didn't seem entirely satisfied and it wasn't hard to realize how difficult things were for the Norwegians, with a powerful neighbour to the south coveting their country as a base for her ships; another across the North Sea, goaded by an aggressive First Lord of the Admiralty; and yet another, Russia, just across the Baltic. Norway was no more than sixty miles wide for the greater part of her length, and Sweden no more than two hundred; and beyond Sweden lay Finland, already deep in conflict with Russia. It wasn't a prospect that could ever please Norway whose chances of preserving her cherished neutrality were growing more slender every day.

'Keep your boats out of the fairway,' the harbourmaster warned. 'There are a lot of ships leaving on the tide in the morning. Four general cargo and one fish oil tanker under the escort of the patrol boat, *Jens Roschmül*. There are also three Baltic traders due to follow.'

Doubtless, Magnusson thought, like the general cargo vessels, all full of Swedish ore destined for Germany.

That night, the red ball of the sun was obscured by a low violet-grey bank. Then, as darkness fell, the stars glinted with unwinking frosty clarity. Only the movement of launches about the harbour set up a ripple, making the lower yards groan and the blocks rattle against the masts. By morning the mercury seemed to have dropped out of the barometer, and dawn was obscured by great banks of mist rolling up like clouds of gas, enveloping the ship in a vapour that left half-frozen globules everywhere, turning the breath to smoke and making the crew shiver with the cold. Then slowly, the sun paled and the fog arrived, creeping in insidiously. One minute there had been nothing except violet tendrils of mist; then they were surrounded by a thick grey bank that shut off one end of the ship from the other and blocked out all sight of land.

Peering anxiously into the fog Magnusson's brows were down and he was listening nervously. As the ship lifted gently, the rigging dripping water to the deck, it was like swaying inside an opaque ball. From time to time he heard the thump of a propeller and the low boom of a siren. The water looked darker ahead than astern and a dim shape moved through the gloom which he studied closely. He caught Campbell watching him, his narrow face bleak and puzzled, as if he found it hard to understand that a non-naval man could be so concerned. All at once, Magnusson felt like the Old Man of the Sea.

The fog lasted only a day; then a breeze got up and the fjord cleared. Many of the ships had gone, but already others were arriving to take their places. Narvik was busy, the air filled with the roar of winches and donkey engines.

Soon after breakfast, they saw a boat leave the side of *Cuxhaven* and head towards them.

'Nobody but the Finns on deck,' Magnusson said. 'Get the rest aloft, Campbell. Get 'em rigging ratlines and greasing the braces and halyards.'

The Germans were smart, erect and friendly, and they looked round *Oulu* with only the faintest sign of contempt on their faces.

'*Cuxhaven*,' the older of the two said. 'We are carrying nitrates from South America and the war caught us far from home. We had to take the northabout passage to Narvik. I am Johannes Boch, master. This is Erich Wolff, first mate.'

Magnusson decided he didn't like the Germans. They had hard faces and cold eyes, and Boch looked like one of the picture-book Prussians he'd seen so often as a boy in magazines illustrating the other war, with a thick neck, blond hair, even a duelling scar on his cheek. The bastard only needed a monocle, he thought, and to speak like Erich von Stroheim – 'Zo! Ve meet a-gain!'

'Magnusson,' he said. 'First mate. The captain died in New York.'

The story came out pat now and the Germans seemed to accept it, but Magnusson noticed their eyes were all over the vessel, studying the rigging with special care.

He took them below into the Café Royal atmosphere of the saloon with its red plush and brass and offered them akvavit. Only Boch accepted, Wolff saying he didn't drink.

'Here's to us,' Boch said, as he lifted his glass. 'We sailing ship men are all brothers of the sea.'

'*Skål!*'

'There aren't many of us about these days,' Boch went on. 'Perhaps we are lucky. *Cuxhaven* was a training ship before the war but I think sail training ships are out of favour since *Admiral Karpfanger* disappeared last year. They say she struck an iceberg. Now, since the Reich badly needs nitrates, *Cuxhaven*'s naval officers have left her and she, too, has been pressed into service.'

Despite his words, Magnusson guessed he was a naval officer himself. He had the same self-possessed air that Campbell and Admiral Cockayne had.

Boch smiled. 'Your countrymen in Finland are putting up a splendid fight,' he said. 'Especially since there are only a few of them and there are so many Russians. It is the old Russian steam-roller again.'

Wolff laughed. 'Trust the Russians to attack in winter,' he said. 'You'd think they'd have learned something from Napoleon's campaign of 1812. The Führer would have more sense.' He gestured towards the men in the rigging. 'I think you had a difficult time with the weather. It does not deter us, of course. Like all ex-training ships, *Cuxhaven* has an auxiliary.'

'I thought you had a lot of men aboard,' Magnusson said cheerfully. 'You'll need them for shovelling all that coal.'

Boch's face stiffened. 'It is diesel-driven,' he said.

'Must take up a lot of space in the hold which could have been better filled with cargo.' Magnusson sniffed. 'Auxiliaries don't really belong in sailing ships, do they? No auxiliary ever came within striking distance of a record passage.'

Boch's face was like granite. 'Why are you here?' he demanded coldly.

Magnusson smiled, suddenly enjoying himself. 'Nearest landfall for the Baltic,' he pointed out. 'We had to keep out of the way of the British destroyers.'

The Germans glanced at each other. 'There are three of us here,' Boch said. 'It is most unusual. But I think we are all orphans of the war. It is bad to be so far north at this time of the year. With ice about, here is no place for a sailing ship. We're going south when spring comes. And you?'

Magnusson shrugged. 'Different ships, different long-splices. We go as soon as we've finished our repairs.'

The Germans were smiling as they left, but when Magnusson suggested returning their call Boch's face stiffened again.

'It will be difficult,' he said firmly. 'We have much gear on board from the training ship days.'

Campbell stared, narrow-eyed and bleak-faced, as the boat headed back to *Cuxhaven*. 'I'd sell you a hundred of that bastard any day,' he said. 'Cheap, too. They didn't want you aboard.'

Though it was unlikely they were being watched from the shore, Magnusson kept everybody at work. He had two of the younger Finns, slung in bosun's chairs, smearing the wire braces and halyards with tar, graphite grease and paint, and two more scraping the masts. Several others were chipping paint from the iron deck and pulling up old planking for the carpenter to renew. It was bone dry and smelled of pine in a way that made Magnusson itch for the land.

They waited for a boat from *Kosciuszko* to arrive, but the Poles were keeping to themselves, making their plans and nursing their hatred, and when another launch appeared during the afternoon, they almost fell into the sea in astonishment at the sight of the girl standing by the engine hatch. She was tall and blonde with the same opal eyes that Magnusson had, and even from the deck it was clear she was a beauty. She wore trousers and heavy boots and gloves; perched on her blonde hair was a red woollen cap and she was huddled in a heavy sheepskin-lined jacket.

As the boat bumped against the ship's side, she reached for the ladder and climbed up it nimbly and expertly as though she had done it thousands of times before.

Magnusson met her as she stepped on deck and she gave

him a smile that made his day. '*God dag. Hvordan star det til.*'

'*Bare bra, takk.* I am Magnusson, *förste styrman.*'

'You are Norwegian?'

'No. Finnish.'

'You have a Norwegian name.'

He shrugged and she dumped a pile of magazines on the hatch. A few were French with girls on the cover. *Country Life*, he also noticed, and *Feld Krigs Röpet, Officielt organ for Frålsningsarmén i Finland.* Good old Salvation Army, he thought. You could always bank on *The War Cry* with its mixture of godliness and honest kindliness.

'I will send more,' she said. 'Also warm clothing. I expect you have heard of me. I visit all ships that are new to Narvik. If you have any Norwegians on board or any who have been in here before they will know our hut. It isn't much but we organize dances and provide food. Sometimes it is fish balls or fish puddings made with eggs, but usually it is labskaus. And good labskaus, too. I don't recommend it in small restaurants where it's made with old sausages and potatoes, but ours is excellent.'

A wild fantasy was growing on Magnusson. It couldn't be, he thought wildly. It couldn't possibly!

'You couldn't be – ?' he began and she gave him a brisk, no-nonsense smile.

'*Ja,*' she said. '*Jeg heter Annie Egge.* I am Annie Egge, Missions to Seamen.'

7

For a while Magnusson couldn't think of anything to say. For weeks he had had in his mind a picture of a tough old battle-axe big enough to flatten any drunken sailor who argued, and here she was, a Nordic goddess with bright eyes, a winning smile and legs that seemed to end somewhere under her armpits.

'You're not what I expected,' he managed.

Her smile grew wider. 'I never am, I find,' she admitted. 'We provide food, cater for homesickness and try to prevent the Poles from *Kosciuszko* murdering the Germans. We have to watch them all the time because the one thing they would like is to catch a few down the dark alleys near the harbour. You are very welcome to visit our mission hut.'

Studying her, Magnusson considered it might be a very good idea and hurriedly suggested a drink in the saloon.

'It's cold,' he said. 'A glass of akvavit wouldn't come amiss.'

She dazzled him with another brisk smile and agreed that it would be a very good idea.

Campbell and Willie John had appeared alongside with remarkable speed, Willie John beaming all over his ugly, ravaged face and making signs that he wished to be introduced. As they settled themselves in the saloon Campbell began pouring drinks. For once his naval reserve had slipped and he was staring goggle-eyed at the girl as he handed round the glasses.

As they drank, she looked at them all. 'Are you all the

officers there are?' she asked. 'I expected someone more senior.'

'You'd be surprised how experienced I am,' Magnusson said.

'With girls, no doubt,' she said, suddenly frosty. 'I was thinking about ships.'

'I know the job.'

'I hope you also know the responsibilities of what you're here for.' Her smile had vanished with her friendly manner and she had become sharp-edged and efficient.

'I have a list here of shipping movements,' she went on. 'We have a contact in the office of the harbourmaster and director of shipping, as we also have in the office of the fish oil factory and at the ore jetty.' She tapped the list. 'It has all the names of ships, nationalities, cargoes and destinations. Six of them are British and two of them, *Mabel Eccleston* and *Clydebank*, are due to sail.'

She placed a chart on the table. 'You will have seen the patrol boats opposite Djupvik,' she said. 'They are both old and armed with 50-mm guns. There are numerous gun emplacements about the harbour – ' her finger stabbed at the map – 'here and here and here, but many of the fortifications marked on the chart don't in fact exist. The intention is to provide guns, but so far they haven't arrived. We are also expecting the coastal defence ships, *Eidsvold* and *Norge*. *Norge* is the flagship of Commodore Askim, the senior naval officer in the north. They are both ironclads but they mount two 8.2-inch guns and six 5.9-inch guns.' She smiled. 'That is quite substantial, so if your ships have to come, they had better make sure they don't get in the way. *Norge* will be in telephone touch, through shore headquarters, with our Naval High Command. There is also an infantry depot at Elvegårdsmoen here on Herjangsfjord. It contains the stores and reserve ammunition for four infantry battalions, as well as engineering and bridging material for the northern forces. They were mobilized when the Finnish war started. The depot is unoccupied except for a token guard, and if the

Germans come, they must be prevented from capturing it.'

Magnusson was watching her carefully. He felt she ought to be someone's wife or girl friend, waiting ashore with a big smile and a warm room, perhaps even a warm bed, not behaving like a business executive dispensing facts. Even Wren Dowsonby-Smith, efficient as she was, had had more warmth and femininity than this. Though Admiral Cockayne had been wildly wrong in his picture of her, he had been dead right about her efficiency. Even her smile belonged in a boardroom or at a conference table, brilliant, beautiful, but curiously devoid of warmth.

'Norwegians are very pro-British,' she went on briskly. 'And very anti-German, but they don't wish to be brought into the war. However, we are under no delusions but that the Germans will invade us if they feel it necessary. The British and French, too, for that matter, if it suits them.

'We have strong cultural links with the Germans.' Her voice was sharp now, and she sounded increasingly like a schoolmistress lecturing a particularly dull class. 'In the nineteen-twenties, when there was famine in Germany after the first war, their children were sent to live with us. In the thirties, their *wandervögeln* tramped and sang their way through the country, taking photographs and making sketches. They said it was their love of nature but their love of nature was of a curious variety. The sketches they made were of bridges and crossroads, and the picture postcards of the harbour that they brought probably went into files at Army Headquarters, because they were mostly young men with straight backs and fine telescopes. When they came in 1939, they were no longer poor either. They had money – doubtless government money – and they swarmed ashore from the ferry boats. It was only after Poland that we remembered.'

'And now?'

She frowned. 'Norway has practically no military forces. Our fortifications face not Germany but Sweden – because Sweden has always been the traditional enemy – and they were built in the last century. Our coastal defence ships are mostly old whalers armed with popguns and there is no standing army – only a permanent cadre of around two thousand officers and NCOs whose job is not to fight but to train the boys who come every year for their military service. We have built a good home in Norway but we have neglected to put a fence round it to keep out the trespassers.'

She picked up the glass of akvavit, then put it down again. 'The respect for law and order has always been too great. In Norway we spent our time concentrating on good manners. Everybody says "please" and "thank you" and greets you by raising the hat. Great God, how they greet you with the hat up here! Sometimes, the self-satisfaction is too much to bear.'

Magnusson was curiously impressed by her tempestuous truthfulness, but she seemed to see some criticism in his expression and continued angrily. 'You think we are moronic idealists, no doubt! But the Norwegians peopled Normandy and much of England, as well as Iceland and probably even America. Norway has always produced virile people.'

Willie John lifted an eyebrow and she swung round on him. 'You laugh at me! But we are proud of our country and I don't see much pride in England just now! The only casualties you have suffered so far in the war are from the blackout! Your troops are short of weapons, the top age limit for conscription is as low as twenty-six and it is impossible to volunteer. All you do is sing about hanging out your washing on the Siegfried Line. Even the Finns regard your promise to help as overblown!'

She pushed the akvavit aside. '*Ta det bort*! Take it away,' she said. 'I don't like it. I never did.' She bent over the chart again. 'I have counted nine ore ships in the last month. We have also heard that the German whaling-factory ship, *Jan Willem*, is due, and we also expect other German merchant ships.'

'Is that significant?' Campbell asked.

She gave him a contemptuous glance. 'Of course it is significant,' she said. 'The Germans are given to boasting and sometimes, when they have had too much akvavit, they say what they shouldn't. One of them told me that these merchant ships carry arms. Why arms? We are not at war with them! And why should a whaling-factory ship come in here? She is big enough to cope with any weather that exists and she does not carry iron ore.' She paused. 'I have some other news for you, too: *Graf Spee*'s prison ship, *Altmark*, has been reported near the Faeroes.'

Suddenly they were interested. 'Coming here?'

'Perhaps.'

'Does she have *Graf Spee*'s prisoners on board?'

'The Germans think so.'

Magnusson exchanged glances with Campbell.

'Can we get advance information when she's due to arrive?'

'*I* shall give it to you as soon as I get it. Come to my hut in three days' time. By then –' she smiled, her eyes suddenly mischievous – 'like so many other seamen, you will probably be anxious to see me again and it will give you the excuse you need.'

The fog disappeared and the sun returned. The weather was still bitterly cold, however, and the water black in the windless fjord, the atmosphere crystal clear and only slightly warmed by the brilliant sunshine during the day. The snow was dazzling and crunched metallically on the deck under the feet, and the birches and pines were motionless and silent as if afraid to break the strings of diamonds with which the hoar frost had sprinkled their boughs. The buildings of the town had thick caps of snow and, in the sunshine, their façades were ablaze with the glitter of hundreds of icicles.

Ashore there was a strange atmosphere of tension as though everybody was sitting on a time bomb. The Norwegians were nervous and the sailors from the German ships were arrogant. The French and British kept to themselves, avoiding the trouble that the Germans seemed eager to stir up, and occasionally Magnusson met men from *Kosciuzsko* with agony and loathing for the Germans in their eyes. There had been a few brawls, he heard, but the Norwegian police, determined to keep the peace, had set up a squad of men for no other reason than to watch the Poles and keep them apart. The Germans were not watched, he noticed, and they appeared to be taking things easy. Little work was being done aboard *Cuxhaven* and, as Campbell had said, there seemed an enormous number of men in her.

The telegraphists kept up their listening watch all the time. By some means known only to himself Willie John was managing to get a supply of akvavit on board from the shore.

''Tis cold in yon hold, boy,' he complained. 'A feller hass to keep warm just.'

It wasn't long before they caught the German ship transmitting and Willie John reported eagerly, his accent thickening, as it always did when he was excited. 'In code,' he said. 'And, poy, 'tis a plutty powerful set, yon!'

After three days, Magnusson hailed a passing launch and begged a lift ashore. Narvik was an attractive place flanked by the waters of two smaller fjords. The grey rocks and windswept plateaux, cold and forbidding at any time, were covered with a blanket of snow. Both inside and outside the town, great pathways had been cut by snow-ploughs through drifts eight feet deep and the snow was piled in the streets and against the sides of houses, while tall spirals of blue smoke stood straight up in the still air against the white hillside.

Annie Egge's hut was close to the water's edge near the fish oil factory, with the words, *Sjømanns Misjonen*, on a lighted board over the door. The interior was warm and cheerful. Several seamen were drinking coffee and tucking away food with the delicacy of mechanical diggers, and Magnusson recognized German, Norwegian, Swedish and Finnish being spoken. A dance was going on with local girls to partner the sailors, and somehow, after *Oulu*, their very cleanness made them look frightening, with their hair so neat and their lips so red. The men were curiously shy, only the German sailors dancing, strutting round the floor in that curious march that passed with them for a quickstep.

Annie Egge handed him a coffee and suggested he sat in the office with her to drink it. It was a warm room, the walls lined with pitch-pine, the chairs covered with red cushions. On the wall was a text, beautifully embroidered.

Må ej din hand
Så hardna uti striden
Att den till bön ej knäpps,
Då dag år liden.

'It is Swedish,' she said. 'It is a good text for sailors and a better one for our mission. It means "May hands never be too hard-worked to prevent them from being clasped in prayer when day is done." '

'A fine sentiment.'

'Norwegians are a devout people. We are Lutheran, but there are a few Catholics at odd villages down the coast. Up here in the north – ' she smiled – 'there is even talk of trolls, huldrefolk and oskurei.' She paused and pulled out a sheet of paper from a drawer. 'But you didn't come for a talk on religion. Your two ships which left here three days ago have been torpedoed. They were caught within two hours of each other and less than four hours after leaving Norwegian waters. The submarines were waiting for them.'

'Who warned them?' Magnusson asked. '*Cuxhaven*? My radio officer thinks *Cuxhaven* has a powerful transmitter.'

She gave him a cool look. 'I think so too,' she said. 'But I have never seen any sign of it.'

'You've been aboard her?'

'Of course!'

'They didn't invite *me*.'

'I have a few advantages over you. There are a great many men aboard her, and I don't think all of them are sailors. I have known sailors all my life and these don't move like men who follow the sea.'

'What about *Altmark*?'

'We're wondering if she's going straight to Bergen, and from there to Kiel or Hamburg. I'll let you know if I hear. It's thought she passed undetected between the Faeroes and Iceland during the bad weather a few days ago, but she must make a landfall soon, and it ought to be somewhere in northern Norway. We think she will hide during the day and move only at night.'

Nothing had been heard when the signal came.

Willie John appeared in Magnusson's cabin with an excited look on his face. 'We're on the move, boy! The code letter's arrived.'

'Right. We'll go with the tide at first light. There's a fresh wind that'll take us down the fjord.'

Picking up a launch to Narvik, Magnusson sought out Annie Egge again. The hut was being run by the old man who handled her launch, so, discovering where she lived, Magnusson headed through the narrow streets of painted wooden houses up the hill. The night was sharp and frosty and his feet crunched in the packed snow. Small windows glowed yellow through the darkness, and here and there under the overhanging eaves of the bigger buildings he saw the notices that heralded the approaching thaw – 'Beware of falling ice.'

For some reason, he hadn't expected her to have a family, assuming from her temperament and the work she was doing that she lived alone. But the door was opened to him by a man with the weathered face of someone who worked constantly out of doors. With the grave courtesy of the Norwegians he introduced himself as Annie's father and invited Magnusson inside where, almost at once, they were joined by Annie's mother and grandmother. They all had the opal-eyed, northern attractiveness of Annie herself, who was the last to appear.

Magnusson had expected to be able to talk to her alone, but this was clearly going to be impossible as the whole family pressed him to sit down and join them in coffee and cake.

'I was a sailor, once,' Herr Egge said. 'I came here from the Lofotens. My son is a sailor. He is serving his period with the Navy in a patrol vessel stationed at Oslo. We have a nephew who is a sailor too. He is in the coastal defence ship, *Eidsvold*. I think he is fond of Annie.'

It surprised Magnusson to learn that Annie Egge was warm enough to have someone fall in love with her. He glanced quickly at her, but she was pouring coffee, remote, sure of herself, contemptuous of his opinion, and he wondered what it needed to rouse in her emotions other than hatred for the Germans.

Herr Egge was still talking. '*Eidsvold* is due here in Narvik soon. When she comes, we shall have a celebration because my son will be coming on leave soon afterwards also and we shall have the whole family with us.'

They sat around making small talk for an hour until, growing desperate, Magnusson said he would have to go. Annie immediately reached for her coat and the red woollen hat she wore.

'I'll come to the end of the road with you, Captain,' she said. 'The dog needs a walk.'

Outside the air seemed twice as biting as before and they walked in silence until they were away from the house. She came straight to the point.

'It's thought that *Altmark* will not come here now,' she said. 'She's believed to have arrived off Norway and to be doing as we expected and hiding in one of the smaller fjords, or behind one of the islands, and moving only after dark. If she's seen, we expect she'll pose as a warship and claim immunity for the legal limit of seventy-two hours, which is enough for her to pass down the Leads. I think your navy has lost her.'

'I thought I'd better check.'

She gave him a cool glance. 'I suspect you were also checking that I lived alone and were hoping that I did.'

Magnusson shrugged. 'It crossed my mind.'

'Doubtless you would prefer even to be in my bed.'

Magnusson smiled. 'I'm not all that big,' he said. 'I wouldn't take up much room.'

She frowned. 'I do not think you are approaching your job in the right spirit,' she snapped.

'The British were always noted for their lightheartedness.'

'Not with me!' For a while she studied him, then spoke in her usual crisp manner. 'I think your country has let us down,' she said. 'We asked for help. Not once but many times. When the Abyssinian war started and you applied sanctions against Italy, Norway took them seriously and, while your country didn't suffer, we paid dearly for our conscientiousness with rotting fish we couldn't get rid of. When the German tourists came in 1939 we tried to warn you they were here only to take photographs and spread their propaganda. When the war started we arrested German spies and sent them home. What did *you* contribute? You sent us British officials who knew so little Norwegian they could scarcely say "*Skål.*" '

It was a depressing litany of truth and she spared nothing. 'Finally, when we decided something must be done, and told you the Germans were passing information from here to their submarines and asked for help, all we got in return were three amateurs who think war is a game to be played like football. No fouls. No bad language. All very sporting. I'm sorry your captain had a heart attack. Perhaps he would have had more sense of responsibility than you have.'

8

The breeze was blowing from the east as they made sail the following morning. Narvik was outlined against the yellow glow of the sun, with snow-covered roofs and the spire of a tiny church. Behind the hills, trees rose like a dark curtain. Out of the sun the water looked black.

With the anchor aweigh, *Oulu* began to pay off before the wind until, as she gathered headway, the square sails rattled down. As the wind fell aft, the topsails and foresails were sheeted home and the jibs lowered. Glancing up at the arches of canvas above him, with the salt wind on his face, Magnusson found himself thanking God that Cockayne had picked him for this job, because there was nothing so beautiful as a ship under sail.

Oulu was sluggish at first, then slowly she began to edge down the coast towards the sea. As they left Ofotjord, the sea route widened and the mountains fell back. Willie John was on deck as they slipped out towards the Leads, his hangdog face corpse-white from the cold.

'Have you coded the signal?' Magnusson asked.

Willie John turned. 'Did I no' spend half the night o'er the bluidy thing?' he said.

As they left Vestfjord behind them and the humps of the Lofotens began to dwindle, the radio behind the grain sacks in the hold began tapping out its message. Willie John reappeared on deck, pleased with himself.

'Gone, boy,' he reported. 'No problems at all.'

Spring had still shown no signs of arriving in the northern

latitudes, and the land to port – towering walls of black rock and snow, with patches of green and the darker verdure of pine trees – was depressing. There were coils of thick mist about that made visibility uncertain, and a surprising amount of traffic in the Leads.

In the afternoon, the breeze freshened and the weather began to look threatening. Dark clouds swept down on the ship, and as the sea came bubbling into the lee scuppers the air was filled with the clang of ports.

They made a good passage towards Bodø however, though the weather steadily worsened. The sea rose and there was an awe-inspiring sunset with the ship driving towards a wall of storm cloud tinged with ochre where the sun caught it. The sea looked muddy, as if its bottom had been stirred up, and at intervals everything was blurred by squalls of rain and hail, hard and painful as they struck the face. The sun still fought to break through the masses of torn cloud but, finally the royals came in and all hands were called to furl the mainsail.

'Ooh-ah! Eee! Ooh-ah!'

They hauled with all the traditional cries of sailing ship men on a rope until one of the young Finns, trying to take in the fore upper topsail, found that the buntlines and half the robands securing the sail had jammed. Working with the spar pointing at one moment down to the boiling sea and the next upwards to the sky, he lost his grip and the wire leech of the sail started battering him about the head and shoulders. Then a block broke loose and began to flail the air like a bomb on a string, threatening to brain everybody within reach. As it swung, it tore away Willie John's aerials.

The wind was immense now, no longer merely blowing but roaring as if it were trying to tear apart the very atmosphere. By midnight, with only the topsails on her and her upper and lower yards naked and gleaming like old bones in the last of the light, they were hurtling along at thirteen knots.

Because of the weather, they had to head west away from Bodø and the next morning they passed a black-hulled ship hard to see against the mistiness of the land. She lay just to the east of them, heading south through lifting seas. She had a weary appearance as she beat against the weather, a blunt dark shape with the water humping over her bows.

'She's in a hurry,' Magnusson said, watching the distant shape creeping among the islands that hung like a chain of beads off the coast. 'Who is she?'

As the squall passed over them, the clouds thinned and they got a better view of her. Standing by the wheel, soaked by the drizzle in the dim, chill silence, Magnusson stared through his binoculars.

'She looks bloody shifty, too,' he said. 'As if she didn't want to be seen.'

Campbell was standing alongside him, tense and excited, also watching the distant ship through his glasses, and suddenly Magnusson heard him draw in his breath with a thick hissing sound.

'By God, no wonder!' His words burst out of him excitedly. 'It's *Altmark*!'

His handsome young face was alert and lit up with a vision of naval glory, and Magnusson saw that in his hands he had the silhouettes Cockayne had given them.

'You sure?'

Campbell gave him a cold look, as if it were impossible for a naval man – a *real* naval man – to be wrong. 'If she's not *Altmark*,' he said, 'then she's her spitten image.'

They were studying the other ship intently now, and Campbell drew in another sharp breath.

'I can see the name on her stern,' he said; 'I can just make it out.'

Magnusson lowered his glasses. 'Get Willie John up here.'

They were scudding before the wind now and the land was dropping behind them, the strange ship growing smaller as it headed away.

'You going to warn the Home Fleet?' Campbell snapped.

'They've been looking for her for two months.'

'It'll probably give our own game away.' Magnusson was undecided. 'We've been told not to transmit unnecessarily.'

'You're surely not going to allow her to pass southwards unreported?' Campbell was quivering like a terrier at a rat-hole. To him the issue was clear. There was the enemy in the open sea, and nothing else mattered. No man can do wrong who lays his ship alongside an enemy, Nelson had said, and for over a hundred years the Navy had lived by Nelson's precepts.

Magnusson was still trying to make up his mind when Willie John joined in. 'Ye've probably forgotten, boy,' he said coldly. 'We havenae got a bluidy aerial at the moment, anyway.'

'Then get a new one rigged, dammit!' Campbell snapped.

Willie John glared, but Magnusson gestured, faintly resentful that Campbell was usurping his own position as captain.

'Fix it, Willie John,' he said.

Willie John made a real effort but, while his men were used to stringing aerials, they weren't used to doing it on a sailing ship heaving about as *Oulu* was heaving about at that moment. Lumpy rollers were building up behind her and she was lifting stem and stern like a rocking-horse as she raced before the wind. When one of the telegraphists slipped and broke his wrist, Willie John decided enough was enough; they had better wait until the wind had dropped a little.

'For God's sake,' Campbell snapped. 'We're losing an opportunity!'

Willie John gestured at the swinging masts. '*Dhia*, have I no' already injured one of my fellers?' he snapped back. 'What happens if I injure the other, boy? Who's goin' tae work the bluidy sets?'

'For God's sake, what's a man's limb against an opportunity like this?'

Willie John stared at him, shocked, and in that moment

the differences in their backgrounds were glaringly obvious. Willie John, a civilian playing at being part of the Navy, had lived throughout his career by the saying, 'One hand for yourself, one for the ship.' To Campbell, there was no question of self, no question of safety. He had lived *his* life to a background of naval thinking in which a man could never be considered important against the destruction of an enemy.

The atmosphere in the saloon that evening was tense, with Willie John and Campbell staring at each other with hatred in their eyes.

'My God,' Campbell said, 'we'll never get a chance like this again!'

'Why do ye no' *swim* then,' Willie John snarled, his sad, good-natured face distorted by his dislike. 'I'll tie a message tae y'r bluidy leg if ye like. Like a carrier pigeon just.'

As Campbell swung round in frustrated fury, Magnusson pushed him aside.

'Shut up,' he snapped.

'Nelson said – '

'To hell with Nelson! I'm not Nelson and neither are you! I'm an amateur with a lot of experience. You're a professional, so far with very little. We're supposed to be working together. That means using our loaves.'

The morning came with a thin grey light as they passed Vassafjord. It had a narrow entrance, barely visible against the dark mountains behind, but Campbell's sharp eyes were everywhere and it was he who spotted the ship lurking there.

'She's there,' he snapped. 'It's *Altmark* again! She's lying up where she can't be seen during daylight. We should lay alongside her.'

'And get ourselves blown to smithereens for our trouble?' Magnusson said. 'For Christ's sake, talk sense! It's believed she mounts guns. All *we*'ve got are a few small arms in the hold and a crew of Finns who aren't even involved in the war with the Germans.'

He stared at the entrance to the fjord and the dark curved

bulk of the German ship, then swung round to the man at the wheel. 'Bring her about, helmsman. Get the canvas off, Campbell. There's more than one way of killing a cat.'

As the canvas came off, *Oulu* slowed.

'Let go the starboard anchor!'

The German ship was already frantically flashing morse at them as the ship swung, blocking the entrance. Campbell was staring towards her, his mouth twisted in a grim smile, his eyes gleaming with triumph and elation at the prospect of action.

'Dulce et decorum est pro patria mori,' Willie John said solemnly.

Campbell's head jerked round. 'What's that?' he said, only half-hearing.

'It means, boy, that it iss sweet an' fittin' tae die for yer homeland. And it iss also a load of balls! It isnae sweet an' it isnae fittin', and it willnae make much bloody difference tae the war.'

Campbell's eyes glinted. 'You're a novice,' he said. 'A mere bloody novice, motivated by nothing else but self.'

'Dry up,' Magnusson said. 'What about that aerial?'

''Tis finished just,' Willie John growled. 'But we cannae send from this position, boy. They'll pick us up straight away an' blow us oot o' the water.'

'If we bottle them up, what will it matter?' Campbell said.

'We can't bottle them up,' Magnusson said. 'Not here. Not even if we were sunk. The water here's Christ knows how many fathoms deep.'

Campbell looked startled. 'The wreckage in the entrance would stop them!'

'She's three times our length and ten times our weight. She'd brush it aside without even noticing it.'

Turning, his eyes glowing with rage, Campbell stared again towards the bulky shape of the German ship in the entrance to Vassafjord. The rain was falling in a thin veil of blue-grey between them, blurring its shape and making wavery lines of its masts and rigging.

Then his anger burst out of him in a broken-voiced shout. 'There are three hundred Allied sailors aboard her! We should lay alongside her!'

'And do what, for God's sake?' Magnusson snapped. 'For Christ's sake, clear your bloody head of glory and think sense! The thing to do is force her out and leave her to the fleet. She's gone in there to keep out of sight but you can bet your bottom dollar, with us blocking her exit, the one thing she'll decide is that it's safer at sea. And when she's gone, we can signal her course and position. Answer them, Willie John.'

Campbell's mouth opened and shut as if he were about to protest but instead he turned and stared once more at the German vessel in the shadow of the land. She was flashing them again.

'They're askin' what ship we are,' Willie John said.

'Give him our name: *Oulu*, of Mariehamn. Nothing else.'

The signal lamp clattered and the German ship began to flash once more, the pinpoint of light piercing the greyness of the early morning.

'He says,' Campbell translated coldly, 'that we are blocking his exit.'

'I thought that'd worry 'em. Give 'em the same again: *Oulu*, of Mariehamn. Then tell them we have trouble. Just that. No more. Campbell, get the Finns up the mast and make it look as if we *have* trouble. That buntline block did plenty of damage. See that it *looks* as if it did.'

As he'd half expected, with the constant reiteration of their name, the Germans in the fjord were growing impatient, and they saw a launch leave the side of the ship, bouncing in the lifting seas and clinging to the shelter of the land. The German officer who scrambled on board was soaked with spray and very angry.

'Get your ship out of our way,' he exploded.

Magnusson looked blank. 'We are Finnish,' he said in English.

The German switched languages. 'You are blocking our

exit,' he snapped.

Magnusson looked stupid. 'We have trouble.'

'We wish to leave.'

Magnusson shrugged and grinned. 'We think you are sheltering like us,' he said cheerfully. 'Perhaps you would like a whisky?'

The German officer's face grew dark. 'If you don't move your ship,' he said, 'we shall ram her.'

'We have trouble,' Magnusson persisted. 'We have lost the fore upper topsail. We have a man with a broken wrist.' He laid a hand on the German's arm. 'Are you sure you will not take a whisky?'

The German officer brushed him aside and wrenched at the pistol he wore at his waist. 'Get this ship moving,' he repeated. 'Or I'll shoot!'

Magnusson gaped at the pistol, still affecting stupidity. 'We are not at war with Germany,' he said indignantly.

'Get it moving!'

'You have no right to threaten us! We are a neutral ship.'

It was only when the German began to look apoplectic, and Magnusson felt he was in real danger of being shot, that he gave way. Glancing towards the fjord, he saw that the water round *Altmark*'s stern was already being lashed to foam by the movement of her propellers. She was swinging, and if they didn't move soon they could well be rammed.

'Get the canvas on,' he ordered. 'Stand by the anchor.'

As the ship swung, there were yells from the German launch alongside, now in danger of being swamped, and the officer began to dance with rage. The explanations and argument that followed took another ten minutes, the German growing more and more nervous, the light on *Altmark* flashing unanswered. Campbell had already worked out their position and Willie John, his message coded, was standing by the open hatchway that led to the hold, smoking a cigarette and looking even more stupid than usual.

Altmark, Magnusson noticed, had stopped her propellers

again, clearly deciding that ramming was best avoided if possible. She was facing the entrance now, however, and as *Oulu* finally began to move very slowly across the entrance to the fjord, the German officer shoved his pistol away and clambered over the side. *Altmark* was under way again even before the entrance was clear. As she edged past, her wing bridge only feet from *Oulu*'s lower yards, they could see furious faces on the bridge and uniformed men shouting insults at them. Magnusson enjoyed himself shouting them back.

The German ship – bulky, big and black – stopped only long enough to pick up her boat then she began to head south, ahead of *Oulu*.

'Give us time to get clear,' Magnusson said to Willie John. 'Then get a message off. Campbell, give him her course. In the meantime, we'd better vanish. I wouldn't want them to put a German destroyer on our tail.'

In thickening weather, they headed west and south, widening the distance between them and the fleeing German ship. Within an hour, Willie John had got his message off and appeared on deck brighteyed and cock-a-hoop.

' 'Tis gone just,' he said. 'They acknowledged.'

The day was spent on tenterhooks; then the following morning Willie John appeared in Magnusson's cabin, red-faced with triumph and looking drunk.

' 'Tis spotted by a coastal command aircraft she's been,' he crowed. 'Off Bergen. She's bolted intae Jøsingfjord wi' two Norwegian gunboats in attendance. We're gettin' destroyer signals. 'Tis a big diplomatic scene goin' on with the Norwegians sayin' she hass neither contraband nor prisoners aboard and the Navy wantin' tae take her in for examination.'

Campbell's face was thin and bleak with longing. 'I wish I were with 'em,' he said.

Bodø on Saltfjord was not unlike Narvik. A picturesque

town of parallel wooden streets which had grown inland from the little harbour which was its livelihood, it contained only four thousand people. As they lay down the fjord at anchor, they saw more German shipping and a lot of activity at the German consulate.

The whole ship was on edge for news of *Altmark* but the Norwegian radio was saying nothing. When the harbour-master appeared to inspect the ship's papers, he brought with him two Norwegian sailors and a petty officer and seemed considerably more suspicious than his Narvik counterpart. He first inspected the holds, where Willie John had his radios well hidden, and this was followed by an intense examination of the log and the ship's books. The Norwegian's sharp eyes missed nothing. 'You have been to New York?' he said.

'Yah.' Magnusson nodded.

'Like it?'

'All right.'

'Cargo?'

'Jamaica rum. American wheat. I think Finland has more need for them than England.'

'Where's the wheat come from?'

'I dunno. Oklahoma. Somewhere like that.'

The Norwegian was writing industriously. 'How do you spell "Oklahoma"?'

'I don't know.'

'I see your papers are signed by Sven Aanrud, in Marie-hamn. I know him.'

Magnusson's heart sank. The last thing he wanted were chatty reminiscences about people he'd never met.

'Old friend,' the Norwegian said. 'I used to go into Helsinki a lot and I met him there. I didn't know he'd moved to Mariehamn. Any radio on board?'

'Only for the weather forecast.'

'Any photographic apparatus?'

'Why?'

'There's a war on, in case you hadn't noticed. Both sides

94

are anxious to find out as much about us as they can.'

'No. I've got no photographic apparatus.'

'Any passengers?'

'No.'

'Crew?'

Magnusson spread the crew list on the table. 'All Finns. They want to go home.'

'What's *your* name?'

'Magnusson.'

The Norwegian didn't seem entirely satisfied, but Campbell kept the Finns well in evidence and in the end the Norwegian disappeared over the side, frowning heavily but unable to find anything suspicious.

'The buggers suspect *we* radioed *Altmark*'s position,' Magnusson said.

'And we *did*, boy,' Willie John chirruped. 'Did we not just?'

The reason for the intensity of the search became obvious that evening when they learned from a triumphant BBC announcement that *Altmark* had been boarded by the crew of the destroyer, *Cossack*. A hand-to-hand struggle had followed and after several Germans had been killed, the rest had fled ashore. *Graf Spee*'s prisoners had been found battened down below decks and released to the cry of 'The Navy's here!'

Tuning in to Berlin they found the Germans raving with fury, mouthing oaths at British pirates and swearing to take it out on the British prisoners they held, while a great deal was made of Norway's permitting of the incident in Norwegian waters.

'Propaganda, boy,' Willie John said dryly. 'Tae inflame public opinion. They dinnae mention the three hundred British prisoners battened down below.'

The Norwegian radio was curiously subdued because the Norwegian Navy had examined *Altmark* on more than one occasion and had sworn there were no prisoners aboard. They seemed to prefer merely to call the action a 'grave violation of Norwegian neutrality', demand the return of the prisoners with reparations, and hurriedly let the matter drop.

On board *Oulu* the pleasure at the news of the rescue was tempered by an awareness of growing danger. Magnusson began to see their project as something more than merely a half-baked idea thought up by Admiral Cockayne to irritate him. There was no doubt that their appearance outside Vassafjord had forced *Altmark* to sea from her hiding place, and that without it she might have escaped the searching British destroyers. He'd gone into the adventure thinking it a bit of a lark – after all, sailing ships! – but it was no lark. For the first time, he began to understand what Annie Egge had meant. They hadn't cared enough, and a bit of good old-fashioned naval discipline in the future would probably do no harm. He resolved to have a go at it but then he stopped dead; good old-fashioned naval discipline was the one thing that would send the Finns over the side faster than a panicking rat up a drain.

It was now quite clear the Norwegians suspected *Oulu* of being involved in the *Altmark* affair and equally obvious that their interest was being pushed by German consular officials ashore.

Magnusson wished he could contact the British consul for help but he knew that was the last thing he dared do. He would also have felt happier if he could have left Bodø and headed for Trondheim, but he had a strong suspicion by now that when the time came and the signal was received he might well find that the Norwegians were playing a waiting game and, prodded by the Germans, would produce a variety of reasons to keep them where they were. The Norwegians were in no position to dispute things with their prickly and powerful neighbours, and the German record was too dubious to take chances. Even if they were allowed to leave, there was a strong possibility that they'd now be watched every bit of the way and, once they left the Leads at Kristiansund, would be stopped by a German destroyer whose officers would be a great deal more ruthless and a lot more meticulous in their search for a hidden radio.

The stopping of *Altmark* had changed everything. For the first time Magnusson was beginning to feel enthusiasm for the job and almost wished they could put back to Narvik so he could say so to Annie Egge. The pleasure in her face would have made it all worth while and would have wiped out the distaste she felt at their earlier lack of enthusiasm.

Suddenly, however, it also began to seem a good idea either to slip across the North Sea to Rosyth while there was still time, or to make plans to scuttle *Oulu* and beat a hasty retreat across Norway into Sweden. But Bodø was not Narvik and there was no direct rail link with the border. There wasn't even one with Narvik. To reach Sweden they would either have to sail back to Narvik – which could well be dangerous – or reach the railway at Lønsdal forty miles to the south, take the train to Trondheim and another from there to the Swedish frontier.

He was just wondering if he couldn't slip away unnoticed, when he saw the harbourmaster's launch approaching. The Norwegian's face was expressionless.

'How are your repairs going, Captain?' he asked.

'Slowly,' Magnusson said. 'I hope it won't be too long. Things have changed.'

'Sailing ships,' the Norwegian said flatly, 'never change.' He studied his fingernails. 'What about your crew? Don't they find all this delay galling? I heard you had to put into Narvik too.'

Magnusson shrugged. 'We shall probably have to put into a lot of other places as well,' he said. 'But if we reach Mariehamn, then we shall have done what we are attempting to do.'

The Norwegian gave a cold smile. 'I shall have to muster and count your crew before you leave,' he said. 'Too many ships have been leaving men behind lately.'

It wasn't difficult to recognize what was taking place. The

game of official pretence had started. There would be problems over the crews, somebody would decide that stores they had bought had not been paid for, fresh incidents would be devised, and time would be wasted. The Port Health Authorities would insist on checking the galley and discover the ship needed evacuating and delousing. Something would be missing when they needed it and an application would have to be made to the Ministry of the Interior. As a last resort, the Norwegians would wait for one of the crew to go ashore and arrest him, with or without reason, for being drunk and an international incident would be staged. At a pinch, one would even be manufactured round some key figure like one of the officers or the bosun, and a major case drummed up. It wasn't hard to think of ways to hold a ship in port.

It seemed to Magnusson to point to only one thing. The Germans were intent on some sort of action in Norway, and it seemed imperative that they should put to sea and radio the information.

When the code letter was received, however, as he'd half expected, the harbourmaster decided that *Oulu*'s crew was incomplete and that Magnusson needed another three men.

'According to my information,' the harbourmaster said, 'you are about to sail with three men short. There's also –' he gave a little shrug '– a small question of a bill from one of the town's chandlers.'

Magnusson scowled. 'I've bought nothing from anyone.'

'They say you have. It will take a few days to sort this out, you understand?'

The problem of the crew members was sorted out within three days and the chandlers discovered they had debited the wrong ship with goods, but permission to leave was still not granted.

'The war in Finland has started to go badly for you,' the harbourmaster pointed out. 'The Russian offensive on the Karelian Isthmus has brought their forces close to Viipuri and the Finns have evacuated Kovisto. I'm afraid the Russian attacks are wearing down the gallant resistance of your countrymen and the war is coming to an end. My government thinks the Russians might well sweep into Sweden and eventually into Norway, and insists that all Finnish ships be detained until it's discovered just exactly what's going to happen.'

9

The harbourmaster's prophecy proved to be correct. As February changed to March, the Finnish war ended.

The news set the forecastle by the ears. The Finns accused the British of not giving sufficient help, and the British said they'd offered but that the Norwegians and Swedes had refused passage. It ended up in a fist fight, with a black eye for Able Seaman Myers and a cut lip for Astermann. Magnusson decided if they didn't leave soon there was going to be trouble with his crew.

The harbourmaster remained apologetic.

'Other Finnish ships are moving,' Magnusson fumed. 'We've had reports of them.'

The harbourmaster refused to budge. 'My instructions regarding your ship are quite clear,' he said. 'Until I receive instructions from Oslo I cannot change them.'

'May I see your instructions?'

The Norwegian frowned. 'It's not the policy of Norwegian officials to allow government documents to be perused by non-nationals.' He smiled and gestured. 'Of course, you could always approach the Finnish consul. Perhaps *he* will do something to help.'

He spoke with the self-assurance of someone who knew Magnusson would never do any such thing.

As March dragged into April, Campbell seemed subdued by the waiting but Willie John remained as undiminished as ever. He was drunk and singing as he came aboard.

'If it's thinkin' in yer inner hairt
    The braggart's in ma step,
    Ye've never smelled the tangle o' the Isles. . .'

Magnusson grabbed him by the collar and dragged him into the saloon. There he cursed him until Willie John went pale.

'By Christ,' Magnusson snarled, 'if I ever see you drunk aboard again, I'll toss you over the side with a block of concrete strapped to your feet! You're jeopardizing the life of every man aboard with your brainless bloody drinking! From now on you stay sober! Understand?'

Willie John, his body huddled inside a twisted oilskin, stared at him, his face pale, seedy, ugly and worried.

'Lissen, *bodach*,' he said, 'I promise. 'Tis a damn fool I've been just, but I'll swear off it. *A dhuine*, I've never been teetotal – God help me if I had tae be – but I swear this time I will be.'

Fortunately no one had heard the carousing, but the Norwegian officials were not letting up on them and were always ready with another excuse to hold the ship. They had no sooner sorted one out when they found another, and finally the Finns took a hand.

Ek Yervy appeared in Magnusson's cabin, red-faced and smiling as usual, but there was an element of sadness about his big face.

'I vould speak med you,' he said.

'Okay, speak away. What's on your mind?'

Yervy frowned. 'De Finnish boys vant to go home,' he said.

Magnusson pushed a glass forward and Yervy sank the contents at a gulp. 'You mean they want to leave the ship?'

'Dat vot dey say.'

'We can't sail the ship without them!'

Yervy shrugged.

'What'll happen to them?'

Yervy shrugged again. 'Dey seely fockers. Dey go back

to sea, I expect. Dey seamen. You go to sea. You come back. You go to sea again. The tide comes in, the tide goes out. You can't change it.'

'But what about the ship?'

Yervy shrugged. 'Dey have girls, wives, mudders, liddle vuns. Dey are vorried. Russians have drop bombs on Viipuri and Helsinki. Dey want to see dere families.'

It was a disturbing thought and Magnusson tried talking to the Finns, giving it them man to man. But there was a new element of distrust about the ship and the word 'bastard', used hitherto as a term of friendliness, suddenly took on deeper tones. The British and the Finns no longer played cards at night, and the naval ratings no longer taught the Finns uckers. The Finns were tight-mouthed and their smiles were gone. They had been happy to go along with the ship while the chances of returning home were slim but, now that their war was over, they were concerned only for themselves.

The code letter came regularly, but there was nothing they could do, because it was impossible to send the lengthy explanation that the situation required without drawing attention to themselves. Finally, a Norwegian torpedo-boat was stationed within a quarter of a mile of *Oulu* and it was possible, even with the naked eye, to see the radio direction finding apparatus on her bridge. They were being watched and from then on they didn't even acknowledge the exasperated signals that kept arriving.

It was while they were pondering what to do that Magnusson received a letter from Annie Egge in Narvik. It arrived, as arranged, via the *poste restante*, and she was clearly disturbed that they had not left. Obviously she had her informants in Bodø and was growing worried. It seemed to be time to speak to her.

Going ashore, Magnusson telephoned from the office of her contact in the town. He was surprisingly pleased to hear her voice.

'Why haven't you left?' she demanded, suspicious at once

of his motives.

'They're on to us,' he said. 'They're trying every trick in the book to keep us here. It's pretty obvious that pressure's being applied by the Germans. I think they're up to something.'

'So do I.' She sounded nervous and worried. 'I think they have designs on Norwegian independence. I think both sides do. We know you have troops ready.'

'*We* wouldn't come except to stop the Germans coming.'

'That is exactly what the Germans are saying, and I think they might be one step ahead of you, because the cargo ships, *Rauenfels* and *Alster*, and the tankers, *Kattegat* and *Skagerrak*, are due here. Why? *Rauenfels* is carrying ammunition, I've heard, and the tankers are deep-loaded. They will not be discharging here, so why are they coming? Also, we now have news that the whaling factory ship, *Jan Willem*, is due any day from Murmansk. Why is *she* coming? She doesn't carry ore, but she does carry large quantities of fuel oil. Why so much fuel oil suddenly in Narvik? And why does she carry twice her normal crew? I have heard also that Colonel Sundlo, the military commandant here, sympathizes with the Germans and may even be a Nazi himself.'

She'd obviously got good information, Magnusson thought; Cockayne had suspected the same thing.

The following day, 4 April, they became aware of a sudden exodus of German ships from the port. Some of them had been there for some time, some had only recently arrived. As they left Bodø, Magnusson noticed that they all headed north.

Just as suddenly the Norwegians seemed to lose interest in *Oulu* and it was clear that they were beginning to grow nervous. Magnusson stared about him. There was a strong breeze from the east blowing down the fjord, and they could see it stirring the snow from the trees. Behind them was a patch of black forest and he guessed that against it *Oulu*'s hull and spars were virtually invisible.

He made up his mind. Something was on the move and

the mission had now become dangerous. He stood on deck, staring at the shore. There was a smell of mud and crude oil, and a tang of damp and wet pine trees. There were a few fishing boats about, as well as some ships at the coaling jetty, and the line of marker buoys in the fairway dwindled into the distance like the corks on a fisherman's nets. The RDF torpedo boat had moved away a little and he had long since noticed that after generations of peace the Norwegians' discipline was not what it ought to be.

He called the other two officers to his cabin. Campbell was set-faced and stiff but there had been no more querying of orders.

'How about the water tanks?' Magnusson asked. 'Are they full?'

'Practically.'

'Radio frequencies?'

Willie John shrugged. He had kept his promise to stay off the drink, but he was clearly not enjoying it and his face was grey and more haggard than ever. 'Bang up tae date, boy,' he said.

'Admiralty charts?'

'Amended to the minute.'

'Let me have the times of the tides and moonrise and moonset. I'm going to slip away tonight.'

During the day, Magnusson made sure they were seen ashore in Bodø. Leaving Willie John aboard with a grieving expression, he and Campbell spent a lot of time about the bars. Campbell's enthusiasm for the deception was such that he even pretended to be drunk.

'Don't be a damn' fool,' Magnusson snapped. 'You're a rotten actor. Leave it to Willie John.'

Noticing that certain faces kept cropping up regularly about them, he made a great show of mentioning how long they were staying.

'All winter, if necessary,' he said. 'There is only a lost war to welcome us home.'

That night the atmosphere aboard *Oulu* was tense. Magnusson assembled the whole crew and told them what he intended. To his surprise, the Finns, whom he had thought might insist on being put ashore, raised no objections. With the wind whistling down the fjord from the north-east, they would need only a little canvas to carry them to the open sea.

Orders were given quietly. The anchor chain had been shortened; as the tide rose it lifted the ship and the anchor with it, so that the need for the winch was reduced, and the few metallic clinks as it turned were muffled by a sheet of canvas laid over it.

'Up and down,' Campbell called out softly.

'All right,' Magnusson said. 'Loose the topsails.'

Oulu was slowly beginning to slip away down the fjord, the dark patches of forest hiding her black spars, and they had gone a mile without a sign of movement from the Norwegian patrol boat.

'Get the foresail on her and let's have the anchor inboard.'

As the extra canvas filled with wind, *Oulu*'s speed increased. Once clear of Saltfjord, it was Magnusson's intention to continue before it in a westerly direction. Any attempt to continue to do their job in the Leads now was clearly pointless, and they obviously couldn't head further south because they'd be detained at Trondheim as they'd been detained at Bodø and there the Norwegians would probably be more meticulous.

The weather had deteriorated by the time they reached the open sea. The clouds had come down, dark and threatening, and the night was ugly, the seas racing past *Oulu*'s sides as they tore along under shortened canvas.

When morning came conditions were atrocious, with heavy seas and opaque snow squalls reducing visibility to nil. The wind had increased considerably and shifted to westerly so that it grew more and more difficult to make any way westward. By midday, the ship was battling against a gale and great rolling breakers were crashing over the unprotected bulwarks.

In an excess of affection for the Finns for sticking to the ship, Magnusson allowed them rum. There was a lot of laughter and a warm stink of tobacco, spirits, oilskins and unwashed clothes in the forecastle when Willie John appeared, his face gloomy.

'We have tae gae aboot!' he announced.

'What the hell for?'

'We've been told tae watch for *Jan Willem* and yon other German ships.'

They put *Oulu* about, everybody now in a bad temper, but then a staggeringly beautiful sky cheered them all up once more. A bank of black storm cloud edged with bright gold lay across a yellow sea that looked as if it were boiling, and to the south was an enormous rainbow as a squall of rain and hailstones struck the ship. Magnusson glanced at the barometer. It was falling steadily and he saw the air was filling with more huge masses of cloud as the sea surged and lifted.

In the late afternoon the heavy chain to the fore royal parted and they just managed to get the sail in before it blew itself to shreds. As the wind increased and the seas rose higher, *Oulu* began to labour once more. Even as they rushed out on deck they saw the sky darken still further, menacing and ugly.

'*Alle man på däck! Resa upp*! Everybody out!'

The seas were charging up behind them, one after the other, filling the air with slashing spray as their heads tore away from *Oulu*, to leave her in a trough polished and veined like green marble. Below deck, they could hear the crash of crockery and tins from the galley. Squalls of hail that bit the flesh hit them, the chips of ice rattling against the sails and piling up in the scuppers like miniature snowdrifts. The sails were buckling and flogging in the wind, and there were already two men on the wheel.

The spray was coming over the ship now like streamers of grey silk and the shrieking wind made them speechless. To look into it was impossible, and it was difficult to give or hear orders.

The pandemonium increased, and the dim winter light could hardly penetrate the gloom so that they could see no more than a few yards of grey-green sea and white foam which vanished instantly in the spindrift astern. As the wind caught the ship again, she was laid over in a sea that looked like a whirlpool. Four sails had blown out, the foresail flailing in tatters round its belt rope.

The strength of the wind was unbelievable. It seemed possible to lean on it, and its shrieking mingled with the shuddering and groaning of the hull and the roar of water thundering over the deck in torrents. As Magnusson watched, the poop sank into a trough and the whole horizon astern was blacked out by a towering marbled wall of water. Just when it appeared to be about to smash down and inundate them, the ship lifted and the wave burrowed beneath her, so that she slid, yawing, into the next trough. They were now running north-east and had almost reached the shelter of the Lofotens, with the worst of the storm behind them, when Magnusson's attention was caught by a shout from Campbell. The sheets of the jibs had worked loose and the sails were flapping wildly in the wind.

'Down haul! Out and make fast!'

No one wanted to go out on to the jib-boom because it was see-sawing wildly, one moment pointing at the sky, the next down towards the waves. Then Worinen grinned and, jumping the rail, he climbed out with hands that were as familiar with the work as they were with eating and drinking. Astermann joined him.

The ship was tossing in the cauldron of the sea and the two Finns were already soaked to the skin. One hand for the ship and one for yourself, Magnusson found himself saying under his breath. And make sure it's the stronger one for yourself. They were working like madmen, lashing the gaskets wherever they would hold, crawling about the dripping boom with the assurance of men who knew their job.

Magnusson sniffed. The wind had changed and he turned
to Yervy who was on the wheel with Myers. 'Starboard', he
said. 'A quarter-point'.

Slanting rain, driven before the wind, obscured the horizon. A big sea roared and fumed about the deck and every
few minutes another wave hurled itself sickeningly against
the windward side of the ship. Then, astern, he saw a mountain of water leaping towards them like a charge of cavalry,
its forward slope streaked with white.

'Hang on!' he yelled. 'Warn those two forrard!'

But the wind blew the words from his mouth, and the
green monster swept down on them just as the two men on
the boom completed their task. Making fast with stiff fingers, they had finished their lashing and were just turning
to edge back along the footrope when the wave hit the ship
with shattering force. Curling over the side, it hung there
for a moment, then dumped itself on deck with a roar. Men
grabbed for the lifeline, their feet in the air as it swept
across, breaking almost to the mainyards. *Qulu* seemed to
stop dead, shivering from stem to stern, and as Magnusson
glanced round, counting heads, he heard the cook shrieking.
'Man overboard,' he was yelling. 'Two! Two!'

Men dropped from the lifeline like flies off a ceiling and
forced their way to the port rail. There had been no time to
stow the ropes, and buntlines and clewlines lay in confusion
everywhere. Several were flung overboard but there was no
sign of anybody in the heaving hissing sea.

'Who is it? For Christ's sake, who is it?'

Campbell appeared, stumbling through the draining
water, soaked to the skin, his oilskin ballooning in the wind.
There was a cut on his cheek, the blood mingling with the
sea water that ran down his face.

'Worinen and Astermann,' he yelled. 'They were just
coming off the jib boom!'

Men were hanging over the side of the ship now and for
a moment they saw two heads appear. The Finns were close
and Worinen tried to grab the side of the ship. Blood started

as the nails were torn from his fingers.

Astermann managed to clutch a rope, but the ship was hurtling along at a good twelve knots and he was swung against the side, blood on his face. Then he was swept away again, and as the next huge wave roared by, the two men vanished from sight, hidden by the crest. As it thundered on, they reappeared further away, clawing at the air, their mouths open and yelling, but it was impossible to reach them, impossible to do anything but watch them drown.

Wearily they pounded the cast-iron canvas, all of them taking more care than before.

Magnusson found himself cursing Admiral Cockayne. The lark they had been enjoying when they had left Falmouth had finally vanished. Suddenly the venture was grim and ugly.

'The whole bloody idea of using a sailing ship was ridiculous,' he snarled.

'For God's sake,' Campbell said, unexpectedly consoling, his stiff face coated with rime, 'they were the most experienced men on the ship. They'd been in sail all their lives.'

As Magnusson brooded, Yervy appeared alongside him. Magnusson stared angrily at him, expecting confrontation, an accusation that he didn't know his job. Instead, Yervy's voice was gentle.

'I yoost want you to know,' he said, 'dat dere is no blame. All men below know it not you, *Skepparen*. Yoost big sea. Sometimes dey come.'

The relief that flooded over Magnusson made him feel weak.

'I don't think it was anybody's fault,' he said. 'The ship was well under control. It was a freak sea.'

'Yah. Dat is it. A freak sea. De Finns t'ink you good *styrman*. Dey not angry. All same,' he paused and ended with a shrug. 'I t'ink dey leave you soon.'

10

They reached Vestfjord again in the late afternoon of 6 April, sneaking past the pilot station at Tranöy and into the fjord without being seen. The weather was still overcast and the wind was blowing ferociously, driving the low cloud past the mastheads at speed and bringing squalls of snow. In the gloom, they entered the narrow channel to a subsidiary fjord and dropped anchor in the lee of an island at the entrance to a small lagoon, allowing the ship to swing against the dark shadow of the land. They were all nervous and ill at ease, and Magnusson left a look-out on the deck with strict instructions to report if the harbourmaster's launch was seen.

They were close to the shore where they could see a stream clattering down the hillside, a black wriggling snake through the snow. The sea line was littered with fish-boxes that had floated in, shattered fish-baskets, and the usual old shoes, tins and sea-worn timber. The wind continued to blow hard, and the coarse winter grass along the shore bent under its blast. The smell of the snow filled their nostrils with dampness.

Worried by the fact that they were back at Narvik when he wished to be at sea, Magnusson prowled round the ship. During the early evening the wind grew even stronger, setting the halyards slapping and the rigging humming. A furled sail broke loose and started to flap, and he had to send the sullen Finns up to secure it. Then the snow came again, soon developing into a tremendous whirling blizzard that shut out the land.

He was still bothered by the deaths of Worinen and Astermann. He knew it wasn't his fault, but the fact that they
had died in a war that wasn't their own – and because the
ship had been sent north again instead of being allowed to
return to safety – was constantly in his mind.

As he went on deck next morning the day was misty and
grey, and Campbell was pointing at the fjord. Several ore-
carrying tramp steamers were moving out, and passing them
towards the harbour was a big whaling factory ship carrying
the German ensign.

'*Jan Willem*,' Campbell said.

'Well, they were expecting her,' Magnusson said. 'Now
they've got her.'

There was a cluster of houses on the headland, and he
reckoned there must be a telephone by which he could
contact Annie Egge. He was worried about their isolated
position and by the fact that the Norwegians were suspicious
of them. Some officious officer might well decide to inquire
what they were up to and, as at Bodø, find an excuse to
keep them there.

He had himself rowed ashore and found a farmhouse
where the farmer agreed to allow him to use the telephone.

Annie was startled to hear his voice. 'You should be in
Trondheim,' she accused him at once.

'We couldn't go there,' he said. 'The Germans in Bodø
decided we radioed *Altmark*'s position.'

'Did you?'

'Yes. She was spotted by aircraft.'

There was a long pause then the cool voice came back
calmly. 'I think the Germans will use it as an excuse to
violate our neutrality. Why did you return here?'

'We were ordered to. We lost two men in the storm.'

There was a long pause. 'Perhaps it is our fault,' she said
slowly. 'We took many German children into our homes,
but they took advantage of our kindness to spread their evil
gospel, and some misguided people began to think the Ger-

man way was the way that indicated strength and confidence.'

Magnusson couldn't find an answer and for a long time there was silence. Then, even over the wire, he heard her draw a deep breath, almost a sigh, as if she were struggling to control her indignation.

'The factory ship, *Jan Willem*, has arrived,' she said. 'I've been aboard her with magazines and woollen comforts. She would be ideal for refuelling German warships and she has too many men aboard.'

'How do you know?'

'You think because I'm a female I don't know the size of a ship's crew? I've been aboard more ships than I can remember. They say it's because they're working a double-watch system, but I've noticed there are a lot of binoculars aboard and a lot of men who don't look like whalers, and they are very interested in everything that's going on in the town; particularly in *Eidsvold* and *Norge*, which have also arrived since you left. I am wondering if she has munitions aboard too.'

'Can't you get your customs people to inspect her?'

'They have done. They found nothing suspicious. They think she ran into a British warship and came here to dodge her, but I have heard that the Dutch attaché in Denmark has told the Danes that the Germans are about to invade them.'

'What have the Danes done?'

'Nothing. Their old men are as tired and blind as ours. I've also heard that a German troopship was torpedoed this morning south of Bergen.'

'Going where?'

'Where *could* she be going, but to Bergen?' The voice sounded harsh and bitter. 'Many soldiers were rescued by Norwegian fishing boats. They were in full uniform and they said they were on their way to protect us against the British and French.'

'Whose side are you on?' Magnusson asked bitterly. 'Ours

or the Germans?'

'I am on neither side!' she snapped. 'I am on *Norway*'s side. I don't care whether the British beat the Germans or the Germans beat the British so long as Norway is safe.'

There was a long silence and he heard her draw another deep breath. 'I will try to find out what has been heard. It might take a day or two. I'll get word to you.'

It was with a feeling of unease that Magnusson headed back to *Oulu*. The bloody war, he decided, was becoming complicated.

It was snowing again when he climbed aboard, and *Oulu*'s decks were white, her yards picked out against the iron sky. Below, it was cold and the crew wore their thick jerseys and heavy boots. The evening meal seemed worse than ever and Magnusson went to bed because, to his surprise, Campbell and Willie John were playing a game of draughts in the saloon and as it grew noisy he felt he needed to think. Instead he fell asleep immediately.

He was awakened in the early hours by Marques's hand on his shoulder. Seeing the petty officer towering above him, he sat bolt upright, the blankets sliding to the deck.

'What's up?'

'The Finns, sir.' Marques answered him calmly. 'They've gone. They lowered the starboard boat and went.'

'Didn't the watchman see 'em?'

'They hit him with a sock filled with sand. He's just come round.'

'Where are they heading?'

'Djupvik, he thought, sir. They'll be there by now.'

'Is it because of Worinen and Astermann, Chief?'

'Shouldn't think so, sir. They just want to go home.'

'Then why the hell didn't they leave us in Bodø?'

Marques shrugged. 'I suppose because in Bodø there's no railway to Sweden. Narvik's connected directly by rail. It's only twenty miles to the frontier, and from there you can get directly to the Baltic coast and pick up a connection into

Finland.'

Magnusson sighed. 'Well, thanks, Chief,' he said. 'Call Mr Campbell and roust out the rest of the crew.'

As they appeared on deck, blinking and sleepy-eyed, scratching at beards and shrugging hastily into jerseys, lumber jackets and gloves, Magnusson explained what had happened.

'We've still got enough to handle her,' Campbell said, undaunted and itching as always to do his duty. 'You and me, Marques and four seamen. Willie John and the telegraphists can give us a hand on deck while the rest of us handle the sails. There are enough to get us to sea.'

Magnusson glanced at the sky. The wind was still ruffling the water and sending it slopping against the sides of the ship. The shrouds and stays were whining and occasionally gusts of spray were whipped over the bow and low clouds scudded over the mastheads.

'Not in this weather,' he said. 'Not without the Finns.'

During the next afternoon, the snowstorms grew fiercer. Nobody came near them but Magnusson wasn't kidding himself it was because of the weather.

Willie John confirmed his suspicions. 'We're pickin' up traffic from the direction o' Kiel an' the Jade River, boy,' he said. 'The German radios there are chatterin' like guests at an Irish weddin'. There iss somethin' in the wind.'

They watched throughout the day, their eyes nervously on the weather. By evening the wind was still blowing from the south-west, noisy and fierce, sending the spray across the ship to frost the decks with ice. Towards midnight, however, it dropped a little and Magnusson guessed that if it fell away completely there would be fog, and he was hesitant to take a short-handed ship to sea in it.

'We'll go tomorrow morning,' he said. 'As soon as we're clear of the Lofotens, we'll radio and hope to Christ the Navy does as it promised and comes to the rescue.'

They were gloomy as they ate their evening meal.

'I didn't think it would turn out this way,' Magnusson said, and he realized he was disappointed.

He arranged for a look-out to be on deck all night in case the Norwegians started to investigate. If the harbourmaster appeared, he was prepared to up-anchor and chance it.

He was awakened in the early hours by Myers breathing in his face.

'Sir,' he said in an urgent whisper. 'Destroyers!'

Magnusson sat up. Myers looked scared and Magnusson's heart leapt hopefully.

'Whose?' he asked. 'Ours? Or Norwegian?'

Myers did a curious little embarrassed shuffle and coughed to clear his throat. When he spoke again, his voice came harshly and twice as loud.

'Shouldn't think neither, sir,' he said. 'Not flying the bloody swastika.'

PART TWO

Southwards

1

As Magnusson hurried on deck, he was joined by Campbell.
Most of the ship's company were lining the rails, staring
across the misty water. A flotilla of large destroyers, in line
ahead, was just passing the end of the inlet, heading eastwards into Ofotfjord towards Narvik. Their navigation lights
were burning but obscured occasionally like the lighthouse
on the point by the flurries of snow. At their sterns flew the
red, white and black swastika ensigns of Nazi Germany.

'They must be invading,' Campbell said.

The Germans, intent on what lay ahead, seemed not to
notice *Oulu* against the trees. Through his glasses Magnusson could see the officers' faces all staring down the fjord.
Near Ramnes, one of the ships slowed to a stop and a boat
went ashore loaded with sailors and men in the heavy pot-
shaped German helmets.

Opposite Djupvik were the two small converted trawlers,
Michael Sars and *Kelt*, on outpost duty, and one of the
German destroyers broke out of the line. As it approached
the Norwegian ships they saw a string of flags flutter to her
yard-arm.

Willie John appeared from below in a hurry. 'The Norwegians are radioin' tae base in plain language, boy,' he
said. 'They're sayin' they're in touch wi' German destroyers!'

The German ship had closed with the Norwegians now,
and they could hear the iron voice of a loud hailer coming
in fits and starts on the wind. As the other destroyers van-

ished from sight round the headland by Djupvik, they saw a puff of smoke burst from one of its guns and a few seconds later heard the dull thud echoing across the narrow waters of the fjord.

'If this isn't an invasion I don't know what it is.' Magnusson was frowning, wondering what the hell his job was supposed to be now.

They were still watching the German destroyer alongside the Norwegian trawlers when they heard another shot coming from beyond the curve of the land.

'Must be *Eidsvold* or *Norge*!'

A red Very light drifted above the headland, and soon afterwards they heard four heavy thuds and a thunderous rolling explosion. Almost at once a cloud of brown smoke rose over the trees. There was the sound of gunfire; someone somewhere was putting up a fight. The German destroyer had now left the Norwegian trawlers and was heading up the fjord. She was just picking up speed when they saw a sailing ship creeping through the curling banks of mist along the south shore close to them, laying as near to the wind as she could so that her canvas was on the point of flapping. Her top masts were missing but, as though to defy the Germans, she flew at the yard-arm the red and white flag of Poland. It was *Kosciuszko*.

The German destroyer spotted her at the same time and leaned over to the water as she swung on to a new course. Closing to within a few hundred yards of the Polish ship, she opened fire at once without challenging. She was at point-blank range and the shell struck the deckhouse amidships.

There was a blinding flash and *Kosciuszko* seemed to bulge in a shower of splinters. Men were dashed aside like lead soldiers, the deckhouse disappearing in a whirl of flying planks. A second shell struck the starboard bitts, and fragments flayed the deck and tore sails to shreds. The third shell struck her at the base of the foremast, bringing down spars and rigging in a tangle of wires and ropes. The fourth exploded amidships, and more planks flew through the air to splash into the water. Immediately, flames began to spread with lightning speed, running up the shrouds and setting light to the furled sails. In no time, tar, tallow and grease had caught fire and the whole ship appeared to be ablaze.

The mainmast began to bow forward, slow and dignified, with the yards dipping even further to hang suspended before they too crashed down. Men were running along the deck, shouting hoarsely through the smoke as the Germans moved in even closer and swung broadside-on so that they could fire with everything they possessed.

The Poles were still trying desperately to sail their ship and for a little longer she continued to move forward, a mass of wreckage trailing alongside, even as the shells were tearing into her hull. Then the remains of the foremast and mainmast fell, the canvas draped over her side, smoke curling up as further shell bursts set it alight.

There were still a few men on their feet, hacking and cutting, trying to tip the flaming mass into the fjord. But the ship seemed to be littered with dead, the wheel gone and the masts and bulwarks all beaten flat. By the time another salvo had splintered the stump of the foremast, *Kosciuszko* had settled until her decks were almost awash and the surviving Poles reduced to shaking their fists at the hated enemy. One of them had produced another flag and stood waving it defiantly until a shell lifted him into the sea, the flag settling over him like a shroud until the weight of the water in its folds carried it under and him with it.

By now there was virtually nothing left of the ship and the Germans turned their machine-guns on the bobbing heads in the water, apparently determined to extinguish even this feeble flame of resistance to their Polish conquest and not let a single man live.

At last the firing died down because there was nothing left to fire at. The German ship moved closer to the burning wreckage and a final shot sent it to the bottom. Then she swung away and headed down the fjord towards Narvik.

Silently, the men on the deck of *Oulu* stared at the debris-littered fjord. Then they realized there was a single man swimming in the water, trying to make his way towards them, crying feebly as he lifted an arm to attract their attention.

'Lower the boat,' Magnusson said. 'Have him out!'

The Pole was a pale-faced, bullet-headed boy of about nineteen and for a while he sprawled on the deck gasping and shivering like a stranded fish. Then he sat up, his eyes blazing, the blood dribbling from a cut on his forehead to mingle with the water on his face, to shout some unintelligible Polish watchword and shake his fist at the retreating destroyer.

'Tadeuz Wolszcka,' he finally introduced himself. 'Cadet.'

Magnusson drew a deep breath, almost unable to speak for his loathing for the Germans.

'Find him clothes, Campbell,' he managed. 'And sign him on. We have one more hand.'

As he turned away, he saw the German destroyer had swung back on her course and Willie John's voice broke in on his thoughts.

'She iss signallin', boy,' he pointed out quietly. 'She says she iss sendin' a boat.'

As the German ship drew closer, Wolszcka glared at her, his eyes red with hatred.

'Get him below deck, Chief,' Magnusson said to Marques. 'And keep him out of sight or they'll probably take him and shoot him out of hand. And have a club handy because if he gets a chance he'll break out and try to murder a few of them.'

The German officer who stepped aboard was tall and fair and very correct. Licking his lips nervously, Magnusson was glad he hadn't shaved and that he was wearing an old jersey and a stained donkey jacket.

'*Guten Morgen, Herr Kapitän,*' the German said.

Feigning stupidity, Magnusson answered in Finnish.

'Magnusson,' he said. '*Förste styrman.*'

The German frowned and tried again in German. Magnusson frowned back at him and answered stubbornly with the same words. Then he pointed at Campbell. '*Andre styrman,*' he said. He gestured at Willie John. '*Tredje styrman*' – at Marques ' – *timmerman*' and at Myers – '*doonkey.*'

The German was still frowning. 'You speak English?' he asked.

It gave Magnusson a lot of pleasure to force him to use the language of the enemy.

'A little,' he said.

'What ship are you?'

'*Oulu*, of Mariehamn. We try to go home. That is all. *Skepparen* dead in America. We have cargo of grain for England but we decide perhaps Finland want it more.'

The German smiled. 'That is a very good idea,' he said. 'We are in command here now, not the Norwegians. They were stupid enough to try to resist. All they got for their trouble was the loss of two of their ships. We sank them with torpedoes.' He sniffed. 'They were destroyed at once. They were only old ships. Perhaps you will do well to take heed of what happened and do as we tell you.'

Magnusson's hatred boiled inside him. 'If we don't?'

'Then we must take measures to see that you do.'

'As you did with the other ship?'

'They were only Poles.' The German spoke as if the Poles were an inferior race fit only to be exterminated like cockroaches. 'Jewish-run. Germany has no time for Poles. How many crew have you?'

'Ten. Yesterday we have twenty-two but they leave.'

'Why?'

'They go home to Finland by train.'

The German smiled. 'I think they have much to learn from Germany,' he said. 'We are here to protect the Norwegians from the British and the French. It will be done peacefully. We expect the Norwegians to help us.'

'*Ikke alle hester blir solgt,*' Magnusson said.

'What does that mean?'

'It's a proverb. Not all horses get sold. Perhaps this one won't.'

2

Annie Egge watched the Germans arrive.

The day before, when she had read in *Aftenposten* that the British and the French had informed the Norwegian government that mines had been laid in Norwegian waters to prevent them being used by German ships, her heart had sunk. Norwegian neutrality had received a nasty knock.

There were rumours of a German invasion in the paper and she knew it was more than possible now. Then the radio had given the news of men and horses being washed up on the shore from the sunken troopship south of Bergen. If there was a troopship off the Norwegian coast, where could it have been going but to Norway? Her father's reaction to the mine-laying – 'Now look what they've done! They've dragged us into a war!' – only irritated her because he seemed not to realize that the Germans were already making their preparations.

That night there was a blackout and the air-raid sirens sounded, but there were no aeroplanes and the lights came on again quickly. She went to bed early, tired of her father's complaints and desperately worried about the news of the torpedoed German troopship. They had its name now, *Rio de Janeiro*, and she took the trouble to look it up in the shipping register. It told her nothing very helpful but she knew it implied something terribly important. An exceptional amount of iron ore had been passing steadily through the town for months and at that moment there were twenty-five ore ships in the harbour, most of them German. She had also heard that leave had been stopped for *Norge* and *Eidsvold*, so that it was obvious the naval authorities were also suspicious and on edge.

Early in the morning, she was awakened by the crash of gunfire. Then the windows rattled as the house shuddered under a tremendous explosion, and she heard snow, dislodged by the vibration, slide heavily from the roof and thump to the ground outside. Dressing quickly, she snatched up a heavy coat and her woollen cap and gloves and was heading for the door as her father appeared, half-clothed, her mother close behind him.

'Something's happened,' he said.

Her reply was tart. 'Of course something's happened. Something's been on the point of happening for ages but everybody's been too blind to see it.'

He didn't seem to hear her. 'It must be from the iron company,' he said.

'Of course it's not from the iron company,' she snapped. 'It's from the sea.'

They moved to the window and, snatching back the curtains, saw that the dawn was heavy with fog. The lightening sky was also obscured by a looming shadow and she realized it was a vast column of dark smoke that curled and coiled over the water down the fjord not far from the town.

'Is it war?' her mother asked.

'No.' Her father's tone was one of certainty. 'It can't be anything to do with us. German ships must have been chased into the fjord by the British.'

Annie hadn't the slightest doubt in her own mind what it was and, cramming the woollen cap over her hair, she headed for the street. It was snowing hard as she slammed the door behind her.

The sky was just beginning to grow paler as she made her way to the centre of the town. As she moved down the narrow street, a soldier from the guard post on the peninsula ran past shouting that the shooting was from Germans. Suddenly the cold seemed twice as fierce and she shuddered inside her clothes.

As she reached the Ore Quay there was another explosion that seemed to rock the street and she saw a second huge column of brown smoke rise into the sky. As she began to run, a man pulled her into a doorway. 'Wait,' he said. 'There's shooting. It's not safe!'

'What's happening?'

'German ships! They've blown up *Eidsvold* and now *Norge*. They're putting troops ashore in Herjangsfjord.'

'Well, why don't we stop them?' she demanded. 'There are five hundred men at the Elvegårdsmoen depot.'

The man merely shrugged. 'The Germans are already coming into the harbour,' he said. 'They'll be here soon.'

She stared over the roofs at the rising smoke. Her cousin in *Eidsvold* was a fair boy scarcely out of his teens who spent all his time ashore with his eyes on her, mutely adoring, and she guessed he would not have survived. He was a born victim, gentle, kind and shy. In any rush for safety he would allow himself to be pushed aside. She sighed, wondering how his parents would take it. They had always had high hopes for him and had set their hearts on a match between them.

As the firing died down, she moved cautiously towards the waterfront near the Post Pier. There seemed to be soldiers everywhere, most of them in German uniforms watched by a few Norwegian troops, mainly boys. She ran forward and grasped the arm of one of the Norwegians.

'Why aren't you using your rifles?' she demanded.

'We've had our orders.' The boy glared at her, a look of shame and misery on his face.

She stared about her, bewildered and as ashamed as the soldier. Middle-aged men were standing with their hands in their pockets, watching the Germans.

'What's happening?' she asked.

The man she addressed spat out a cigarette but seemed curiously unmoved. 'They came ashore and organized a truce. They're using it to post machine-guns. The German officer said "I come to greet the Norwegian army." I heard him.'

She stared at the Germans. They were placing weapons to cover the Norwegian gun posts, shouldering the leaderless Norwegian boys out of their way.

She ran to a Norwegian sergeant. He was a grizzled, middle-aged man who was glaring fiercely at the Germans.

'Why don't you shoot them?' she demanded.

He brushed her aside. 'I've got my orders.' His frown deepened. 'Or rather, I've not got my orders. No one seems to be running the show.'

'But what about the officers?'

'They're waiting for the colonel. And he's too old and likes the Germans, anyway. They say he's on the telephone to headquarters now.'

'Why? You don't have to ask permission to fire on invaders!'

Her voice had risen in her anguish and one of the German NCOs came towards her and pushed her away roughly.

'Go on,' he said in Norwegian. 'Get away!'

'You speak our language,' she spat. 'I expect you learned it here as a child when you were given shelter after the other war!'

The German looked uneasy but he continued to push her away. Inspired by her fury, a few of the watching men started to catcall and jeer and the German unslung his gun and began to jab at her with it.

An officer appeared, shouting, 'Go back to your homes! There is nothing here for you! Move!' When there was no reaction, he began to grow angry and drew his pistol. 'If you don't move I shall fire!'

As his men began to unsling their weapons, the Norwegian she had first spoken to pulled her away.

'Come on,' he said. 'Or they'll fire!'

'And you're afraid?' she snapped. 'I'm not.'

But she went nevertheless, depressed, miserable and shocked, unable to see what she could do.

German troops were occupying the railway and, as she neared the water's edge, she was stopped again by a man with a rifle. More Germans, many of them still green from seasickness, their uniforms stained by sea-water and vomit, were climbing ashore. The snow was coming down again now, plastering their greatcoats.

She looked at her watch. It was only six a.m. Out in the harbour, she could see the smoking wreckage of *Eidsvold* and *Norge* floating on the water, flames still flickering about it. A few rowing boats and small fishing vessels circled it, picking up living and dead. Around her, people were still rubbing their eyes, asking themselves where their northern troops were and knowing that no other troops had been mobilized. The crowd included bewildered children and a few angry students.

'I offered to fight,' one of the students was shouting. 'I offered my services straight away but they turned me down because I've had no training! How can I have training if they won't accept me?'

'*Pretend* you've had it,' Annie snapped at him. 'You can always learn after they've given you a rifle.'

In the market-place, a large open quadrangle faced by the old post office and telegraph building, people were gathering. The bronze lamps on the bridge had once been the pride of the town until it was discovered they'd been purchased secondhand from a town in the south which had bought better and larger ones and the pride had disappeared. The railway tracks ran under the bridge, fanning out towards the harbour, the ore in huge conical heaps between them. She could just see the steamers in the harbour but could hear none of the roaring rumble of ore streaming into the hulls which normally went on night and day.

There was a sound from the people around her like a sigh, and she saw that German swastika flags were being run up over the telegraph building and the town hall. One of the Germans was trying to commandeer a bicycle from a messenger boy, and the boy was fighting back. 'It's mine,' he yelled.

'The Führer says we take what we need,' the German shouted. 'If you want to argue, go and see the Ortskommandant.'

Norwegian soldiers were being hustled into the market-place now, but, as Annie watched, a few managed to slip out of the column and vanish between the houses. It wasn't much but it lifted her heart because, like the messenger boy's spirited defence of his bicycle, it indicated that somewhere there was still the will to resist.

The Germans were forming up now, carrying strange weapons she had never seen before, grenades dangling from their waists. They were marching with a grim bearing and the precision of expert, experienced troops. The Norwegians watched them, numbed, as they placed guards on the station, the quay and the principal buildings. Following them angrily, she wondered wildly why nobody had thought of shooting Colonel Sundlo, the Norwegian commander. He had always been known as a reactionary with a sympathy for fascism, a short, stocky man with a formless face who wrote for the newspaper on the danger of communism.

Tears of humiliation and fury trickled down her cheeks. The long decades of peace had turned the army into an inefficient and inflexible fighting machine, and in recent years military men had even come to be hated by the working classes so that it was difficult to be an officer.

More Germans were climbing ashore at the piers and jetties, and began to march into the square after the others. They were carrying placards in Norwegian, saying 'Be calm. We come to help you against the English'. Roused by the shooting, people were peering sleepily through the windows of their houses into the thickly falling snow, clearly attaching greater importance to the machine-gunners than they did to the placards.

A lorry filled with soldiers with slung rifles rumbled past. A machine-gun poked out of the rear from among the hard-muscled, stony-faced men. A pro-German youth acted as self-appointed guide, complete with home-made armband and, as they passed, a chic, blonde woman whom Annie had known for months as a German sympathizer waved and smiled. German flags were floating from all the public buildings now and soldiers were billeted in the Realskole, watched by the infants who should have been going there later in the morning.

For a long time, she wandered about aimlessly, almost as if she were torturing herself by the sight of the Germans, then she decided it would be a wise move to clear her office. But the Germans had already taken over the building as a billet and she was refused admission. For a quarter of an hour she argued, knowing that in her desk there were documents which showed without doubt that she had passed information on to the British, but the German officer refused to allow her to enter, like the rest of them nervous and uncertain of what the Norwegians might decide to do.

Returning home, she found her father listening to the radio, his face anxious.

'The Germans have invaded Denmark,' he said. 'Their army didn't fight.'

'They've invaded Norway too!' she snapped at him. 'Here! In Narvik! And *our* army didn't fight either! We should be ashamed!'

He looked at her with the same bewildered expression she had seen in the town, and she was sorry for her anger because he was obviously at a total loss what to do.

'They're in Oslo, Kristiansand, Trondheim, Bergen and Stavanger too,' he said, 'and they seem to have taken over the radio.'

'Then try to get Stockholm! The Swedes will give us an unbiased picture.'

The triumphant braying of the Germans had not mentioned that in other places they had suffered heavy losses. At Oslo, the out-of-date fortress of Oscarsborg had even managed to sink the German cruiser, *Blücher*, with the loss of a thousand men, while the pocket battleship, *Lützow*, had been put out of action. There was a faint trace of triumph in the Swedish announcer's words, as if the Swedes, no less vulnerable than the Norwegians, enjoyed seeing the German plans go wrong.

The British radio was more wary, giving little away, and offering no indication that they were about to send help. It seemed desperately important to find out what was happening elsewhere, but everyone was as bewildered as she was and the picture she put together was one of confusion and complete surprise.

Her mother was in tears, preparing to go to the hospital to give what help she could. It was packed with dead and wounded Norwegians.

'Germans, too,' she said.

'They should let *them* die,' Annie spat.

'They're behaving quite well.' Her mother seemed to be trying to excuse the Norwegians' own behaviour. 'They had no Norwegian money for the cab drivers who took them to the Grand Hotel, but they promised they'd pay all right.'

'*They murdered Norwegians!*' Annie snapped.

By evening, to her surprise, the first signs of resistance were being shown. The sweet-starved Germans were buying up all the chocolate and the shops were retaliating by hiding their stocks, while bakers were claiming they had no flour and were not baking any more pastries. But the radio said that an unknown politician with a doughy face and a total lack of humour by the name of Quisling had been made prime minister, backed by the Nazis, and that the invaders were already striking out in requisitioned buses to the unsubdued districts.

There was still no sign of help coming from anywhere and, sick at heart, feeling that somehow Britain ought to have followed the Germans down the fjord and wiped them out, she began to wonder what she ought to do. Her days in Narvik were numbered. The Nazis had never shown much mercy to people who opposed them and she knew she had to get away.

But where to?

Rumours were already coming in that Norwegian troops stationed further north were moving on the town, but the snowstorms were hampering their movements and already the Germans were setting up road-blocks and were in control of the railway. She wondered if there were any chance of one of the British ships escaping, and, as she used her binoculars, she remembered *Oulu* in the entrance to the fjord. As far as she knew, the Germans hadn't yet noticed her.

Her father was standing by the telephone when she returned home and her mother was sitting on the settee, weeping. Her grandmother had her arm around her, comforting her, but was dry-eyed and frozen-faced.

'What's wrong?' she demanded. 'Have the Germans been?'

Her father lifted his head. 'Your brother Jens's ship has been sunk. The Germans blew it up. One of the petty officers who got ashore telephoned. Nothing's known of Jens.'

She tried to comfort her mother but somehow she seemed already to belong to a different world. Numbed by what had happened, shaken and afraid, the only thought in her mind was still that she must go. After a while, she went to her room and packed a haversack; then returning, she kissed her parents. Her mother and grandmother wept a little but they didn't argue. As she left the house, the snow was coming down faster than ever. Making her way into the town, she saw what seemed to be hundreds of Germans, standing in groups everywhere, clutching their weapons, their eyes shaded by their helmets in the gloom. A few lost-looking Norwegians still wandered about but, for the most part, now that the shock of the invasion had sunk in, they seemed to have disappeared to their homes and were staying out of sight. One or two shops were open, trying to do normal business, but there were no customers and most of them were already closing their doors. The harbour seemed to be full of ships. The huge *Jan Willem* towered over everything, and everywhere she looked there seemed to be a German destroyer – heavy vessels, more powerful than anything Norway possessed – and picket boats were crossing and recrossing the dark waters of the harbour to the quay.

The wreckage of *Eidsvold* and *Norge* still lay in the water, and a mat of small boats still circled it, searching for survivors. She noticed that none of them was German.

She seemed to be looking at her home for the last time. To her surprise, the place didn't seem to have changed. Vaguely she had felt it would look different. But, apart from the Germans, it was exactly as it had been before, throughout all her life. Yet it *was* different, and she knew there was nothing there for her any more.

Sighing, she hitched the pack over her shoulder and, walking swiftly to the stop near the Ore Pier, caught the bus to Djupvik.

3

During the day *Oulu*'s radio picked up the broadcasts from Oslo, and soon afterwards, learning by morse from a passing German ship that the Germans had taken over Narvik, they started making plans to slip away in the night.

'It's going to be difficult with only ten men,' Campbell said.

'Eleven,' Magnusson said. 'We've got the Pole. He's just been round the world on a training ship, for God's sake! If *he* doesn't know what to do, nobody does. The experts can do the work aloft and the amateurs can pull the ropes. You'd better gen them up on what's a hoist and what's a downhaul.'

The topsails were bent on and furled, as if for a neat harbour stow, with the heavy weight of the sheet taken as far in towards the mast as possible. The body of the sails was then hauled up and beaten down in a neat packet on top of the yard, and the rope gaskets passed round the sail and secured ready for easy slipping.

The Polish boy, Wolszcka, worked like a madman, as if by so doing he could cleanse his system of its loathing for the Germans. His eyes black with hatred, he seemed to move twice as fast up the rigging as everybody else.

Towards evening a small trawler appeared, creeping almost shiftily towards them along the line of the shore. Opposite Ramnes, it anchored and a boat was lowered. Three men climbed into it.

'That's Vinje, the harbourmaster,' Campbell said, watching with narrow eyes.

Magnusson frowned, wondering what was coming. 'Get all the non-Finnish speakers aloft out of the way,' he ordered. 'And tell Willie John to send his radio operators with 'em. They can make it to the main spars, surely to God.'

There were two Germans in the boat, one of them an officer, one a petty officer. The harbourmaster's expression had changed; the official face he wore was bleak now and angry.

As they climbed aboard, Magnusson met them.

'I am to inform you,' Vinje said stiffly, 'that you will be allowed to leave, but that your departure is to be delayed for a day or two. It may be necessary to search you.'

Magnusson brought out the bottle of whisky and offered it round as he ushered them into the saloon. The petty officer remained by the ladder, fascinated by the men on the main spars above his head.

The Norwegian was bitter at what had happened and didn't hesitate to let it show in his expression. 'Are you still intending to head for Mariehamn?' he asked.

'That's the idea,' Magnusson said cautiously.

'Will you be able to get away?'

Magnusson eyed him warily. 'It would be better with a few more hands.'

'With more hands, you could make a quick getaway?'

Magnusson sensed that he was trying to find out something. 'Depends on the hands,' he said. 'This isn't a ferry. It's a sailing ship.'

Vinje nodded, slapping his gloves against his thigh. 'I must inspect your hold,' he said.

'Why?'

'It is normal.'

Hoping to God Willie John's men had left the radios well hidden, Magnusson led the way. The German seemed to be enjoying the whisky and Magnusson pushed the bottle closer. The German smiled.

'It is dirty in the hold,' Magnusson said in English. 'You

understand?'

The German nodded and pointed at the deck. 'I stay here,' he said. 'With the whisky.'

Opening the hold, the Norwegian began to climb down the ladder. Halfway down, as Magnusson was about to follow him, he looked up.

'Stay there,' he ordered, and Magnusson stood on the ladder with his head and shoulders above the deck.

'When I speak to you, bend down and point,' Vinje said quietly. 'If the German petty officer comes near, we are talking about the cargo of grain. You understand?'

Magnusson nodded.

'You are Finnish and neutrals,' Vinje went on. 'The Germans will not stop you leaving. They already have enough on their hands. They have the town, but they also have ten destroyers here all in urgent need of oil, and they are expecting the British to retaliate. You understand?'

Magnusson bent down and pointed. 'I'm getting the drift,' he said.

'Do not put into any other Norwegian port. They might try to hold you.'

'To hold a Finnish ship could provoke an international incident.'

Vinje's face became red and angry. 'What do you call the occupation of Narvik? They had the place within half an hour of the expiration of their ultimatum and only three quarters of an hour after it was handed in.'

Magnusson bent and indicated the sacks, talking loudly in broken English and explaining how it was stowed.

The Norwegian's face was still angry. 'Norway is full of small sailing vessels,' he said. 'I can guarantee you plenty of help. Every Norwegian knows all about sail. I myself was in sail before I joined the Navy and I know of three others in Narvik at least.'

Magnusson smiled. 'And *you* would be the help?'

The Norwegian's face was bleak still, but it was softening. 'I do not wish to remain under German domination.'

Magnusson bent again, talking loudly about the cargo once more, then he dropped his voice. They were fiddling about like dogs round a lamp-post, trying to decide which should lift his leg first. 'I'll tell you something,' he said quietly. 'We aren't heading for Mariehamn. We're heading for Rosyth in Scotland. And this isn't a Finnish ship. It's a Royal Navy ship, and I need your help as much as you need mine.'

The Norwegian managed a thin smile. 'Just as we suspected,' he said. 'It was you who directed your ships to *Altmark*, no?'

He began to climb the ladder. 'I will come back,' he said. 'Watch the point after dark. I will flash a light. Can you put a boat in the water to pick me up?'

'Yes. But no women, children or cripples. Only able-bodied men who can work, and carrying no luggage.'

'Very well. Now, I must go. We've talked long enough about your cargo. They'll be suspicious.' Vinje raised his voice. '*Det var nok i orden alt sammen.*'

The German officer had just reappeared from the saloon as the Norwegian emerged.

'*Alles ist in ordnung?*' he asked.

'*Jawohl. Alles.*'

Magnusson watched silently as they headed for the ladder, collecting the petty officer en route. With the boat heading back towards the trawler, he called Campbell towards him.

'We have the hands we need,' he said quietly. 'Norwegians who wish to leave. Sailing ship men.'

The BBC early evening news was full of the day's events. Having occupied Denmark without interrupting their stride north, the Germans had control of several points on the Norwegian coast. But the Norwegians were beginning to resist strongly and the king, the government, the country's gold reserves and the Foreign Office papers had vanished northwards. The Luftwaffe was flying into Sola near Stavanger and it was expected that when the king and the government were found they would be bombed.

During the day *Cuxhaven* left, towed by a Norwegian tug flying the German flag. They watched her pass, her yards shortening as she came beam-on to them. There were no waves from the Germans, and the binoculars that studied them seemed to gleam with heavy suspicion. The deck was singularly empty of crew and they guessed that many of the men she'd had aboard were now ashore, probably dressed in heavy boots and steel helmets, guarding strongpoints about the town.

'I hope she runs into a British ship.' Willie John watched the German vessel gloomily. ' 'Tis somethin' in the wind there iss, boy. There iss a gey lot o' signallin' off the coast. I've identified Home Fleet, a cruiser force and Second Destroyer Flotilla already.'

It was growing dark when they spotted a small rowing boat heading out to them from the bay where the village of Djupvik was situated. The figure at the oars wore a red woollen hat, a dark-coloured lumber-jacket and gloves. It was only as it drew nearer that they saw it was a woman at the oars and, as it swung to come alongside, they realized it was Annie Egge.

She made the boat fast to the ladder, shipped the oars in seamanlike fashion, and scrambled aboard. She was perspiring and pink in the face with exertion as she wrenched off the woollen hat to let her blonde hair fall free. When she removed her gloves, they saw her palms were covered with blisters.

'I wish to come with you,' she snapped.

Magnusson was startled. 'With *us*?'

'Why not? And if you have any sense you will leave at once because the Germans will soon find out about you.'

Magnusson explained that they were hoping for the harbourmaster to bring extra hands, and unwillingly she agreed that they should wait.

'But you must be clear before tomorrow morning,' she

insisted. 'They have the crews of five British merchant ships which were in the harbour held prisoner in the whaling ship. Soon they will be looking for you.'

Magnusson looked uneasily up the fjord. The mist was coming down again as the wind dropped.

'Better come into the saloon and have a drink,' he said. 'You're probably cold.'

'After rowing from Djupvik?' she snorted. '*Herre Gud*, don't be stupid!'

Magnusson shrugged. 'Better have a drink, anyway,' he said gently.

As Campbell poured her a whisky, she stared at the glass, emptied most of it into another glass, then lifted what was left and swallowed.

'To Great Britain and France,' she said. 'I cannot believe they will allow those beasts to stay here. They have put the British and French residents in Oslo into the Nedre Moller-gaten prison and they are now rounding up others who fled into the country. They will do the same here soon. Quisling and the Nasjonal Samling Party have formed a government. He's a traitor, of course. We regarded him only as an eccentric politician with no backing, but now he's got the support of Hitler.'

'Will he keep power?'

'With the king chased by the Germans, and the government running for the countryside? Of course he will! Until the Germans decide to take it off him.' She managed a shaky smile. 'Our only consolation is that we did not lose our honour. We sank their *Blücher* and damaged the pocket battleship, *Lützow*, and I have heard that your navy has damaged *Gneisenau*. But they have taken many Norwegian lives here and the traitor, Sundlo, told his men to lay down their arms.' She looked bitter. 'It is ironic that one of the few untrustworthy men in Narvik was the military commandant.'

She paused and sat back in her chair, looking exhausted as she lifted her eyes to stare at Magnusson. 'I think the

Germans will soon be searching for me,' she said. 'It seemed safer to leave. I took a bus and borrowed a boat at Djupvik.'

Magnusson leaned forward. 'It was a long way to row,' he said quietly.

She studied her hands ruefully and sighed again. 'There is nothing much we can do now. But Norwegians can ski and can shoot, and if they can't fight as an army they will fight as guerrillas.' She sat up, caught by the fire of her own blazing enthusiasm. 'And our merchant ships will go to the free world! We have the third largest merchant marine in the world, two hundred and seventy-two of them tankers, all modern! They will be worth their weight in gold!'

It was impossible not to be swept up by her excitement, even dulled as it was by her eternal statistics.

She indicated the chart on the table. 'You mustn't delay,' she went on. 'The Germans are worried because their ships are short of fuel. There are ten destroyers in Narvik and the only supply they have at the moment is the whaling ship. Her cargo's furnace fuel oil for the destroyers and diesel for U-boats, but there's insufficient to top up everything and they've been ordered to leave in case the British come. But she has only a slow pumping capacity and it would take at least seven hours to fill two destroyers, one on each side. So they can't leave tonight, and they've decided to wait for twenty-four hours. They're afraid to send them in groups because it would lessen their chances of breaking through.'

'What about their army?'

'Third Mountain Division!' She rapped out the information with her usual brisk efficiency. 'But they're worried they might not be able to hold the town against our soldiers or whatever the British will do. They're going to leave two of the destroyers to support them.'

'What are they doing now?'

'Refuelling and repairing damage caused by the gale. That means there are four destroyers in the harbour at once, all vulnerable to air or surface attack. You must inform your Admiralty. The rest are dispersed in the smaller fjords.

They're so worried your navy will come they're sleeping in their clothes.'

She had done her homework well and was even able to give names. 'They are two thousand-four-hundred-ton ships with five-inch guns and a speed of thirty-eight knots. They brought two hundred troops each, with light weapons, mountain guns and motorcycles. They landed at Ramnes and Hamnes, the Post Pier and the Ore Quay. When they blew up the *Eidsvold*, the fog looked like a sea of flame. There was a general and his staff aboard *Jan Willem* as well as troops. Some of the mountain guns they brought were wrenched overboard as they came by the gale and, with the growing resistance that's already beginning to come from the hills, they're worried because they have no anti-aircraft guns or field guns and no reserves of stores or ammunition. The freighter, *Rauenfels*, is due, however, and if the mist holds, she'll hug the southern shore. You'll have to slip out close to Tjeldöy.'

'You know your stuff!' Magnusson said.

She gave him a cold look. 'My father was a sailor. My brother was a sailor. My cousin was a sailor. He was in *Eidsvold* and he didn't survive. My brother was in the armed whaler, *Pol III*, at Oslo. *Pol III* has also been destroyed. My brother is missing.'

Her blazing hatred for the Germans was making her shake with emotion and it occurred to Magnusson that she could be a dangerous character to cross.

'We're ready to sail,' he assured her. 'The wind's in the right direction. You'd better get those hands bandaged and perhaps have something to eat.'

She sat meekly at the table while he cleaned up the raw palms and applied ointment and bandage. After a while he glanced up at her and saw she was watching him carefully.

'Have you the determination to escape?' she asked.

'Why do you ask?'

'You have always seemed to me too – how shall I say it? – too light-hearted for the job you were doing.'

'Everybody always thinks the British take too light-hearted a view of war. *We*'re inclined to think everybody else takes too gloomy a view.'

'You are a *good* sailor?'

'You should see me in uniform.'

She gave him a smile and for the first time it was warm and genuine.

'I think perhaps you are.'

He fastened the last of the bandages as Myers appeared with a plate of stew. It looked an unappetizing mess but she tucked into it willingly. 'Perhaps,' she suggested, 'I will now have the rest of that whisky.'

Magnusson watched her eat, wondering if Vinje – far from a likeable man at the best of times – was intending to betray him. Having extracted the knowledge that *Oulu* was a British ship, was he waiting the opportunity to lead the Germans down to him?

When Annie had finished, they went on deck. Almost immediately, they saw a light flashing from the point.

'Get going, Campbell,' Magnusson said. 'Take the whaler. Marques, you take the Norwegian boat. There might be more of them than we expected and it could save us a second journey.'

There were seven Norwegians, and Vinje's face was bleak. When he saw Annie Egge his jaw dropped.

'What are you doing here?' he demanded.

'I am escaping as you are,' she said stiffly.

The Norwegian turned to Magnusson. 'You said no women.'

'I didn't have much choice,' Magnusson pointed out.

They pushed the Norwegians into the forecastle and gave them the bunks of the vanished Finns. They reappeared soon afterwards, dressed in jerseys and lumber-jackets, prepared to work.

The rest of the night was spent in tense waiting, with Magnusson prowling about the ship, making sure everything was ready and that there was nothing left undone to delay them when daylight came.

Campbell met him in the thinning darkness of next morning, bundled into heavy clothing, his face taut and alert, eyes bright with a sense of being able to do something worthwhile.

'How's the tide?' Magnusson asked.

'High. Stream's slack. Wind's nor'-nor'-east.'

Magnusson wasn't sorry to be leaving the inhospitable coast of Norway and it was with a sense of relief that he watched the crew running along the deck in the light of lanterns, struggling with ropes. On the yards, men were casting off the gaskets that secured the furled sails. As the wind caught them they bellied out and were sheeted home by the men on deck. With topsails set on main and mizzen, *Oulu* began to gather way.

'Mainsail,' Magnusson said.

More canvas billowed out and they began to move faster, followed by flurries of snow. Behind them, the first ferry was preparing to leave Narvik, its lights shining against the blackness of the mountains.

Magnusson was still staring over the stern when Myers at the wheel touched his arm and pointed ahead. Staring in the direction of his pointing finger, Magnusson saw a ship just coming through the murk of snow and fog. Behind her there was another, then another, and another and another, all with the high, peaked silhouettes of warships.

'Christ, what's going on?'

He had just decided that the Germans had learned about them leaving and that destroyers had arrived to capture them, when Myers spoke again.

'Sir, them's H class ships.'

'British ships?'

'I was in 'Avoc before the war, sir. Thirteen 'undred tons, four four-point-sevens. The one in front's 'Ardy, the flotilla leader. She's a bit bigger. That's Second Destroyer Flotilla, sir.'

'You sure?'

'I've seen 'em drunk, sir, and I've seen 'em sober. I'd swear to it.'

Magnusson stared at the approaching ships a moment longer. They were approaching warily, steaming in line ahead, and it suddenly occurred to him that they might well mistake *Oulu* for a German ship.

'Shove the ensign up,' he yelled. 'The British one this time! They've come to retake Narvik from the Germans!'

4

The word flew round the ship and they all cheered as the destroyers passed them. Magnusson was standing towards the entrance to the fjord, waiting for the transports bringing troops and the big-gun ships of the back-up force, but as the destroyers slipped away astern it dawned on him there were *no* troopships, and no back-up force. He began to wonder what the five destroyers could hope to achieve against ten Germans, all bigger than they were, and came to the conclusion that *Oulu* would probably be safer outside the fjord and in the lee of the Lofotens.

The destroyers were disappearing into the mist and *Oulu* was gathering speed as the breeze filled her sails. Then as they made their way along the coast he realized that Annie Egge had appeared alongside him, frowning.

'Where are the others?' she demanded. 'The transports full of soldiers and guns. They cannot capture Narvik with five destroyers.'

He didn't reply, pretending to be occupied with the business of the ship. The destroyers had vanished and as Annie moved in front of him, her eyes angry, doggedly determined to get an answer, they saw a white flash of flame light up the curling vapour astern and a moment later heard the crash of an explosion.

The roar was followed by another, and as the mist turned scarlet they knew that in Narvik ship after ship was being hit. Gunfire was rolling round the narrow confines of the fjord, echoing and re-echoing down to where *Oulu* sped along close to the shore. Silhouetted against the distant trees they could make out anchored ships and faint shapes moving swiftly in front of them that they guessed were the British warships.

'Whatever they're up to, they seem to be making a good job of it,' Campbell said excitedly, his eyes alight. 'That's the Navy in action – the *real* Navy!'

Oulu continued to pick up speed, the water hissing along the side of the ship as she leaned to the wind. The gunfire still rolled behind them from the direction of the town and every now and again Magnusson saw the mist leap, as though the atmosphere had emptied and filled again as the shells exploded.

Willie John clambered out of the hold, his hang-dog face grinning. 'They're comin' out, boy,' he yelled. 'They've finished! They've just made "I am withdrawin' westwards." '

As they swung south-west towards the Lofotens, they were losing a little wind so that Magnusson edged to starboard in the hope of picking it up again to carry them clear into the open sea where they could use their radio to call for help. With Willie John's transmitter blasting out its appeal, he felt the destroyers couldn't fail to escort them to safety.

Turning to watch for the British ships returning, he was still congratulating himself that their luck had changed when he heard a shout from forward and saw a merchant ship heading straight towards them. She was only two hundred yards away, bursting through the mist that swirled about her blunt bow. There were men on her bridge, shouting and pointing at the white ensign and the heavy bow started to swing to starboard even as Magnusson grabbed the wheel and began to push with Myers.

'Hard-a-starboard,' he yelled. 'Campbell, get everybody out from below! She's going to hit us!'

He could read the name, *Rauenfels*, on the freighter's bow as it swung, and see the German flag at her stern. Then the ship was thundering past them, big as a cliff face, her port side scraping the length of *Oulu*'s hull. As her flying bridge caught the foresail, the yards were wrenched round with a crash and the splintering of timber and the screech of steel. Wire stays twanged and parted and the topmast teetered.

The collision had dragged *Oulu* close against the other ship, crushing her starboard rail, so that she was shouldered aside like matchwood. Boats swung out on davits caught the mizzen yards, wrenching them free, tearing the canvas and hooking in the shrouds to break rigging screws. Because she had been swinging as she had struck them, the freighter's blunt bows carved deep into *Oulu*'s hull by the foredeck and for a moment the two ships lay locked together, the barque dragged backwards by the inertia of the heavier vessel. Then *Rauenfels*'s siren went in three long blasts and she began to back away.

As she went astern, her projecting upperworks wrenched again at *Oulu*'s tortured shrouds. The barque seemed to shriek with agony and spars leapt as the masts jerked and heaved. There was a violent twanging sound and the topgallant masts began to bend as if made of whalebone. Amidst the crash of falling spars, Magnusson saw sails flogging, chain sheets knocking sparks out of steel yards; then everything started to come down by the run as the lifts and ties were carried away.

He heard Annie Egge cry out and saw her bolt for the shelter of the poop, the men running after her enveloped in the folds of the spanker as the mizzen topmast collapsed and brought the gaff with it. Vinje, the harbourmaster, lay groaning in the scuppers. He had been struck by a falling block and had crashed against the donkey engine.

Rauenfels had drawn clear now and she disappeared into the mist even as Campbell was fighting to get off a rocket.

'Save your breath,' Magnusson panted. 'She'll not turn back to help us. She's carrying ammunition for the Germans in Narvik and, judging by what's been happening, they'll be needing it.' He swung round, his eyes everywhere, assessing

148

the damage, all too aware there was little he could do. 'Leave it, Myers,' he yelled to the wheel. 'You're wasting your time.'

The ship was already listing and the deck was becoming increasingly dangerous with flying chains and writhing wires. Annie was about to run to the groaning Vinje by the donkey engine but Magnusson caught her as she passed and, with his hand on her shoulder, pushed her roughly back to the shelter of the poop.

'Get back!'

'But – '

'Be quiet!' he roared. 'Stay there where it's safe!'

At that moment the main topmast, topgallant and royal backstays came crashing down across the port davits, where they had hoisted Annie Egge's boat, binding it to the skids. Marques was struggling among the wreckage, finding a new and unprintable name for every one of the stout wires and many of the smaller ones. He remained full of fight but his vocabulary seemed to be almost exhausted.

By now *Oulu* was wallowing lopsidedly in the water. With most of her starboard shrouds and stays carried away, the masts hung crookedly to port, pulling the ship over at an angle. All round her, wreckage floated on the water, grinding up and down in the swell, threatening to smash the hull plates and break the vessel up altogether. The main topmast, which had snapped off at the cap, was now acting like a great battering ram in the lurch of *Rauenfels*'s wake. Already it had crunched a hole and if this was enlarged into a gash the ship would go at once, tilting to port to bring down what was left standing and swamp the only boat they had left.

It was clear that *Oulu* was finished. Magnusson looked up the fjord, hoping against hope that the Navy was returning, but the whole wide stretch of water seemed to be filled with thick rolling black smoke as though someone had laid a smoke screen. Above the sounds of *Oulu*'s torment he could still hear the thud of guns and could see grey ships manoeuvring at speed in and out of the murk. It was impossible to tell whether they were British or German, and he realized it was up to them to save themselves.

'Get the boat launched,' he said to Campbell. 'This bloody ship isn't going to last much longer and if we leave it too late, we'll have to swim for it.'

Marques was trying to shove the folds of canvas, which had fallen to the deck, over the ship's side to form a fender against the assaults of the topmast. As Magnusson picked his way along the deck, he saw that the bulwarks were gone on both sides of the mainmast forward, allowing the sea to sweep in unhindered. There was a wire entanglement in front of him and, up to his knees in water, he began to pull it away.

Campbell reported that they had freed the boat.

'Get her in the water,' Magnusson said. 'Myers, get the girl from the poop and bring anybody else forward you can find.'

The ship was leaning further and further to port now, the boat against her side, held close by the men in her.

'For Christ's sake, hurry,' Magnusson yelled.

He glanced upwards and saw the wrecked masts towering over him, at an even greater angle than they had been. Once she started going, there would be no holding her, and if they wanted to escape they had to get the boat away.

Myers appeared, pushing Annie Egge in front of him and followed by two of the Norwegians.

'Get aboard,' Magnusson yelled.

He could hear ominous creaking now and he almost flung her into the boat. The others began to follow.

'Take her away!'

'There are more to come!'

'Take her away! If we wait, we shan't *have* a boat.'

Instinct told him there were only seconds left. As the boat was released it drifted from the side of the ship, and as the oars splashed into the water, Campbell took her to a safe distance. One of the Norwegians, Wolszcka and Petty Officer Marques were throwing gratings into the sea for the men left aboard.

'Get in the water,' Magnusson yelled. 'She's going!'

He could hear deck planks splitting and iron plates twisting and groaning. More rigging came crashing down, narrowly missing his head. He splashed his way aft to yell at Marques, who nodded and headed for the break in the side of the ship. As Magnusson scrambled over the wreckage of the gaff topsail and its spar, he saw the white ensign they had run up lying under the tangle of ropes and blocks and, without thinking, he retrieved it and tied it round his waist.

Vinje was still lying in the scuppers near the donkey engine, swilled about with water in which splinters of wood washed backwards and forwards. As he tried to pick him up, the harbourmaster screamed and fainted. Without attempting to be gentle, Magnusson hoisted him to his shoulders in a fireman's lift. Stumbling among the ropes and wires, he was aware of frantic splashings, oaths and shouts from men in the sea, and felt the deck tilting more and more.

As he reached the side where the water lapped against the ship, he heard the thud of gunfire again. Then he felt the air about him expand and contract and saw the mist where *Rauenfels* had disappeared turn crimson. The gunfire had stopped but the air was filled with the roar of a vast explosion. The mist had been torn into swirling tendrils and an enormous cloud of brown smoke was lifting out of the grey veil over the sky. Something there had met a violent end.

Flinging the Norwegian into the water, he flopped in after him. Coming to the surface, shocked and breathless at the cold, he spluttered and blinked until he had his breath back then, reaching out, began to drag Vinje after him towards the boat.

'Hurry,' Campbell was shouting. 'She's going!'

He felt hands grab him and was hauled aboard, sprawling on his face in the bilges among feet which trod on his hands

151

as they tried to make room for him to sit up.

'Where's the bloody Navy?' he demanded.

'Myers said they went past five minutes ago,' Campbell announced with a faint trace of bitterness. 'Only three of them, two in bad shape, one with its bows bashed in.'

'No more?'

'That's all. They must have been too busy to pick up Willie John's SOS.'

Magnusson spat out sea water and stared about him, recognizing Marques, Wolszcka and Willie John. Hoisting himself upright, he saw the boat was packed. One or two of the men in it had blood on their faces from head wounds, and Vinje was lying at his feet looking as if he were dead. He began to count noses, noticing as he did so that Annie Egge was crouched, white-faced, next to Myers.

'Where are your telegraphists, Willie John?'

Willie John lifted his head wearily. 'They didnae make it,' he said. 'I saw them goin' intae the forecastle. I havenae seen them since.'

Magnusson frowned, finding it hard to take in. The two telegraphists had both been mere boys, keen, easy-going and certain of their luck. What had they thought in that moment of terror when the inhuman cold of the rushing water had choked the life out of them and they had realized at last that their luck had failed?

It had been undiluted disaster. At least two of his party had been lost and some of them had been injured, two of them badly enough to need hospital. He had lost his ship, his radio equipment, which was the sole reason for his being there, and almost his self-respect.

He turned stiffly. *Oulu* was lying at an angle of forty-five degrees now and rigging kept falling into the water where a few moments before he had been swimming. He stared at her, a tremendous sadness overwhelming him. First *Kosciuszko* and now *Oulu*. It seemed the end of all sailing ships. In another five years there would be no high sails left, nothing but their ghosts moving before the westerly winds, nothing but the shapes of dead vessels littering iron shores. They had often been cursed by the men who sailed them but they had been things of beauty and individuality, and he wouldn't have believed it possible to see the death of two of them in so short a time.

Then, as he watched, *Oulu* lay over on her side as if she were tired. The bow went down and she slowly slid beneath the black water to leave only a lifting mat of spars and wreckage. That bad luck which had dogged her all her life had claimed her at last.

5

Magnusson stared grey-faced towards the land.

They had sorted themselves out and were making slow progress towards the shore. The men at the oars, warmed by their exertion, had handed over their outer garments to the men who had been in the water, and these and the press of bodies in the boat helped to keep them from freezing.

Magnusson was cold and furious, and suddenly anxious – not to escape, but to do somebody some damage. They had decided it was pointless heading for the island of Baröy, and instead had turned south towards a dimly visible cluster of houses.

'I think he's dead,' Marques said suddenly and Magnusson turned his head slowly to see he was bending over the injured harbourmaster. Vinje's head had fallen sideways and his face looked grey, while his eyes seemed to have become disconnected and were staring in different directions.

'Leave him,' he said. 'We'll bury him ashore.'

'What happens now?' Campbell asked as the land drew nearer.

'Christ knows,' Magnusson said.

'We can't stay here,' Campbell said. 'Not with the Germans all round Narvik.'

'Your bloody intellect dazzles me!'

Campbell frowned, suddenly stiff and naval again. 'Well, have *you* got any ideas?' he asked.

They landed on a rocky shore that lifted rapidly to the

hills where the fir trees hung over them, making the day dark with their gloom. Magnusson could feel his wet clothes stiffening in the frost. Several of the men were shivering uncontrollably, their teeth chattering, and he saw Annie Egge strip off her heavy lumber-jacket and slip it over an injured seaman's shoulders. They had to find some shelter from the biting wind before they all died of cold. Dragging the boat up the beach and turning it upside down, they wedged it on a group of rocks to make a roof. It was hard work; their fingers were numb and the rocks they stood on were covered with snow and ice and slimy with weed.

Sending off Campbell and Myers to find help, Magnusson got the others pushing more rocks up to the boat to form a windbreak, and they placed the five injured – four Norwegians and one of the naval ratings – in its lee. Annie, her blonde hair blowing about her face, was trying to make them comfortable and had begged handkerchiefs and shirt tails to bind up their wounds.

'It will suffice until we can get help,' she said. She looked at Magnusson. 'I am sorry your ship is sunk.'

'Not half as sorry as I am,' Magnusson said angrily. 'What do we do now?'

She shrugged. 'We cannot go back to Narvik. The Germans will be looking for me and the other Norwegians and, by this time, perhaps for you also.'

'Can't we take the railway south?'

'There is no railway to the south. From Narvik it runs only to Sweden and on into Finland.'

'What about the roads?'

'In April there is too much snow and they are impassable.'

'Couldn't we get across into Sweden? It can't be more than thirty miles away.'

'Twenty along the railway line. But the Germans control that. Otherwise, it is a climb over the mountains and at this time of the year that would be impossible.'

He looked at her to see if she were being sarcastic but she was deadly serious.

'Go on then,' he said. 'What *do* we do?'

'A bus runs from Bognes and Ulsvåg. There is a ferry at Bognes and the bus then follows the road to Lønsdal. From there we could take the train to Trondheim and catch a connection into Storlien, fifty miles away, in Sweden.'

'How about money?'

'I can find it. In Narvik.'

'That means going back there.'

'I know Narvik better than the Germans. And if I *don't* go, *nobody* will escape.'

'Clothes?'

She smiled. 'You are beginning to think at last of everything.'

He frowned. 'I want to get home.'

'To rest on your laurels?'

'No,' he growled. 'To get hold of the biggest gun I can find and use it to blow some bloody German's head off!'

Three freezing hours later, Campbell and Myers reappeared, bringing with them five men from a farm they had found, all of them wearing coats and heavy sweaters against the icy wind.

'Come,' one of them said. 'You will be warmer in the barn. We have not a big house, but the barn is dry. There is a hay loft with cattle below. It does not always smell nice but it is warm from the cows. The wounded we will put in the house.' He smiled apologetically. 'Perhaps we must put two in each bed, but they will be safe, and we can find clothes from our friends. I think you are lucky. It is lonely here and you will not be found.'

They covered the dead harbourmaster with stones and stuck up a crude cross; one of the Norwegians conducted a short service. The British joined in with the Lord's Prayer.

'*Hvil i fred*,' Annie said. 'May he rest in peace.'

'It is a good way to die,' one of the Norwegian officers said. 'For the glory of one's country.'

She turned angrily. 'To ascribe glory to the violent death

of anybody loving life,' she snapped, 'is nonsense and a failing of human wisdom.'

'God ordains our end.'

'Perhaps God is merely something man invented to re-assure himself when he comes to face death!'

Her face was pink with anger and Magnusson watched her approvingly. There was an incandescent spirit about her, a fearlessness that was heart-warming.

They began to climb the slope, stumbling through the snow and the close-growing pines above the frozen shore-line, helping the five injured between them. The snow was deep but the Norwegians knew where to tread and they avoided the worst of it. At the top of the slope, they reached a road where the snow was packed as if vehicles moved along it.

'The road to Korsnes,' Annie said. 'It is no more than twenty kilometres away.'

'Sailors aren't good walkers,' Magnusson said. 'Like piles, bad feet are an occupational hazard among them.'

'Please?'

He shrugged. 'I think we'll need transport.'

They reached the farm at last and carried the injured men upstairs. The condition of the naval rating and one of the Norwegians was serious. The other three were suffering from shock.

The Norwegians seemed bewildered by the events, and Annie got them tearing up sheets and clothing for bandages, and taking down curtains to wrap round the wet and shiv-ering men. The farm was made up of detached buildings – living quarters, a cook-house, stables, store rooms, even a schoolroom for the neighbourhood – and the barn had an outside ramp leading to an upper floor which was big enough for everybody.

'We have used it for wedding feasts and for dances,' the farmer explained.

He was plainly troubled by what had happened, but proud

that the Germans had not occupied Narvik without casualties.

'One of the British destroyers is beached near here,' he said. 'And another sank in mid-channel further west. But two German destroyers were sunk and five damaged. The others are all short of ammunition and fuel, and only a few of the merchantmen are still afloat. There were twenty-five of them. Another ship, *Rauenfels*, was blown up. She ran into the destroyers as they left. She was carrying ammunition and went sky-high.'

'Serve the clumsy bugger right just,' Willie John said with bitter satisfaction.

The following morning they woke cold, tired and hungry. The barn window was patterned with rime, and a bucket of water by the door was frozen solid. As they went outside, the air, thin and icy, hit them like a blow in the chest, searing their lungs as they drew breath. They could see the fjord from the door, a black lake of water under a cold grey sky and surrounded by snow-clad hills. There was no sign of the Germans and the farmer brought the news that they were still occupied with clearing up the debris in Narvik harbour.

'They say the British fleet is off the Lofotens somewhere,' he said, 'and the pilot station at Tranöy reported two British destroyers to the north of Baröy. I think they are still waiting for the Germans to try to escape.'

His sons had already gone south to report to what there was of the Norwegian army between Oslo and Trondheim, and he was expecting to go himself as soon as he could make arrangements for someone to help his wife and daughters look after the farm. Other men like him in the area were doing the same thing.

It was clear, however, that escaping south was not going to be easy. From Trondheim, Bergen, Kristiansand and Oslo, the Germans were already fanning out, setting up road blocks to stop the movement of civilians, and bus services were coming to a halt. They were now wondering if it wouldn't be possible to get hold of a fishing vessel in Djupvik and escape at night towards Trondheim, putting themselves ashore there to pick up the railway to Sweden. The problem was chiefly money, food and the depth of the snow. The blizzard which had been blowing on and off ever since the Germans had first made their appearance had loaded the branches of trees and lay in drifts several feet deep. A visit to Narvik seemed imperative.

It wasn't difficult to get a lift in the back of a timber lorry, but it was bitterly cold and Magnusson and Annie huddled together out of the biting wind. Her face was pinched and white-looking, and when he put his arm round her and pulled her to him to keep warm, she didn't object. As they crossed the causeway to the railway station, the place looked grey and sombre under the leaden skies, the buildings black against the whiteness of the land. The Germans had already placed guards about the centre of the town and it seemed wiser to keep well away from it.

It started to snow again as they climbed from the lorry and walked towards the harbour. Houses caught by the blast from exploding ships, after the fight on the 9th, looked like death's heads, their empty windows like the eye sockets of a skull. Roofs were missing and several buildings were mere shells streaming smoke, while the narrow waters in front of the Post Pier and the Ore Quay were filled with the wreck-age from damaged ships. The big whaling factory ship, *Jan Willem*, appeared to be untouched but her starboard side was a confusion of hoses and wires hanging into the sea, and all round her the water was full of sunken vessels. Of the twenty-five merchant ships which had been in the harbour, only *Jan Willem*, a big freighter, *Lippe*, and two British ships, *North Cornwall* and *Mersington Court*, still seemed to be afloat. On the east side of the fjord a British destroyer lay beached and on fire, her ammunition still exploding.

The German destroyers had suffered dreadfully and the survivors were still struggling to save their ships. Superstructures were distorted and large areas of deck were burned out. Several seemed water-logged, and boats were ferrying between them and *Jan Willem*, crammed with cutting gear and men, while on the other side of the factory ship a submarine was refuelling hurriedly.

As they recovered from the shock of invasion, the faces of the Norwegians had assumed a stubborn unyielding expression that showed their unwillingness to accept the Germans as 'protectors'. Sturdily independent of authority at any time, they were now rigidly following only the directions of their own town officials and avoiding helping the invaders. Though they were cut off from the rest of Norway, they had better sources of information than people further south, because the reception from the Swedish radio was good in Narvik and news of Norwegian resistance came regularly over the air from Tromsø. There were no reports of fighting in the north but men on skis were bringing across the mountains information from other parts of the country. Tromsø radio had urged evacuation of the town, and in spite of the German efforts to stop them, young men were still slipping away across the fjord.

Keeping to the back streets, they managed to find their way to the Egge home. The door was opened by Annie's father. Behind him was his wife who flung herself into her daughter's arms, her eyes full of tears. Herr Egge grasped Magnusson's hand and squeezed it.

'We thought you were dead,' he said.

Annie turned. 'Do the Germans also think we're dead?'

'Yes.'

'It won't be long before they change their minds,' Magnusson warned. 'They'll find the boat and Vinje's grave, and eventually the injured will have to be brought in.'

Annie's parents had fled with her grandmother to the basement during the naval battle and were still in a state of shock.

'The radio said the British had been repulsed,' Annie's father said. 'But there were hits on the ships in the harbour.

They say the German commander was blown up with his ship and there are floating corpses and German wounded everywhere.'

While Annie and Magnusson ate a hurried meal, Herr Egge went hurrying among the neighbouring houses and returned with his pockets full of money. 'It isn't much,' he said, 'but it will help pay your fares. We can't supply food for the journey because we haven't got much. The Germans have shut all the shops and banks. They've organized ration cards, though, and there must be a lot less people than there were. I've heard the dead at the hospital are lying up the cellar steps and the mayor's asking the Germans to bury them, because we can't do it.'

They spent the night at the Egges's house, Magnusson sleeping in the bed of the missing son, and the following morning they were all up early.

They had to get back to the farm before it grew dark, and they set off intending to beg a lift. The surviving German destroyers were humming with activity and it looked to Magnusson as though they were expecting trouble. One of them, disabled, had been secured to the jetty and German sailors were stacking ready-use ammunition as if she were to be employed as a shore battery. Another cripple was being escorted out of the harbour, while the remainder were raising steam.

Then, as they reached the Beisfjord causeway, they heard shouts from behind and saw people beginning to run and scatter. As they stopped, bewildered, a car skidded to a standstill alongside them.

'Get out of town!' the driver yelled. 'The British are coming! The pilot station at Tranöy telephoned and they're clearing the place! They say one of the ships is a colossus!'

As the car drew away with screeching tyres, they heard a rumble like thunder from the seaward end of the fjord.

'That's gunfire,' Magnusson said and they began to hurry after the other people crossing the causeway.

The gunfire was heavier already than anything they'd

heard before and a young man running towards them yelled that the fjord was swarming with ships. German troops were hastening already from the occupied areas of the town, except for the few who remained behind for the defence of the harbour. The firing increased, punctuated by tremendous blasts, the sound echoing backwards and forwards across the water to remind Magnusson of the story of Rip Van Winkle hearing the giants playing at skittles in the mountains. The whole fjord seemed to be expanding and contracting with the sound.

'Come on,' he said and, grabbing Annie's hand, began to run. As they reached the trees at the other end of the causeway they heard a roar like an express train approaching, and as he pushed her down into the snow a shell exploded in the town.

Tiles and timber hurtled through the air, and they felt the blast wash over them. As they lifted their heads, smoke and a cloud of pulverized snow was drifting away towards the south and they could see flames leaping up. Men, women and children were hurrying into basements and towards a half-built subway in the hillside belonging to the ore company. A few remained on the slopes on either side of the fjord, indifferent to the danger in the exhilaration of seeing the hated Germans suffer. Soldiers were running about, bent double, their arms about their heads, showing all the signs of panic. Another shell roared past and smashed into the town.

'Poor bloody Narvik,' Magnusson said. 'First the Germans, now us!'

Annie's head came up, her eyes bright. '*Poor* Narvik?' she said. '*Proud* Narvik! We don't expect to regain our freedom without blood. It's like being the princess in the fairy story with the black knight and the white knight fighting for her.'

Above the racket of small arms, they heard the sound of an aeroplane engine and, looking up, saw a British Swordfish, lumbering and slow with its double wings and fixed undercarriage, circling just to the north where they had seen the crippled destroyer limping away. Then they saw nine destroyers – some of them large Tribals, Magnusson noticed at once – followed by the majestic shape of a battleship, square, ugly and menacing, her huge guns lifting. Stark and black against the white background of snow, he recognized her at once.

'It's *Warspite*,' he said.

The ships were emerging from the smoke, the British destroyers circling to look for targets. One of the German destroyers shuddered from torpedo hits which lifted great columns of water above her forward and aft. Then *Warspite*'s great guns fired. The tremendous crack came across the water as they saw the long tongues of flame leap from the barrels. The German vessel, already on fire where the torpedoes had struck seemed to leap in the water and pieces of deck flew through the air. Guns were going off everywhere now, the British destroyers firing everything they possessed. The German ship burst into flames along her whole length and men could be seen jumping overboard into the water.

The Swordfish was passing sedately over the town now. It was already becoming impossible to see across the fjord for the burning buildings and the drifting smoke from *Warspite*'s guns. Around Annie and Magnusson, young Norwegians were dancing and yelling excitedly.

A German shell, fired wildly in the confusion, landed on the slope below them and the blast waves tore through the trees, uprooting several. Another tremendous explosion enveloped the destroyer moored at the quay as a floating battery. One of the British destroyers had closed her to board but had been driven away by heavy firing from the shore. As she went astern, the German ship blew up. A group of Germans running for their lives were swept away by a flying iron spar and what few windows had not already been destroyed in the battle on the 9th fell in. By this time the British destroyers had disappeared down the narrow fjord to the north of the town beyond the Ore Quay. The rumble of gunfire and explosions continued for some time; then they saw the British ships retiring seawards, and Magnusson began to curse and pound his fist against the trunk of a tree. He turned to find Annie staring at him, bewildered.

'That's the second time they've been in here and I've had to stand and watch 'em leave without me!' he stormed.

A man came out of a near by house, his eyes excited. 'They've got the lot,' he yelled. 'They trapped them in Rombaksfjord! My brother saw it all and telephoned!'

It seemed there wasn't a single one left of the ten German destroyers which had steamed in so arrogantly only four days before, and the Germans ashore were all dead, captured or in flight.

The town was covered by the pall of smoke that now hung over the fjord and they could dimly see vehicles moving out towards the east. For a while the Norwegians round them watched; then, unable to resist, they began to recross the causeway into the town. Magnusson looked at Annie and she looked back at him, her eyes bright. He knew she wanted to go too.

As they entered the town again, houses and buildings were burning; there didn't seem to be a single undamaged window or roof. The air was thick with the stench of fuel oil mixed with the acrid smoke of burning timber, and they could hear the crackle of flames. The whole town seemed to be a confusion of bomb craters and rubble, with splintered wood and bent steel everywhere. The Norwegians showed no bitterness at the bombardment, but the Germans were half-delirious, – laughing, crying or singing – and when they were told they were finished they could only answer, '*Ja, ja! Kamerad! Kamerad!* Pardon!'

Already they were streaming out of the town in flight to the mountains, some of them mere boys of no more than eighteen, their tunics unfastened, their hands devoid of weapons, sheer terror on their faces, as they stumbled through the snow towards the trees and the mountain that loomed over the town.

'For God's sake,' Magnusson said, as they watched. 'If we could only put troops ashore now, we'd have the place!'

The Germans continued to stream past them, dropping personal belongings and equipment as they went, many of them wet through and looking like half-drowned cats, tramping a path through the snow like a dark curving snake. One youngster, small and wearing an oversized helmet, stopped to speak to them.

'Which is the way to Sweden?' he asked.

Annie immediately pointed towards the slopes.

'Up there,' she said. 'That's the way.'

Her eyes were bitter as he moved on. 'It takes them into the mountains,' she said. 'Perhaps they'll starve up there or die of the cold.'

The streets were empty with just an occasional truck moving about, filled with bodies brought from the shore under tarpaulins, and one elegant old limousine with tasselled curtains, marked by a red cross, that was picking up wounded. The Missions to Seamen was littered with German bedding and equipment and the remains of meals but otherwise it was empty and Annie stood silently looking at it, her face pale and sad.

Shells with delayed fuses were still bursting in the town and the harbour was a graveyard of wrecked ships. Flocks of gulls screamed over the water, diving from time to time on the floating corpses. The pier was a heartbreaking sight. The new cold storage plant, of which Narvik had been so proud, had collapsed, and the creamery at the other side of the square had lost all its windows. Wooden jetties had been blasted away, the pillars projecting from the water like decayed teeth. Parts of ships lay everywhere among the timber, logs and cleft rocks, like the playthings of destructive monster children.

The windows of the town's great stone church had been smashed and its slender spire had lost some of its tiles.

Graves were being dug in the cemetery, even as others had been laid open by shells, and the mortuary chapel had been blown to pieces, the debris scattered among the headstones.

The town was deathly quiet. There was no electricity because the power station had been hit. The destruction was immense but among those few Norwegians still in the streets there was a strange leaping enthusiasm. Despite what had happened to Narvik, it had been a victory, and some of them were singing 'Tipperary' – the only British tune they knew.

A few more Germans drifted past, also singing, but it was looted Norwegian brandy, not self-confidence, that stirred their voices. Some of them wore scraps of Norwegian uniform or civilian clothes, and one of them, staggering with drunkenness, took an angry pot shot at a cat, the bullet striking a stone and whining away into the sky.

Watching them, Magnusson stood on the wrecked jetty near the smoking remains of the destroyer that had blown up. Then he stared down the fjord in the crazy half-hope that by some miracle of telepathy he could let the situation ashore be known.

As he turned away, he found a German officer staring at him. He was tall and good-looking in the best Aryan manner, his face white and tense, his jaw jutting forward, his hand holding a pistol. He clearly imagined Magnusson was a Norwegian, and for a moment, before Annie grabbed his hand and pulled him away, Magnusson thought the German was going to shoot him.

'I can tell you one thing,' the German choked, turning on his heel and following the others out of the town, 'and that is that your friends, the British, will never come! Never!

6

That evening the BBC and the Norwegian free radio announced that the Allies had made landings on the Norwegian coast. There was a yell of delight from the listening men.

'We can join them when we know where they are,' Magnusson said.

'Perhaps they're at Narvik by this time,' Annie smiled.

But a discreet telephone call to the Egge family revealed that no troops had arrived there. The following morning, they learned that British troop transports were anchored off the Island of Hinnöy to the north and immediately began to debate whether it would be possible to reach them. But Hinnøy involved a circuitous journey round Narvik.

'We must warn the British ships somehow,' Annie insisted. 'The place is simply waiting to be captured.'

'We might pick up a puffer in one of the fjords,' Magnusson said, 'and go by sea.'

'Puffer?' Campbell looked puzzled. 'What's a puffer?'

'Some Scot must ha'e first called them that,' Willie John explained. 'After the steam puffers o' the Western Isles. Two-masted, high in the bow an' wi' a big wheelhouse aft. They make a noise like a traction engine gaein' uphill. You can hear 'em for miles but for ability to keep the sea there iss naethin' ta beat 'em.'

Trying to decide what to do was almost as difficult in the confusion that surrounded the situation as doing it. It was clear that somewhere to the south Norwegian forces were still resisting the Germans, and that young men were trying to reach them by every means at their disposal. A few others were trying to reach Narvik, expecting the Allies to land there at any moment, but there appeared to be no movement at all from the men at Hinnöy, and from the stories that found their way across the fjord it seemed the Allies were still trying to make up their minds what to attack.

'For Christ's sake,' Magnusson said in a fury. 'All they've got to do is walk in and take the bloody place!'

They decided to wait one more day, especially as the injured men seemed to need a little more time. It wasn't easy, tempers were frayed by the disasters and there was no unity to bind them together, no discipline, none of the years of working together, officer and man, that held a ship's company together in times of stress. They were only half a dozen regular Navy men, a group of Norwegians, a half-mad Polish boy who could only mouth thoughts of vengeance, and a girl.

That afternoon, Magnusson stood outside the barn staring towards the north. The sky was the grey-yellow colour of mud and it looked heavy, as though sagging with the weight of snow. The wind was thin with the dampness that again spoke of more snow, and there was the same indefinable smell in the air they'd encountered as they'd arrived in Vestfjord for the first time.

Stamping on the frozen ground behind him, Willie John swung his arms, slapping his back, and blew on his fingers. His breath hung like smoke about his head.

'I hope tae Christ it doesnae block the roads,' he said. ' 'Tis going tae be awful hard gettin' south as it iss.'

That night they received a message from the Egge family that a group of Norwegian naval officers were intending to board one of the trawlers and head for England with as many British survivors as could be mustered. Many men from the destroyers sunk in the first battle had hidden in the woods north of the town and were hoping to cross into

Sweden, and the Norwegians had by now learned of the loss of *Oulu*. It was decided that Magnusson and Annie should contact them at the Egge house, and they begged a lift from the farmer, hoping to make arrangements for everyone to be picked up at Djupvik.

It was clear as soon as they reached Narvik that Allied hesitation was giving the Germans time to re-establish themselves. According to the radio, other troops were already heading north from Oslo to link up with the troops from Trondheim who, in their turn, were probing still further north to contact the men in Narvik.

They waited at the Egge house, nervous and impatient for the arrival of the Norwegian officers from the trawler.

'If they can't get away, they intend to blow her up and die with her,' Fru Egge said.

Annie turned to her mother. 'What in God's name for?'

'It will be a gesture.' Fru Egge flapped her hands unhappily. 'To show the Germans we won't tolerate them here. They told us so.'

Annie glanced at Magnusson. 'If they told *you*, they probably told others, too, and the others might have included a few Quislings.' She beat her fist against the palm of the other hand. 'They'd have done better to escape into Sweden or join the forces in the north.'

They sat in silence waiting; as the time began to drag on, Magnusson grew worried. There had been treachery in Norway and not all Norwegians were as patriotic as the Egges. Occupied but unsubdued, Narvik seethed like a cauldron, and insecure, their commander killed in the British attacks and with no hope of reinforcement, the Germans were quick on the trigger. Had they also, in self-defence, recruited their Quislings and set them to work?

The charred buildings and the wrecked shipping in the waters of the bay looked dark and ugly against the snow. Staring through the windows, Magnusson couldn't sit still, and in the end they decided, for their own reassurance and for the safety of the Egge family, that they could stay no longer but must see for themselves what was happening.

People were waiting by the station, and Magnusson eyed the railway line as it swept eastwards along the coast. Beyond the hills it rushed in and out of tunnels and cuttings and over high bridges to the Swedish frontier only twenty miles away. Just outside the town, there were half a dozen canvas-covered freight cars. They didn't look like iron ore cars and he wondered if they carried guns because he'd heard the Swedes had been forced to allow the Germans to pass through their territory. In front of them was a locomotive damaged in the battle, festooned with bizarre ice sculptures fashioned from leaking steam by the intense cold.

The Germans seemed to be everywhere, and in a vicious mood. As Annie and Magnusson reached the Ore Pier, a launch full of soldiers was just leaving. It headed out into the harbour, trailing an arrowhead of wake across the black water, towards a trawler at the entrance to Herjangsfjord. As they watched they saw the red, white and blue flag of the Norwegian Navy break out at the trawler's masthead. A small crowd of Norwegians, hatred in their eyes, stood along the waterfront; then German military police, metal gorgets at their throats, started pushing them away.

'Go home,' the sergeant in charge kept saying. 'Go home.'

The Norwegians began to move reluctantly. Only a few stopped to argue and the gun butts came up at once to jab at kidneys and shoulders. It was obviously not a good time to be in Narvik, and Magnusson decided to leave and try again another day.

They were just turning to go when a shot rang out. There was a cry and a loud 'Aaah' that came like a sigh from the crowd along the waterfront, then the high-pitched wail of misery from a woman. Magnusson reached out for Annie's hand, but she darted away to find out what was happening. It seemed ages before she returned, ashen-faced and with blood on her hands.

'So much for their protection,' she said. 'They have shot

a boy who argued with them. They know the trawler's going to escape. They've sent troops out to her.'

She grabbed his hand and pulled him back into the crowd. The launch was alongside the trawler now, white against her dark hull. As the Germans stood upright to climb aboard, there was a crackle of shots and two of the soldiers toppled into the fjord. Immediately, the launch pulled away, circling to pick up the wounded men. The growing dusk was lit up by flashes as more weapons were discharged from the trawler's decks. The Germans were firing back now, and one of the Norwegians leaning over the bridge rail fell into the water.

'Oh, God,' Annie said. 'Why did they learn about her *today*? Tomorrow we could have been clear.'

The launch was now laying off at a distance, the men in it clearly uncertain what to do. Then they saw movement where the railway from the iron ore depot circled the headland at Framnes. A gun was being pulled into position by a lorry and they could distinctly hear the shouts of the crew across the water. The first shell burst on the shore of Herjangsfjord just beyond the trawler and they saw the acid-white flash among the trees. A groan went up from the crowd, and men could be seen running along the deck; then the Norwegian flag jerked down and fell to the deck.

'So much for their resistance,' Annie said contemptuously. 'Ten minutes! Until the first shot was fired.'

The launch moved in closer again as the flag came down, and they saw German soldiers scrambling to the deck of the trawler. A second launch left the quay and chugged across to join the first one, so that soon the trawler was swarming with Germans. Then, suddenly, the Norwegians began to break free and run. A few shots were fired and two of them fell, but the rest were jumping into the water and swimming away as fast as they could. Almost immediately, there was a blinding flash and, as the thunder of the explosion came across the water to them, the trawler appeared to disintegrate. A huge cloud of smoke billowed out from the centre

of the ship, brown and grey and streaked with the red of
flames. She appeared to swell as the mast went straight up
like a flung javelin, and as it flopped back into the fjord, it
smashed down on the swimming men and crushed the German launch which was struggling to get clear.

'They did it,' Magnusson breathed. 'They blew her up!'

The blast across the water whipped at their faces and
plucked at their clothing. Debris was dropping in a tremendous shower, steel bitts, part of the deckhouse, spars, tan-
gled rigging, the windlass and the anchor winch. Smaller
objects whirled through the air like ashes from a volcano,
and bodies, both Norwegian and German, floated among
the wreckage.

The remains of the trawler were already blazing like a
torch and they could hear the roar and crackle of flames,
their glow reflected on the watching faces, picking out the
planes and angles of chins and cheekbones and foreheads.
Launches and ships' boats, hurriedly dispatched from all
parts of the harbour, were hovering at a safe distance, afraid
of further explosions; of the men who had jumped overboard only a few were still swimming.

Annie turned and buried her face in Magnusson's coat.
One arm round her, he stared at the blazing hulk that was
now settling lower in the fjord and tilting over to one side.
Then slowly, like a tired animal, the trawler finally lay over
on her beam and slipped beneath the water. As she vanished, there was nothing to be seen beyond a rising column
of steam and a few floating scraps of burning wreckage.

They turned silently and were just heading for Beisfjord
when a commandeered lorry appeared, full of steel-helmet-
ed men with iron faces and hard eyes, quite different from
the shocked and defeated troops they'd seen not very long
before. The lorry careered past them, sliding on the icy
surface, and stopped across the road. As they shuffled to a
halt in the snow, Magnusson was surprised to feel Annie's
hand slip into his as she pressed closer to him, and he
realized that inside that tough little frame there were such

emotions as fear, doubt and nervousness.

'Nobody must leave Narvik!'

The German sergeant was standing in front of them, his rifle raised and held across his chest. The people about them came to a stop, and the sergeant was joined by an officer who pointed towards the town.

'Back,' he said. 'Back into the town!'

Shoved, shouted at and threatened, they moved back like a lot of sheep as the Germans herded them into the square. There was a bus standing near the quay, an old battered yellow bus, its engine clattering. The Germans were forcing the driver and passengers to get out and join the crowd. Near the Ore Quay, more people were rounded up and all of them were driven through the town until they reached the Realskole.

Packed inside, some sitting on the desks and others on the floor, surrounded by the childish chalked pictures of ships on the walls, Magnusson found himself still alongside Annie. It was bitterly cold, and he saw her looking at him, her face drawn with strain.

'What are they going to do to us?' she asked.

'God knows. Shoot us all, probably.'

He had meant it as a joke, but her frightened glance made him realize for the first time just how much the work she'd been doing must have taken out of her.

'Not you,' he said.

'They might if they find out about me. What about you, Magnusson? You are a British sailor and you are wearing civilian clothes. They could accuse *you* of spying, too.'

For a while they sat in silence, and as he realized she was still holding his hand, he sighed.

'I'm sorry about your brother and your cousin,' he said.

She said nothing for a moment, then her shoulders moved, almost as if it were something she'd expected. 'Yes,' she said. 'I am sorry too.'

After a while, they discovered why they were there. Somebody talked to the sentries at the door and the story sped round the room.

'They are trying the men from the trawler,' they heard. 'They've set up a court in the mayor's office. They are to be shot.'

Soon afterwards, the Germans ordered them to their feet, and they were pushed outside. After the shelter of the schoolroom, the wind seemed to penetrate their clothing and the cold gnawed at their very bones. There was a warehouse near the quay with a flat brick wall, and they were forced to stand in a large semi-circular group facing it. As they waited, stamping their feet, a lorry arrived. Immediately, Annie's hand slipped into Magnusson's again, gripping it tightly.

From the back of the lorry, seven Norwegian naval officers, still in soaked uniforms, appeared. One of them had his arm tucked into his shirt as though it were broken, and he looked grey-faced and sick with pain. Another had a bandage over his eye and round his head. They were all shaking with the cold. They were pushed roughly into a line against the wall and Magnusson heard Annie draw in her breath sharply. A German officer appeared from a car and stood near the line of men, reading out their names.

'You are officers in the Royal Norwegian Navy,' he said. 'And you have been charged with rebellion. Having accepted German Wehrmacht rulings, you have been found guilty of rejecting them in that you attempted to escape with your ship and killed and wounded German troops. You have been properly tried by a German court martial, and have been found guilty. The sentence of the presiding officer is that you are to be shot to death at once. There is to be no appeal.'

A low moan escaped from the crowd and several women began to weep. The men watched stony-eyed and, as Annie began to sob, Magnusson put his arms round her and pulled her towards him, hiding her eyes.

German soldiers had been lined up in groups in front of the seven Norwegians. In a daze, Magnusson saw the German officer's arm sweep down and heard the crash of the rifles. The Norwegians were flung against the wall, their chests covered with great splodges of blood. The man with his arm in a sling staggered back, his injured limb flung wide, the forearm and wrist hanging limply. Then, like the others, he slid down to a sitting position and toppled forward, leaving a smear of red down the dark brickwork of the wall.

At the crash of the volley, Annie had cringed inside Magnusson's arms, and he heard her cry of anguish. For a long time, after the thunder of the shots had died away, there was silence, in which Magnusson could hear the sobbing of women. Annie was shaking, her face buried deep in his coat.

The German officer turned. 'You may go,' he said coldly.

For a long time, the crowd stood silently, almost as though they didn't understand, then one of the German soldiers pushed at the people at the end of the line, and they began to shuffle off, moving slowly, numbed by the cruelty and the ruthlessness of the execution.

It was as they headed back towards Beisfjord a second time that Magnusson saw the bus. Annie seemed in a state of shock and she was crying softly.

'If only people had listened,' she was saying. 'I knew the Germans would never come just as protectors.'

The bus was still standing where it had been abandoned, small, old-fashioned, high-bodied and yellow. Not far away, the buildings were all wrecked where they had been hit by shells in the battle two days before, small wisps of smoke still rising from them. Heaps of steel, timber and concrete lay together and near them was another bus, charred to ruin, its tyres burned from the rims, the body blackened and twisted.

'Look, Annie,' Magnusson said.

She brushed her hand across her eyes and stared at the little bus. 'It goes to Bognes,' she said wearily. 'If the Germans allow it, of course. It's a private bus and sometimes it doesn't manage it and, after this, they'll probably stop all services.'

'Why don't we take it?' Magnusson urged. 'The Germans are busy just now. They've got a town full of resentful people in a murderous mood. They'd never notice if it disappeared. Come to that, neither would the driver. I expect he's gone for a drink to steady his nerves. An hour from now it'll be too late and tomorrow the Germans'll be watching. They might even have patrols on the roads out of town to the south.'

She stared at him with suddenly bright eyes.

'We could be on the way to Trondheim before they discover it's gone. We could leave it as soon as we see any hint of the Germans, and walk into Trondheim to pick up the train to Sweden.'

Impulsively, she grasped his hand and squeezed it with both of hers.

'Yes, Magnusson,' she said eagerly. 'Yes!' She stared at him and drew a deep breath. 'I'll drive it. Up here everybody doubles for everybody else, I have driven a bus many times.'

Slowly, they walked towards the old vehicle. Inside it was a basket of vegetables and the skinned carcass of a sheep, as if some farmer had been bringing them into town when the battle round the trawler had started.

'Food, too,' Magnusson said. 'We could even sleep in it, if we took turns.'

She gave him a sharp glance that was full of excitement and daring.

'The key is still in the dashboard,' she said.

Glancing about them, they saw that no one was looking in their direction and quietly, without fuss, they climbed aboard. Sitting in the driver's seat, Annie found the choke and pulled it.

'I think,' she said quietly, 'that it is the type that has to be wound up.'

Magnusson was startled, thinking of clockwork; then it dawned on him that she meant the bus had to be cranked.

Climbing out, feeling like a burglar rushing from the scene of a crime into a street full of policemen, he went to the front of the bus. The starting handle was attached to the engine, pushed from the ratchet with a spring. Shoving it in, he looked up and Annie nodded.

It was icy to his touch, biting at his fingers. Giving it a tentative swing, he found there was no response. Guiltily he glanced round and swung again. Again there was no response. This time, in a fury, feeling that God had it in for him, he yanked with all his strength. As he did so, his foot slipped on the snow and he went down on one knee and banged his elbow on the fender with numbing force. But as he picked himself up he realized that the engine was ticking over.

Climbing aboard again, he stood beside Annie as she let in the clutch and the bus began to move, grinding away from the stop, slowly at first but picking up speed all the time. Glancing back, he saw that nobody appeared to be interested, least of all the Germans.

'We've made it, I think,' he said.

They were climbing away from Narvik along the edge of Beisfjord now. Below them the waters lapped at the rocky shores and above them the fir trees obscured the sky.

'We will head south,' Annie said, looking up. 'It's a good road and only snowbound part of the way. We can probably go the whole distance in this. And so far there are no Germans between Narvik and Trondheim.'

'I hope you're a good driver,' Magnusson said.

She gave him a shaky smile. 'I am a very good driver.'

7

They reached the farm near Djupvik late in the afternoon, and the whole crowd streamed out to meet them.

'We wondered what the hell it was,' Campbell said, grinning, his taut, handsome naval face pink with excitement. For the first time since Magnusson had known him he looked relaxed, as though he needed the excitement of war to draw the steely backbone out of him and make him human.

'What's it for?' he asked.

'We're going south in it.'

He described what had happened in Narvik and explained their new plans. 'We can all get in her,' he said. 'We've even got food.'

'The radio says British troops are ashore at Namsos, boy,' Willie John pointed out. He was huddled inside a hideous checked windcheater with enormous pockets for which he had been bargaining with the farmer the whole of the previous day. 'Yon's only a hundred and twenty miles away.'

'We shall not have to go all the way to Trondheim then,' Annie said, her eyes alight. 'We can join them now at Namsos.'

They spent the night with everybody who knew anything about internal combustion engines arguing over the intestines of the old bus. They had hidden her in the barn alongside the cattle and, tramping about in the cow dung and the stained straw, they stuffed aboard what little equipment they possessed.

'We should need no more than one night for the journey,'

Annie said. 'At the most, two. We might even do it in one day if the ferries are running.'

The following morning, however, when they were hoping to leave, they saw that one of the ancient tyres was flat and had to drive the bus to the nearest level piece of land and jack it up. The big wheel and the primitive tools they found about the farm made the work difficult, and it was well into the afternoon before they had the puncture repaired and the wheel back.

'Tomorrow,' they promised themselves.

By this time, it was clear the farmer's family would be relieved to see the back of them. The food they provided had changed from meat to soup; Magnusson guessed they were finding their presence a strain and even becoming more than a little afraid. The British landing at Narvik had not yet materialized and it was clear the Germans were growing more confident it never would.

They were still uncertain where to head. The Germans were to the south and the chances of reaching the British in the outer islands seemed very slender. It subdued them all, with the exception of Wolszcka who continued to plan his own private mayhem, his body jerking with nerves as he muttered in incomprehensible Polish.

According to the radio, the Germans were still searching for the Norwegian king who was sheltering in the tortuous valleys which cut up the country, hiding behind trees like anybody else as German aeroplanes flew low above to use their machine-guns. He clearly had no intention of becoming a puppet of the Germans and had made a proclamation, urging resistance, that lifted their hearts. Already, small but bloody actions were being fought by Norwegian troops in the snow-bound woods, but the Germans had aircraft and experience and, despite the Norwegians' courage, were pushing them slowly deeper and deeper into the forests and the wastes of snow.

At the last moment the farmer's two daughters decided to

join them, and they loaded the bus with tinned food, water and flatbrød, the wafer-thin cakes made from oats that the farmer's wife prepared.

'You must take it,' she insisted. 'We make a year's supply in an afternoon. It never spoils and bread baked for a birth is sometimes produced for the wedding.'

Huddled in a sheepskin coat, Annie was driving, her gloved hands on the wheel, her hair tucked into the red woollen cap she habitually wore.

She had largely recovered her spirits and managed to smile at Magnusson. 'It is like going on an excursion,' she said. 'We often used to go down to Saltfjord and Marsjøenfjord. It is very beautiful down there. Sometimes, if there was a timber trader leaving, we could get a trip on her. This area and the Baltic are sailing ship sanctuaries. There are little ports with wooden jetties all over Norway, Denmark, Sweden and Finland. The ships used to take pulpwood to Britain or Newfoundland, and brought back fish from the West Indies.'

The ferries at Bognes and Sommarset were working, though they had to threaten and finally bribe the operators to take them across. The elderly ferrymen, still bewildered by the invasion, were inclined to do nothing until they received instructions, and the arrival of a busload of refugees worried them. With the assistance of Annie and the Norwegian officers, however, they got them moving and crossed to the road that led south to Lillesjøna, where they had heard there were British troops.

The bus was slower than they'd expected and could only crawl up the hill. At Fauske they heard there were British ships at Bodø, but there was no sign of them in the fjord and they decided that the best thing was to continue on to Lillesjøna. But then they learned that, while the British were certainly in the fjord there, they were only transferring troops to destroyers for Namsos and that both places were being heavily bombed by the Luftwaffe.

The news stopped them dead in their tracks and they

were still trying to decide what to do when the snow came. It started as a menacing cloud in a dirty grey-yellow sky over the flank of the mountains, and seemed nothing more than a cold breath of air out of the north. Then the first gust hit the bus, coming like a demon, and at once the air was full of flying particles of ice and the thickening snow began to plaster the windows.

As the streaming drift whitened out the horizon, in no time it was impossible to see more than a few yards. Every scrap of glass was coated with snow as fine as dust that penetrated every gap and cranny, clinging to garments when they stopped and climbed out, stinging exposed faces with millions of needle-pointed fragments and hissing against the sides of the bus.

They managed to find a small wooden hotel with the basic necessities and a village hall where they were allowed to sleep the night, but the news was discouraging. The Germans were nervous and air attacks were being made against anything that moved. The British were sticking to the trees, but the Germans were throwing a ring round Namsos to prevent any forward movement and the town had been reduced to rubble. With the quay wrecked, the Allies were having difficulty getting stores ashore.

The following morning the snow had stopped, but the roads were appalling, and as they pressed further south beyond the end of the fjord where they had lain near Bodø, they heard that the British Navy had bombarded Narvik; they began to wonder if they'd been wise to head south when perhaps all they need have done was wait on the quay.

Norwegian troops were also operating north of Narvik, but the Germans were recovering from their disasters and were deployed in strongpoints around the town. Aircraft had landed on the frozen lake about ten miles to the north, bringing personnel and ammunition for a complete mountain battery, while the artillery were experimenting with guns brought ashore from the wrecked destroyers and with elderly cannon from the British merchantmen trapped in the harbour. In the end, with the chances of the British capturing the place diminishing rapidly, they decided to continue south.

The following day, the expected spring thaw was put back yet again by another heavy snowstorm and, with steam hissing from under the bonnet, they discovered they had a leaking radiator and had to keep stopping to fill it up with snow which seemed to melt and leak away as fast as they put it in.

They struggled on for another hour at a speed that wasn't much above crawling; then, as they began to descend a steep winding road, one of the girls at the back screamed and someone shouted 'Aeroplanes!'

Swinging round, Magnusson had a brief glimpse of two grey machines heading towards them, following the slope of the hill, and he saw the snow around the bus leaping in little spurts from the road. As Annie wrenched at the wheel, the bus slithered on the icy surface and, as the aeroplanes shot overhead with a deafening howl of engines, it began to waltz towards the snow-covered grass verge. Magnusson could only watch as Annie fought to regain control. For thirty yards they seemed to gather speed; then, with a final pirouette, the old vehicle struck a stone kilometre marker and rebounded from the hard surface into the trees. Amid the crackling and smashing and splintering of branches and shrubs, it rattled and clattered over the uneven surface down a forty-five degree slope. Snow, flung up from the drifts with the force of explosions, spattered the windows while yelling men and girls tumbled about in the aisle between the seats. Magnusson saw a huge branch, broken off by the wind, pointing towards them and coming nearer by the second. Grabbing Annie from the wheel, he pulled her into his arms and flung himself down. There was a tremendous crash as the windscreen was shattered and the bus impaled on the branch. The engine note rose to a scream and finally died, and all that could be heard was the groaning of springs, querulous cries from among the twisted seats, a steady drip-

drip from beneath them, and the hissing of steam.

Slowly, Magnusson became aware that he was lying on the floor underneath the dashboard. His arms were round Annie and her cheek was against his, icy cold, her blonde hair about his face.

'I think you saved my life,' she said slowly in a shaky voice and, looking up, he saw the driver's seat was covered with splinters of glass and that the jagged end of the huge branch had plunged into the padding of the back rest.

As they struggled free, they knew it was the end of their journey south. *Oulu*'s ill-luck seemed to be following them. By the grace of God, however, nobody was hurt and they clambered out of the bus, staring at the sky and ready to run for the trees. But the two aeroplanes had vanished as if they had never existed.

Even as they chattered excitedly, shaken by the disaster but grinning nervously at their escape, the snow started yet again, plastering their clothes and faces while they tried to examine the damage. The branch had stopped the bus dead half-way down the slope, its front wheels lifted from the ground, steam still coming from under the bonnet. Already the snow was coating the windows and roof and beginning to blow through the broken windscreen and build up in little drifts on the seats.

Standing among the whitened undergrowth, still dazed and shivering from shock, they stared at the wreck. It was bitterly cold and their faces were pinched with the frost. They had no ropes and they were talking only for the sake of talking because they had no hope of freeing the vehicle. Huddled together, a dark mass splashed with colour where the Norwegian woollen scarves, gloves or caps stood out against the sombreness of the scene, they watched as Campbell lay on his stomach trying to see under the engine. Wolszcka was standing by his side, his mad eyes red with rage, screaming some Polish gibberish at him until Campbell sprang up in a fury.

'For Christ's sake,' he roared, 'shut your trap, you stupid

Polish baboon, or I'll shut it up for you!'

Wolszcka stared at him, uncomprehending; then, as his hand went to the sailor's knife he wore at his belt, Magnusson pushed them apart. As the Pole turned on him instead, he swung his fist and Wolszcka landed on his back in the snow and was immediately grabbed and disarmed. As he was dragged to his feet, Campbell moved forward.

Magnusson held him back. 'Leave it, Campbell', he snapped. 'He's lost his country, his ship, his friends, his home, his family, probably even his wits. He'll get over it if we give him time.'

Campbell was clearly not in a forgiving mood. 'He wasn't worth plucking out of the drink,' he growled. 'We should have chucked him back. Like you do fish.'

Magnusson sighed. 'Shut up,' he said. 'You're supposed to be a naval officer. Start behaving like one.' He turned to the others. 'Anybody speak Polish?'

One of the Norwegians indicated that he could and Magnusson turned to him.

'Tell him,' he said, 'that nobody wants to fight him. We just want to get him to where he can fight the Germans. But tell him we can't do that if he persists in fighting *us*. Tell him we're sorry for him but if he doesn't behave himself we'll truss him up and leave him where the Germans will find him. We need his help and he needs ours.'

As the Pole listened, the hatred gradually faded from his eyes. Eventually he shrugged off the restraining grips and, moving towards Magnusson, took his hand. Magnusson thought he was going to shake it but instead, to his surprise, the Pole lifted it, bent over and kissed it, jabbering something in Polish.

'He says he will cause no more trouble,' the Norwegian said. 'He just wants to kill Germans and will do as you tell him.'

Turning away, Magnusson found himself face to face with Willie John. The radio officer's ravaged face was grey with cold and fatigue, the lines deeply etched, his nose bright red. He fished in the voluminous pocket of the windcheater he had acquired and produced a bottle.

'Akvavit,' he said. ''Twill warm ye up, boy.'

Magnusson took the bottle. 'I told you I'd throw you overboard with a piece of concrete attached to your feet if I found you with booze again,' he said.

'We are no' aboard, boy,' Willie John said drily. 'Drink, mon. 'Twill warm ye. Everybody else here hass a bottle. Yon farmer wass gey busy wi' us while ye were in Narvik.'

Magnusson shrugged. There was no ship, no longer any reason for their being in Norway. Now wasn't the time to argue and the drink was a help.

Campbell appeared alongside him, his features bleak with strain. 'Hadn't we better get on with it?' he said. 'Somebody's got to get the bloody bus free.'

'Give it a rest,' Magnusson said. 'You're wasting your time. It'll never go again.'

Campbell turned an angry face towards him. '*Somebody's* got to do something. Standing about talking love and kisses won't help us get any further south.'

'We're not going any further south,' Magnusson said.

'Which way then, boy?' Willie John asked. 'North?'

'No. Not north either.'

Campbell's face darkened. 'Then, for Christ's sake, *which* way?'

Magnusson pointed towards the west. 'That's the way,' he said. 'All this balls about going to Sweden! For God's sake, where do we go after Sweden?'

Willie John gave a small grin. 'We could sit oot the war in luxury in Stockholm, boy,' he suggested.

Magnusson jabbed a finger towards the west. '*That's* the way.'

'There's only the sea in that direction,' Campbell snapped.

Magnusson nodded. 'Exactly,' he said.

Annie was standing on her own, separate from the rest of

them. Her back was to them, and he knew it was because she didn't wish them to see her tears or the anguish in her face. Moving towards her, he put his hand on her shoulder. She jumped at his touch and swung round. He was about to put his arms round her when, without a word, she flung herself at him, her face against his chest. Lifting her head, she managed a watery smile.

'I think I have ruined everything,' she said.

'Not at all. It was the aeroplanes. And who wants a bus, anyway?' Magnusson drew a deep breath. 'How far are we from the sea here?'

'We can't be more than four kilometres from Marsjøenfjord.'

'Then for God's sake,' he said, 'let's use it. There are bound to be fishing boats.'

She was blinking away the tears. 'If the weather were good,' she said, 'if the spring thaw had come – you would probably be able to see Marsjøen itself through the trees from the slope there. It's only a small place but it has timber-loading quays where the ships came in.'

'Fishing boats also?'

She shrugged again. 'I expect so. Why?'

He looked at her and grinned. 'We're wasting our time,' he said, 'trying to get south to Trondheim.' He gestured into the swirling snow, towards the west. 'That's the way we should go. We're not soldiers. We're sailors and we have a special ability. The ability to handle ships. For God's sake, let's follow our calling and go back to the sea.'

8

For a long time she stared at him silently, her head up now, her eyes bright, her arms hanging down by her side, the snow in soft little layers on the fringe of blonde hair that had escaped from the red woollen cap. Her cheeks were pink with her exertions and the bite of the wind, and at that moment Magnusson decided she was the most beautiful girl he'd ever seen.

Slowly her mouth curved into a smile. 'I'm glad I met you, Magnusson,' she said. 'You are a good man.'

Magnusson shrugged. 'You should see me with my hair cut,' he said.

They left the old bus where it was, slowly disappearing under its mantle of snow, and headed down the road as it turned towards the west. After a while, they found what looked like a ride through the trees and caught sight of sky as the land dropped away on the other side of a ridge towards the sea. As they reached the ridge, it was almost impossible to see beyond it for the whirling snow, but they were just able to make out a long fissure in the land and black water dotted with lumps of ice. The shores of the fjord were backgrounded by white hills and the cheerless immensity of the higher mountains in a daunting landscape.

Eventually the snowstorm stopped and they began to descend towards the fjord. A colossal amount of snow had fallen and the breeze was lifting flurries from the laden branches of the trees and plucking little whorls from the exposed ledges. Pushing through the forest, they came to a

narrow winding road. It appeared to lead downwards towards the sea and they were just about to step out on to it
when Campbell spoke.

'Germans!'

Through the whiteness, as they scrambled back among
the trees, they could see movement and hear voices.
Magnusson's heart began to thump. The approaching men
couldn't fail to notice their tracks and not one of them was
armed.

They could hear the crunch of boots now on the snow,
and Magnusson saw the tips of slung rifles through the trees.
Some of the men wore peaked grey-green caps, and he was
just trying to decide whether to run for it when Annie put
a hand on his arm.

'They're not German! That's Norwegian they're
speaking!'

Lifting his head slightly, Magnusson saw the group of men
drawing nearer. They were marching briskly, all carrying
rifles but in no military order. They were in ragged groups
of ones and twos, but just behind them he noticed another
group. These men were marching in threes – five files of
them with one man in front – and he recognized the flat,
bowl-shaped British steel helmets and heard an aggrieved
voice complaining about the snow with a string of obscenities that could have come from no one but a fed-up British
soldier.

Without waiting, he stepped out into the road.

The Norwegian soldiers in the lead stopped dead, waiting.
The British soldiers behind had unslung their rifles and,
though they were dirty, unshaven and travel-stained, they
were alert and wary.

As Campbell and the others followed Magnusson into the
road, the man in front, a sergeant, held his hand out sideways, the palm turned behind him as a warning for caution
to his men.

'You English?' he asked. His voice was hostile and suspicious and he kept his rifle ready in front of him, one hand

on the trigger.

'Yes. Royal Navy.'

'You don't look like Royal Navy.'

Magnusson explained but the sergeant remained suspicious.

'What proof have I got?' he said.

'What proof do you want?' Magnusson treated him to a few obscenities he'd learned before the mast and the sergeant grinned.

'Couldn't be anything else,' he said, lowering the rifle. 'I'm Sergeant Atwood, Koylis. King's Own Yorkshire Light Infantry, that is.'

Magnusson grinned. 'I'm pleased to see you, Sergeant. Can you use those rifles?'

Atwood's face tautened. 'You bet we can, sir. We belong to the Unsurpassable Six.'

'What in God's name are the Unsurpassable Six?'

Atwood gave him a cold contemptuous look. 'That's the trouble with the Navy,' he said. 'They're always so bloody concerned with their own tradition, they forget the army's got a bit too. At Minden in 1759, six British infantry regiments – the Suffolks, the Hampshires, the Royal Welch, the Lancashires, the Kosbies and us, the Koylis, the old 51st of Foot – was given the order to advance with the drums beating out the proper time. Against cavalry! We wasn't advancing to receive 'em neither. We was advancing to *attack* 'em. And we routed the bastards too! Three lines of 'em. Eighty-three squadrons. We wear roses every 1 August because of that. We picked 'em as we marched forward.'

'You know your military history, Sergeant,' Magnusson said.

'I'm a regular and they made certain we did. I was attached to the 4th Battalion to lick 'em into shape and I made bloody sure they was good, even if they was Territorials. They didn't know what hit 'em, but they soon found out what I was talkin' about when they got 'ere.'

'Come to that, how *did* you get here?'

'We was sent forward, sir, from Namsos. We 'ad three kitbags of clothes – winter, summer and arctic. When we put 'em on we looked like paralysed polar bears.'

'Mind if we join up with you?'

'Won't do you much good. We got no transport. They just dumped us. How the 'ell the Navy got their ships in, I dunno. Most of 'em seemed bigger than the fjords.'

'What are they trying to do?'

Atwood shrugged. 'Ask me another, sir. The colonel said we could do what we liked because the government in London didn't seem to know what it wanted done. As far as I could see at Namsos, it seemed to be all staff and no war. We had no transport, mortars, ack-ack, or artillery, and the cooks had to borrow buckets and baths to cook us a meal. We was sent to Sticklestead in support of some Norwegians and I reckon nobody got nearer the Germans than we did. But we didn't 'ave radios and 'ad to keep in touch with runners floundering about waist-deep in snow.' He drew a deep breath. 'We got as far as Rora, but we was threatened from three sides and the bloody aeroplanes kept coming down on us. It's a bit unnerving being peppered by a plane coming straight down on you. It takes a bit of getting used to.'

Magnusson nodded. 'As we've discovered,' he agreed.

The sergeant gestured at his men. 'It was the biggest balls-up since Ma caught 'er tits in the mangle. In all me puff I never seen worse. When we got cut off from the rest, we decided to try to head back for Namsos, only now we've 'eard that's gone too.'

'It's a long walk to Narvik, Sergeant.'

'I reckon we can do it, sir, if we have to.'

'How many of you are there?'

'Sixteen, sir, including me. With nine Norwegians. We came here on the off-chance we might just pinch a ship. The Norwegians said they'd know what to do with it. Some of 'em are ex-sailors.'

Magnusson smiled. 'Great minds think alike, Sergeant,

because we came here to pinch a ship too.'

There was no argument. After a short discussion and an exchange of cigarettes, of which the sergeant's men seemed to have hundreds, they fell in together and began to move on again.

'We helped ourselves to the fags, sir,' the sergeant said. 'Naafi. When we started to retreat, they threw it open for us to take what we wanted.'

The road continued to wind downwards through the trees until at last they saw spires of smoke standing up in the still air. After a while, they saw houses and decided to leave the road.

Plunging through the undergrowth, they made their way towards the village down the slope of the hill from where they could see the fjord stretching away to the south-west, curving jaggedly first one way and then the other, the steep sides covered with fir trees.

Marsjøen was a typical Norwegian village of timber dwellings huddled against the hill with, dotted above it, houses and farms where a living was being carved out of the unforgiving earth. They rejoined the road above the place and began to move down it in a long straggling procession, their breath hanging in the frosty air, thirty-six men and three girls, all of them young, all wishing to be away from the hated Germans.

Then Magnusson, who was in the lead, stopped and listened. No one was talking and the woods were uncannily silent, but faintly he could hear a low rhythmic thump almost like the beating of his own heart.

He looked back the way he'd come and the sound seemed to die away again. He said nothing and they continued down the hill. Eventually, he stopped again. The thump came once more and his heart thumped with it. The sound had started a sort of panic inside him. It was unexpected yet familiar. He had heard it before and he strained his eyes through the trees for what he was expecting to see. The sound seemed to die away and he wondered if his ears were playing tricks, if what he was hearing was one of the timber cutters at Marsjøen repairing equipment or hammering at a log. But then the sound came again, too rhythmic to be connected to anything human, and it had a metallic echo, still faint but quite distinct now.

He waited for the others to catch him up. Annie was the first to join him and she touched his hand with hers, almost imperceptibly but in a way that indicated she trusted him. Then Campbell came up, his handsome face heavy with the dislike of walking.

'Do you hear what I hear?' Magnusson said.

'What *do* you bloody well hear?' Campbell growled.

'A ship, my lad. Not a big one, but a ship nevertheless.'

Then they saw her, a small, high-bowed fishing boat with a square white wheelhouse aft. Above, her masts and booms were heavy with rigging but stripped of sails. She was coming down the fjord from the sea, a white speck against the black waters, and they could see the small puffs of smoke that came from the tall stack of her single-cylinder diesel as it thumped, slow, solemn and now very loud – tonk-tonk-tonk. She was heading for Marsjøen and, with the light behind her, they could see the sharp arrowhead of her wake.

Campbell stared, then looked at Magnusson. Magnusson was grinning and he noticed that Annie's hand had grasped his. Their luck seemed to swing from one extreme to the other.

'I was expecting maybe a steamer,' he said. 'Perhaps even an ocean liner or a British destroyer. At the very least a boat with a set of oars. What we've got are puffers and, judging by that one, they look like Mores, which are the best design of the lot.'

PART THREE

Westwards

1

'Suppose,' Willie John said, 'they willnae want tae take their boats across tae England?'

Magnusson stared at him discouragingly, but Willie John refused to be put off. 'Suppose they've decided they like the Germans and want tae stay here? Suppose the captain's wife's due tae ha'e a bairn? Suppose even she iss Swedish, boy? They willnae take very kindly tae any suggestion that they join us in a war that's naethin' tae do wi' them.'

'Perhaps they'll need to be persuaded,' Campbell said coldly.

'What are ye suggestin', mon? Bash 'em on the head and take off wi'oot 'em?'

'There are enough of us.'

' 'Twould create a diplomatic incident.'

'Seems to me,' Magnusson observed, 'that diplomatic incidents have been created right, left and centre in this neck of the woods in the last week or so. I'm prepared to chance it and let the Foreign Office sort it out when we arrive.'

Willie John shrugged and grinned. 'Their Lordships o' the Admiralty'll probably decide they dinnae need your services any longer an' ye'll find yourself back with the merchant fleet.'

'After *Oulu*, you think that'd be a hardship?'

'Perhaps even in a coaster circling England, boy. Maybe a weekly boat, full o' rats and discomfort. Maybe even – ' Willie John's grin widened ' – a dredger in Portsmouth harbour or a sewage disposal barge in the Thames.'

Magnusson smiled back at him. 'Home every night, in a

pub, with a girl round the corner with a warm fire and a warmer bed! In wartime, that's not hardship! Are you coming, or aren't you?'

Willie John grinned again. 'O' course I'm comin', boy,' he said. 'I'm all for dredgers and foo-foo barges. Besides, this iss a bloody cold country and I'm longing for Liverpool with the roadway swimmin' wi' rain an' the Irish and the Protestants starin' at each other across the street itchin' for a fight.'

They stood among the trees above Marsjøen gazing down at the fishing boat now beginning to approach the quay. As it disappeared behind the trees towards the little town, the tonk-tonk of the engine stopped and in the ensuing silence they could hear the calls of the men aboard as they moored.

'Do they leave a man on board?' Magnusson asked.

'Not in their home ports,' Annie said. 'Everybody is trusted up here. Nobody locks things up.'

Magnusson grunted. 'They'll probably have to start now the Germans have come,' he said.

Just above the village there was a broken-down barn in the wood close to the road, which had once been used as a store-shed. It contained the remains of a lorry, an old plough and a few rusty timber-cutting tools. Inside, it felt like a refrigerator and smelled of damp, mould, mice and rust, and the metal of the old junk that filled it was icy to the touch. But the struggle through the snow had exhausted them and they all sank down on baulks of timber, bales of hay, the running board of the old lorry.

Atwood's men and the Norwegian soldiers with them had a few rations and they swopped flatbrød and tinned pork for bully beef. Only Wolszcka, the Pole, remained on his feet, moving about the barn restlessly, occasionally stropping his knife on a stone or a piece of steel.

'Yon mad bugger gi'es me the creeps,' Willie John said. ' 'Tis as jolly as a handful o' worms he iss, the way he moves aboot. What iss he lookin' for just?'

'An aim in life I expect,' Magnusson said. 'He knows

there's something he ought to be able to do but he doesn't know what it is.'

When dusk arrived, Magnusson decided to go down to the village to where they could see the jetty. Atwood was by his side at once, suspicious, as if he thought he was up to something that might affect him and his men.

When Magnusson explained what he had in mind, Atwood immediately said he'd go with him. 'Just to cover you, sir,' he said. 'In case of trouble. There might be Germans down there. I'll bring two or three of my best lads.'

It seemed an unnecessary precaution but, like the rest of them, Atwood had been living on his nerves a long time now and wasn't taking any chances. With them went Campbell, Willie John and one of the Norwegian officers. Annie insisted on going too, in case there was a need to placate the villagers.

'Perhaps they haven't had armed men here yet,' she said. 'And if they see me, they'll not be scared.'

Leaving everybody else in the barn, they moved off through the woods. The little fishing vessel lay alongside the jetty. To Magnusson's surprise, there were no other fishing boats; he had expected at least two or three, and he began to worry how they could possibly cram thirty-nine people aboard, his mind filled with sums as he wondered if they could manage until they could find something else further up the fjord.

The deep snow made walking difficult but its whiteness enabled them to see. The village was silent, the smoke standing straight up in the frosty air into a sky which contained a thin sliver of moon and was full of stars that promised a clear day the following morning. From one of the houses they could hear a radio going, but there was no one about in the single street and Magnusson could only assume that the villagers, still shocked by the invasion of their country, were keeping indoors. The wooden houses with their layers of snow merged into the trees above the fjord, dark shadows with dim yellow lights coming from the windows.

The jetty stretched out into the water, strongly made of timber and steel. Alongside it lay several large dinghies and the single More, the name, *Støregutt*, painted on her stern.

Sergeant Atwood insisted on staying ashore to keep a look-out in case anybody came.

'You never know,' he said. 'Them Germans are right buggers but they know how to fight. They play it big and use both 'ands.'

Magnusson thought he was making a lot of it, since the village was clearly not occupied, but left him in the shadows of the trees. Then moving cautiously, trying to avoid making any sound, the rest of them slipped along the jetty and climbed aboard the fishing boat. After the frosty air outside, the wheelhouse felt stuffy. It was warm from recent occupation, but the bunks had been stripped of blankets. In the forecastle not a jersey or a jacket or an oilskin was to be seen and there was nothing in the food locker but a couple of tins of sweetened milk, a tin of bully beef and a stale loaf. Annie and the Norwegian were staring round them, puzzled.

'But there is nothing to stop us starting the engine,' Annie said. 'We have only to turn on the fuel tap and swing the motor.'

'Talking of fuel,' Magnusson said. 'How about checking the tanks?'

Campbell disappeared aft to the engine-room. As he vanished, Annie looked up. 'Do you think we shall get away?' she asked, and for the first time Magnusson realized it was she who was seeking his advice and encouragement, not the other way round.

'We'll have a good try,' he said.

Campbell reappeared, his face grave. 'She's dry.'

'She must have sails. A foresail, a mizzen and a little triangular mainsail. I've seen 'em using them.'

They found the sails in the hold but Campbell pointed to the open hatch. Above his head they could see the square of sky studded with stars.

'There isn't a breath of wind,' he said.

In the still frosty air, the fjord was silent with the silence of the tomb. There wasn't even the sound of waves, nothing more than the soft slop of water against the hull.

'Isn't there even enough fuel to get us to the end of the fjord?' Magnusson asked. 'We'd pick up a wind there.'

'Bone dry,' Campbell said. 'They must have come in on their last drop. There's another thing, too; there are no fish in the hold. They must have been fishing when they heard of the invasion and decided to come in.'

Willie John had already found the radio in the charthouse, which was behind the wheelhouse. There was a smell of booze about him and Magnusson eyed him suspiciously, though he'd not seen him drinking again. Turning the set on, Willie John bent over it, his head cocked. He was singing softly to himself and Magnusson caught the words.

'When I get oot o' the Navy,
What a wonderful wife I'll make – '

'Get on with it, man, for God's sake!'

'Wait, boy, wait!'

With what Magnusson considered was an unnecessary amount of fiddling with the knobs to show his esoteric skill, Willie John located Stockholm and a news bulletin which told them Namsos had been bombed out of existence, but that British troops were now at Lillehammer. Other areas had been lost, however, and the Germans were heading north in strength.

The report was confusing, and after more fiddling Willie John managed to get Oslo where the radio station was all too obviously in German hands. A triumphant, braying voice was warning the Norwegians to repudiate those men who wished to fight on and dismissing the efforts of the Allies with arrogant contempt.

'The soldiers they have put ashore are cold and bewildered and miserable,' the announcer stated. 'They advanced southward in stolen lorries decorated with such foolishness as 'Tours to the Midnight Sun' and 'See Beautiful Norway'.

Now they are heading for a German prison camp. British bases at Namsos and Lillesjøna have been bombed out of existence and the only plans the British and French who have landed are making are plans to escape.'

As Willie John switched off, they stood staring at each other, as bewildered and miserable as the captured British they had just heard about.

'Seems to me the whole bloody thing's falling apart,' Campbell said stiffly.

The Norwegian officer frowned. 'The British have let us down,' he said. 'Perhaps Norway should get the best terms she can.'

Magnusson looked at him angrily, but as he did so, he felt the deck move and swung round to see Sergeant Atwood push two men in front of him into the chartroom. His rifle was prodding at their backs and the men moved sullenly.

One of them was small and sturdy with a lined intelligent face. The other was big and blond with a face like the craggy shores of his own fjords. Atwood handed over a torch.

'His,' he said shortly, indicating the taller of the two men.

The newcomers were staring round them, their faces suspicious and angry.

'What are you doing?' the big man demanded. 'Why are you aboard my boat?'

There was a long silence and the Norwegian's eyes glowed with fury. 'You are not Norwegian?' he said.

'*I* am,' Annie said quickly. She indicated the naval officer. 'So is he. And there are more of us in the woods. We escaped from Narvik when the Germans came.'

The Norwegian's expression changed. '*You were in Narvik*? We heard about it. Is there much damage? Were the Germans defeated?'

'Twice.' Magnusson was pleased to hear the pride in Annie's voice. 'The British Navy came twice. Ten destroyers and many ships were sunk. The British lost only two destroyers.'

'And the town?'

'It has been badly damaged. Shells landed among the buildings. The dead were mostly Germans.' She paused and looked at the Norwegian in the doorway. 'Why is your boat empty?'

The Norwegian moved to a locker and produced a lantern. Striking a match, he lit it and set it on the table. The yellow light lit their faces.

'I am Mindur Haldursen,' he said. 'I am from Bjugn near Trondheim. When the Germans came I did not like to stay, so with my brother, Leif, and four members of the crew, we set off north. But the sea was full of German ships and we had to creep up the coast. We came here to try to reach Namsos, but then we heard that the bombing had destroyed the town and we did not know where the Germans were. In the end I decided to come in here. I thought I could get fuel because I have a cousin here.' He gestured at the other Norwegian. 'This is my cousin, Lars Orjasaeter. He says there are German sailors down the fjord at Fjållbrakka, and they are systematically taking over all fishing boats and arming them as German patrol boats. The war is almost over.'

'How can you say that?' Annie demanded furiously. 'How can you? The British will drive them away.'

Captain Haldursen shook his head. 'They have no chance. Instead of the guns we prayed for, they arrived with four footballs to a battalion and fifty thousand cigarettes per man. They will not hold out at Namsos for more than another week.'

The bluntness shook them.

The Norwegian shrugged. 'It is hopeless,' he went on. 'They are like sitting rabbits in the snow. They are continuously shelled and bombed. The planes are always overhead and they only have rifles, a few machine-guns and some smoke bombs, none of them much use against aircraft. Everywhere the British move the bombers follow them. They simply destroy every place they stop and the population live in terror of their arrival. Their intentions are excellent but Norway cannot afford allies who have nothing but good intentions. Perhaps we will go with you to England.'

'How soon can you refuel?' Campbell asked.

'They can't.' Orjasaeter, the smaller of the two Norwegians, spoke for the first time. 'There is no diesel here. The Germans took every drum they could find to Fjållbrakka.'

'Have they got the fishing boats up there?'

'No. They all sailed for the Lofotens when they heard of the invasion. Only Kaare Blystad's boat, *Iversen*, was captured. He refused to hand her over so they shot him with his crew. Five of them. They've sent her to Trondheim to have a gun mounted. They're going to seal off the fjords. She's due back any time. There's only one other, *Jakka*, which is lying alongside the German barque.'

'Barque?' Magnusson's head jerked round. 'What German barque?'

'*Cuxhaven*.' Captain Haldursen frowned. 'I passed her as I came in. I know her well. She's carrying nitrates again and heading for Kiel.'

'Then what's she doing here?'

'I think there are technicians aboard,' Orjasaeter said. 'I have heard lathes. You don't need lathes where there is only an auxiliary engine.'

'Where's Fjållbrakka?'

Haldursen produced a chart of the fjord and Orjasaeter's stubby brown hand moved over it. 'There is nothing there except Jensen's timberyard. It is four kilometres as the crow flies, eight by the fjord because it curves, perhaps five by the road over the hill.' His hand moved again. 'There is another loading station here – at Grude, another fifteen kilometres down the fjord. Then there is nothing. Just the sea. You have only to pass the Island of Otno in the entrance and you are in open water.'

Magnusson eyed them worriedly. Why was *Cuxhaven* in Marsjøenfjord? She seemed to be perpetually across their path.

'Are they using her to seal the fjord?' he asked.

Orjasaeter shrugged. 'But they are very thorough,' he said. 'Eventually every fishing boat will need a permit, a certified crew list, registration papers and a certificate stamped by German harbourmasters at every port called at in the last three months. In addition, each crew member will need an identity card and a special permit to enter zones like Trondheim, Narvik and Oslo. There will be look-out posts and control boats for every fjord. Observation and artillery posts are already being established on the high ground.'

'How many of them are there at Fjållbrakka?'

'About forty.'

'Exactly?'

Orjasaeter did a few mental calculations. 'Forty-three,' he said. 'Two officers, two petty officers and thirty-nine men. I counted them. They've taken over the timberyard as headquarters and the ship's captain sleeps in Jensen's house with his officers and petty officers. They've set up a machine-gun post overlooking the road and the fjord and one covering the jetty. They use *Jakka* to ferry them to and from the ship.'

'What about the crew?'

'They are living ashore in the timberyard, apart from a few aboard *Jakka* and a few aboard *Cuxhaven*.'

As they became silent again, one of Atwood's men appeared. He looked about eighteen and very scared. His mouth opened and shut once or twice and Atwood frowned.

'All right, lad!' he said sharply. 'Pull yourself together! That's not the way for a Koyli to be'ave! Get a grip on yourself, do, and make your report proper!'

'Yes, Sarge,' the boy said and it occurred to Magnusson that he was probably far more afraid of Atwood than he was of the enemy.

'Now, lad,' Atwood said. 'Spit it out!'

The boy swallowed, stiffened and his face grew red. 'Germans!' he exploded. 'There's a car coming! It's already at the top of the bloody hill!'

2

Captain Haldursen extinguished the lamp with a quick movement of his hand and they began to scramble ashore. As they ran along the jetty, Magnusson saw the headlights of a car approaching round the bend of the hill like two vast bright eyes.

He turned to the Norwegians. 'Is it the Germans from Fjållbrakka?'

'It must be,' Orjasaeter said. 'They commandeered Jensen's car from the timberyard. And nobody else would come here at this time of night.'

Haldursen was staring up the hill with fury on his face. 'They'll take my boat,' he said. 'All my savings, all my father's savings, my whole life. We haven't even enough fuel on board to heat a cup of coffee.'

They pulled him into the shadows as the car swept into the village. It stopped by the end of the jetty and six armed Germans in naval uniform climbed out. One remained by the car, lighting a cigarette as the other five moved along the jetty. They climbed on to the boat, their hands on their weapons, their boots clomping on the boards.

'They will steal *Støregutt*,' Haldursen groaned as they vanished below.

'There isn't a thing we can do,' Magnusson said. 'We haven't any weapons.'

Atwood coughed. It was an affronted cough. 'Beggin' your pardon, sir,' he said quietly. '*We* 'ave. Rifles, to be exact. What's more, we can use 'em. Quietly, too. They

204

'ave 'eavy butts.'

As they waited, Annie touched Magnusson's arm. Staring up the road where she pointed, he saw a small shadowy shape moving towards them under the fringe of the trees. As it drew near, the thin moonlight caught its face.

'It's the bloody Pole,' Campbell whispered. 'What's the bastard up to?'

They soon found out. Wolszcka had vanished into the shadows at the end of the jetty and for a long time there was silence as they wondered what he was after. Then they saw him reappear behind the German sailor who was still by the car puffing on his cigarette, his eyes on the silent houses of the village, his rifle leaning against the mudguard.

There was a glint of steel in the starlight then a low gurgling cry from the German as he slid to the ground alongside the car. As Wolszcka stood over him, they could see the blood on the blade of his knife. The German was lying by the car, his naval cap with its long ribbons beside him, the blood from his throat black against the snow. Annie gasped and turned her face away, nauseated. Wolszcka began to move towards the jetty.

'For Christ's sake,' Magnusson breathed. 'The bastard's going to take the lot on!'

As the Polish boy headed towards the boat, he passed within a foot of where Magnusson was crouching. Magnusson acted almost without thinking. Reaching out, one hand went over the Pole's mouth, the other grabbing the hand with the knife.

'Give me a hand with the bastard!' he whispered.

Between them they dragged Wolszcka into the shadows, writhing, fighting and spitting like a wildcat.

'Shut up, you mad sod,' Campbell hissed, then Magnusson lost his temper and hit the Pole under the jaw.

''Tis a good footpad, you'd make boy,' Willie John panted.

'I once separated the chief cook and the fourth engineer,' Magnusson said. 'The fourth had a foot-long wrench and the cook had a carving knife.' He looked at Campbell. 'Something that doesn't happen in the real Navy.' He felt the Pole stir. 'Anybody understand Polish, for Christ's sake?'

Wolszcka was already coming round and, trying him with Finnish, Norwegian and a few scraps of the Baltic languages he'd picked up at sea, Magnusson finally managed to get through to him who they were. As he calmed down he began to mutter softly in Polish and Magnusson slammed a hand over his mouth.

'What the hell are we going to do with the rest of the bastards?' he said.

'There's only one thing *to* do, sir,' Atwood said briskly. 'We've got to nobble the lot.'

'Five o' the bastards?' Willie John gasped.

What Atwood had said made sense, however. 'We've done for one of 'em already,' Magnusson said. 'We've got to get the rest now, or they'll get us.'

Atwood picked up the dead German's rifle and handed it to Willie John.

'No shooting, sir, of course,' he warned.

Willie John's heavy face twitched and he regarded the rifle as if he expected it to go off on its own. 'Then what the hell iss this for, boy?' he asked.

'You stick it up their nostrils, sir,' Atwood explained, 'and tell 'em to be quiet. They'll not argue with it. People don't. If you shoot, that lot at this Fall-whatever-it's-called place might 'ear. It's a still night and the sound would carry.' Atwood sounded like somebody who had studied his business. 'And we wouldn't want that, would we? If they *do* argue, you 'it 'em at the side of the 'ead with it. They won't know whether to laugh or sing theirselves to sleep.'

Willie John stared at the rifle in his hands, then thrust it back. 'No' me, boy,' he said. 'Gi'e it to somebody ass blood-thairsty ass yersel'.'

Atwood looked faintly disgusted but Campbell snatched the weapon. 'I'll handle it,' he said. 'What about the others?'

Atwood shrugged. 'We'll attend to the rest, sir,' he said.

Willie John shuddered and, thrusting his fist into the pocket of the hideous checked windcheater he had bought from the farmer at Djupvik, he fished out a bottle. He was just about to raise it when Magnusson turned on him. 'Put that away,' he snapped.

Willie John gave him a sad, defeated look, shrugged, pushed the bottle back in his pocket, and seemed to vanish into the shadows. Because he guessed that Willie John was having a quick nip in the dark despite him, Magnusson was worried by the thought that he was dealing with men he couldn't entirely trust. He turned with something like relief to Atwood who at least seemed to know what he was about.

'What have you in mind, Sergeant?'

Atwood was quite unperturbed. 'Leave it to me, sir,' he said.

He seemed completely in control and Magnusson began to feel easier. 'One of us had better sit on the Pole,' he said, 'or he'll balls everything up.' He gave the job to the Norwegian and turned to Atwood. 'How do we set about it? They'll know we're coming the minute we step on board. The boat'll shift.'

'We're not going to them, sir,' Atwood said calmly. 'They're coming to *us*.'

'How?'

'Just get in the shadows, sir. Move when I move.'

As they vanished into the blackness, Atwood reached through the driver's window of the car and found the horn button. Pressing it, he played a wild tattoo on it that echoed round the hills, then dived for the shadows at the end of the jetty. The reaction was just as he expected. The five Germans burst out of the boat's cabin at the run.

Atwood tripped the first one who fell into the fjord alongside, sending up a sheet of water that was silver in the moonlight. Campbell hit the second with the butt of the rifle. The third went down in the shadows and Magnusson saw three men scuffling in the darkness. The fourth collided with Magnusson himself who kneed him in the groin and, as he doubled up, kneed him again in the face. As he fell, moaning, the scuffle resolved itself into separate panting shapes. There was a whimpering cry and Campbell clambered to his feet.

'That mad bloody Pole,' he said furiously. 'He got free! He's done for him!'

The Norwegian they'd left to guard the Pole was holding his head, and Wolszcka was grinning and wiping his knife. Annie watched him, her eyes sick-looking.

The fifth German seemed to have disappeared and they were just looking round for him when they saw him bolt.

'Catch the bastard!' Atwood snapped. ''E'll give the game away.'

The German was just passing the shadows by the turn of the road as Atwood raised his rifle and worked the bolt. But before he could pull the trigger a figure stepped out from under the trees. They saw the light flash on the object in its hand and there was the sound of breaking glass as the German went down in a huddled heap. When they reached him, Willie John was staring mournfully at the neck of a broken bottle he held in his hand.

'*A Dhia!*' In his grief he broke into Gaelic. 'Ma booze!'

Campbell slapped him on the back and hefted the rifle. 'Now what?' he asked.

Magnusson stared about him. Wolszcka was obviously itching to kill the other Germans but Atwood and the Norwegian were hanging on to his arms, and it suddenly came to him what Wolszcka had done. Loud and clear. When Wolszcka had killed the German sailor by the car, he had started a chain of events that could not now be stopped. There was nothing they could do now but go on.

He drew a deep breath. 'We finish what we've started,' he said.

'What's that supposed to mean?'

'We do for the Germans at Fjållbrakka, and take over *Cuxhaven*.' Magnusson managed a shaky smile. 'I told you

208

we'd find something that blasted Pole would be good at. This is it. Starting wars.'

The German who had fallen in the water was still paddling about beneath their feet, making little bleating sounds.

'For Christ's sake,' Magnusson snapped. 'Get that bloody man out, somebody!'

As they dragged the German ashore and let him sprawl at their feet, gasping and moaning, Wolszcka moved forward, knife in hand. Atwood stepped in front of him, his rifle up.

'Get back, you bastard!' he said. 'You've done enough damage already!'

Wolszcka jabbered away at him and Atwood thrust the rifle upwards until the muzzle was at his throat. 'When I tell you to do something,' he said, 'you do it. Quick-sharp! Savvy?'

Whether Wolszcka understood or not, he backed away, and they dragged the two dead men into the shadows and pushed the other Germans ahead of them on to the boat and forced them below.

Campbell, who had been silent for a while, was having second thoughts. 'Look,' he said, 'I'm no bloody infantry-man! I'm a naval officer. Are you sure we can do it? Taking over a ship full of men.'

'We've got no option,' Magnusson snapped. 'He's started it. We *have* to finish it.'

'Just because that bloody Pole wants to kill every German in the world, up to and including Hitler, is no reason why *we* should get involved.'

'You bloody idiot,' Magnusson snorted. 'We *are* involved. We've killed two already – or at least the Pole has – and captured four. If we don't get the rest, they'll get us. If this lot don't return, they'll come looking for 'em. At the best it means a prison camp. At worst, they could shoot us for murdering their sailors.'

Campbell looked indignantly at Wolszcka, as if he felt

their moves needed better planning than they were receiving. 'The bastard's forcing us into it,' he growled.

'Did we ever have any option really?'

What Magnusson said was right. They were totally committed. Wolszcka had committed them. Like Atwood, he had declared his own private war on the Germans and, though private, it seemed to include everybody else.

Atwood had listened carefully to the argument and now he put his own spoke in. 'You're right, of course, sir,' he said to Magnusson. 'You said it nigh-on as good as I could meself. There's nothing else we can do. But after what they done to us, I'll happily have a go and so will my lads.'

'What you're proposin', boy,' Willie John said, 'needs the Black Watch, the Gordon Highlanders an' the Brigade o' Guards.'

Atwood sniffed. 'You got the old 51st of Foot,' he pointed out coldly. 'My lot.'

'You can't go shooting all over the bloody place, man,' Campbell argued, struggling with his aggressive naval spirit and the need for common sense. 'One shot and the whole place will be alerted.'

'Then we'll 'ave to do it without shooting, won't we, sir? Like we did 'ere.'

'Hit 'em on the head and tie 'em up?' Campbell's scorn was withering. 'They only do that in cowboy films.'

'This isn't a cowboy film,' Magnusson pointed out coldly. 'They're killing British troops all over Norway as far as I can make out, to say nothing of Norwegians. It won't worry me much to give 'em a bit back and I dare bet it won't worry the Norwegians.' He gestured. 'And let's, for Christ's sake, be bloody quick about it, because if we don't get on with it, they'll start to wonder where this lot have got to.' He swung round to Orjasaeter who was keeping well to the back in the shadows behind everyone. It struck Magnusson he was taking no chances of being identified if things went wrong and was probably even looking for a way to get ashore and hide himself.

Neither he nor Haldursen spoke.

Magnusson glared at them. 'Listen,' he snapped at Haldursen. 'We can probably save your boat for you and get you some of that fuel that the Germans took! But we need your help. We need to know where the Germans are at Fjållbrakka. Exactly.'

The two Norwegians exchanged glances and Haldursen muttered something quietly. Orjasaeter nodded.

'I will tell you,' he said. 'There are five in a machine-gun post on the road overlooking the fjord. And four more in a post on the jetty. There are eight in the house where the owner of the timberyard lived: the officers, the petty officers, a mess orderly and cook, a clerk and a driver for Jensen's lorry. There are eight of them billeted in the timberyard, four on the fishing boat, *Jakka*, and at least fourteen living aboard *Cuxhaven*. There were more. But they were machine-gunners and engineers and they were left in Narvik in case of an attack there. They're expected to return in a few days when the Germans come from Trondheim.'

'How do you know all this?'.

'I was at Fjållbrakka when they arrived. They made me carry things. They even gave me coffee. They were boasting because they were getting what they wanted without fighting and without casualties. I saw them set up their posts and saw what went on in the house, because that's where I went to get the coffee.'

Magnusson frowned. 'Go on. What else do you know?'

Orjasaeter shrugged. 'They made me show them round the house and I had to carry the officers' kit ashore. They told me they were taking over the timberyard as a base but that it should go on working normally. They even brought me home at the end of the day in Jensen's car when they came to take the fishing boats.'

'Why didn't they bring *Cuxhaven* alongside?'

Orjasaeter shrugged. 'It's only a timberyard at Fjållbrakka,' he said. 'The deep water quay for loading is at Grude. You can get a big ship alongside there.'

'Why didn't they take over Grude then?'

'There's nowhere to live. Just sheds and the house that Jensen let the watchman have when he got married.'

'And the timberyard at Fjållbrakka? Is it still working?'

'The Germans telephoned Jensen. He's in Oslo. He said we had to do as they ordered. Everybody in Marsjøen works there, so nobody argued.'

'Tell me more about this machine-gun post on the road.'

Haldursen produced a chart of the shore line and Orjasaeter pointed out the road to Fjållbrakka and exactly where the machine-gun post was situated.

'It's a stone building,' he said. 'It was a farm but it was burned out years ago and this is all that's left of it. Jensen used it for storing sawblades. There's a yard at the front for lorries to turn.'

'Right,' Magnusson said. 'That one first.' His hand moved. 'Then the one on the jetty. After that, we move along to the timberyard. By that time with a bit of luck we should have a few rifles and probably a few other items of hardware as well.'

Campbell was looking worried. 'Forty-odd Germans is a lot of Germans,' he said.

'I thought you wished you were in *Cossack* when she boarded *Altmark*,' Magnusson pointed out. 'Well, this is *your Altmark*. They're in small groups. With eighteen stuck on *Jakka* and *Cuxhaven* where they can't help much. Has *Jakka* got a radio?'

'Only for fishing,' Haldursen said.

'Right,' Magnusson said. 'Then we'll take over *Cuxhaven*. She ought to be big enough to carry everyone who wants to leave.'

3

There was a long pause. Then Campbell spoke slowly. 'When do we do it?'

Magnusson turned to Orjasaeter who shrugged. 'They relieve the post up the hill with the car.' He pulled a heavy watch from his pocket. 'They'll be expecting them about now. Perhaps they're the five who came here in the car even. They'll be waiting for them.'

Magnusson frowned. 'Then again we've no option,' he said. 'We do it now.'

'We haven't enough weapons.' Campbell was being particularly stiff and naval.

'We've got six more than when we started,' Magnusson snapped. 'We've also got Wolszcka. He's as good as a couple of tanks.'

'You're being bloody optimistic! There are only eleven of us, for God's sake!'

Magnusson's temper broke. 'Christ, man, there are another twenty-odd in the barn!'

'Half of 'em with no weapons.'

'What do you want, for God's sake? The whole thing set up in naval fashion complete with headquarters and staff and a bloody flag lieutenant? The Germans have weapons. While our blasted politicians were farting about preaching peace, Goering was preaching guns before butter, wasn't he? I'll bet every German who was big enough to carry one had a gun of some sort somewhere. Weapons aren't that important, anyway. It's transport we need. We've got to get to Fjållbrakka fast.'

Haldursen indicated Orjasaeter. 'My cousin has a van,' he said. 'He works the explosives for Jensen. Removing tree stumps. He also works for the quarry at Silvesborg and he uses it to travel about the country.'

Orjasaeter would clearly have preferred to keep the existence of his van quiet, but Haldursen gave him a defiant look. *He* wanted fuel for his boat from Fjållbrakka.

'It's in the shed behind my house,' Orjasaeter admitted unwillingly. 'When the Germans took Jensen's car and lorry, I filled the space by the doors with hay and put the cow in. It looks like a stable.'

'What about petrol?'

'It's full.' The words came grudgingly. 'Sometimes there are emergencies when the thaw comes – landslips that have to be cleared. I always keep petrol in cans.'

'Get it,' Magnusson said. 'Six men in the car and six in the van. Twelve ought to be enough.'

'Not tae get *Cuxhaven*, boy,' Willie John pointed out quietly. 'Ye seem tae ha'e forgotten somethin'. If ye're goin' tae capture a ship lyin' in the middle o' the fjord, ye'll be needin' boats. Unless ye've developed a gift for walkin' on the water.'

Magnusson frowned. He *had* forgotten. 'You can organize that,' he said. He jerked a hand at the dinghies by the jetty. 'When we leave, start this lot towards Fjållbrakka. We'd better also have another group under Marques set off along the road. It's only about three miles and we might be glad of help.'

'Suppose someone starts shooting?' Campbell said.

'It's up to us to see they don't,' Atwood growled.

In his stiff pigheaded way, Campbell still seemed determined to find every flaw he could in the plan, bringing them out with a nagging persistence that exasperated Magnusson. He knew Campbell was right to think of them but he would much have preferred to brush them aside.

'I don't know one end of a machine-gun from the other,'

he admitted, 'but I'll bet Marques, Myers and the others do. We've got a petty officer and four men, all regulars, for God's sake! They'll surely know what to do.'

'You've also got the 51st of Foot,' Atwood reminded him tartly. 'They *certainly* know what to do.'

Magnusson smiled. He had taken a liking to Atwood's no-nonsense approach. In Atwood's mind there was only one way to fight a war and that included cheating, kicking and biting. Atwood had become very conscious at Rora that war wasn't a game of football where fouls were allowed.

'We've also got the 51st of Foot,' he agreed. 'Together with assorted Norwegians all itching to get their own back. If we can't do something with that lot, then we ought to be shot.'

Campbell sniffed. 'We probably will be,' he said.

When Orjasaeter arrived with his van, the hay still sticking to the joints round the mudguards, they crowded into the two vehicles and headed out of the village, leaving Willie John and Annie Egge with Haldursen and the Norwegian officer to guard the prisoners and prepare the dinghies. Marques was waiting for them at the barn and they picked their twelve men carefully.

'We ought to have Wolszcka the Polszcka,' Atwood said. 'The mad bastard'll balls it up.'

'Not if I tell 'im not to, 'e won't. And so far 'e's polished off two of 'em, which is twice as many as the rest of us put together.'

They made their plans quickly, leaving Marques with instructions to follow them on foot as fast as possible, and stopping the car above Fjållbrakka, they crouched in the snow to study the fjord and the timberyard. The thin sliver of moon and stars in the frosty sky gave the place a curiously luminous look, as if it were lit by blue lamps; eerie, icy cold and ghostly at the same time.

Cuxhaven lay at anchor, in the middle of the fjord, her bows towards the sea. Snow covered her decks and clung to her masts and rigging, so that she looked like a ghost ship against the dark water. Alongside her lay the fishing boat, *Jakka*, a quarter of her length, a blunt, ugly little vessel with a dinghy trailing astern in the tide. There was no sign of a sentry.

Lights were on round the timberyard but there was no one moving about. A lorry stood near the gate.

'The bastards have got a nerve,' Magnusson said.

'They will win the war with nerve,' Orjasaeter said bitterly. 'They take risks. The British are still outside Narvik, wondering what to do.'

Edging the car slowly down the road through the trees, they pinpointed the outpost.

'You sure there are only five of them there?' Magnusson asked.

'Five,' Orjasaeter insisted. 'I've counted them.'

Magnusson studied the dark building. There was a single light coming from a window.

'If we was to park the car right in front,' Atwood suggested, 'it'd mask their arc of fire. Then, if we was to rush it, we'd be on top of 'em before they could stop us.'

The others were quiet but nervous, all except Wolszcka, who was honing up his knife on the palm of his hand. Magnusson eyed him uncertainly. He wasn't at all sure of the outcome, but he was glad to be doing something. As he stared at the yellow light among the trees he realized his feet were frozen, and suddenly it seemed almost more important that he should feel warm than that they should succeed in what they were about to attempt. As they had left Marsjøen, Annie had touched his hand.

'I shall pray for you,' she had said, and he reflected that it might need a great deal more than prayer. It might even need a lot more nerve than he possessed, and he was grateful for the few experts they had with them. When he'd been supervising the fitting out of *Oulu* he'd hardly expected anything of this nature, and had even, he remembered, thought how nice it would be to be stationed ashore well out of the way of the war, with no rationing, no shortage of booze or girls, and no blackout. Cockayne had soon disillusioned him on that score, and now he was even about to run a bloody battle. He hoped that God was keeping a sharp eye on him tonight at least.

Atwood was watching him and he got a grip on himself. 'Right,' he said. 'Let's get on with it, Sergeant. Get your men in place. The signal will be a whistle, then we all go in together and, for Christ's sake, since we're coming from all sides at once, let's try not to kill each other. Remember also, we don't want any loud noises.'

'We'll use bayonets, sir.'

'Is that what you usually do?'

'We haven't had the chance yet, sir. But we know how to.'

Magnusson nodded. 'Okay, if that's what you think best. Does everybody know there's to be no shooting?'

'Yes, sir.'

'What about Wolszcka the Polszcka?'

'I think 'e understands, sir.'

'He'll be your responsibility. Better have somebody keep an eye on him, and if the silly sod steps out of line, hit him with a rifle butt. We can't take chances on him giving the game away just because he wants to murder Germans.'

'Right, sir.' Atwood was all efficiency. 'If any of my lot does what 'e shouldn't, 'e'll 'ave to answer to me.'

To Atwood, that threat seemed far stronger than anything the Germans might have in mind.

They took up their positions, Magnusson to the north, the Koylis and the Norwegian soldiers facing the machine-gun in the belief that they'd know how best to handle it, Marques to the west, and the Norwegian sailors to the east. It seemed a good arrangement, but by this time Magnusson was numb with apprehension, and thankful that he had left placing the men to Atwood. Apart from anything else, Atwood, it seemed, had the gift of producing a piercing whistle between his fingers, something Magnusson had never mastered.

He waited, shivering and full of foreboding for the sergeant to return. From time to time the frost made the trees
crack and little cascades of snow fell on them, so that he
began to think not only how cold he was but also how
hungry. He was still worrying about whether he'd be able
to make his frozen limbs move when Atwood came back.

'Right, sir,' he said briskly. 'Everybody in position. Now
we drive up to the door. Bold as bloody brass.'

Magnusson swallowed and started up the car. Moving
slowly to the brow of the hill, he allowed it to run down
under its own weight towards the yard. As it did so, the
door of the outpost opened and the light streamed out,
catching the boles of the trees. Atwood, sitting alongside
him, unfastened his door.

'One of 'em coming to see why 'is relief's so bloody late,'
he breathed. 'Leave the sawny bastard to me, sir. 'E won't
know what 'it 'im. Just park away from the door in the
shadows.'

He was gone from the car almost before Magnusson realized he was going. Without him, Magnusson felt bereft.

It was too late to back out now, however. A figure had
appeared in the doorway and was moving towards them
even as he stopped the car and pulled on the brake.

'*Wieder spät am Tage,*' the German was saying bitterly.
'*Immer spät.* Always late.'

As he approached, Magnusson's heart was thumping.
Then, behind the German, he saw a small dark shadow
move and he guessed it was Atwood. The shadow merged
abruptly with the dark shape of the German and there was
a faint gasp and a cry, then Atwood's piercing whistle almost
made him jump out of his skin.

'Come on!'

They scrambled from the car and began to run forward.
At the entrance to the building, Magnusson crashed into a
German petty officer who was on his way out and they fell
to the ground together. Groping in the darkness for the

German's right hand to stop him reaching his pistol, Magnusson had just got a grip on the man's sleeve when he collapsed in his arms, limp and silent. Looking up, he saw Atwood standing over them.

'Thanks, Sergeant,' he said. 'What did you do it with?'

Atwood held out his hand and Magnusson saw a bayonet in his fist, red and shining with blood.

''E won't argue no more,' he said.

'What about the others?'

'Two dead – ' Atwood nodded at the petty officer sprawled on the floor ' – including 'im. The Pole got the other. Slit his throat neat as you please before anybody could stop 'im. The poor bastard was trying to surrender, too. There's also one with his 'ands in the air, one 'oo got a kick in the goolies, and one 'oo got a smack in the chops with a rifle butt. They won't argue.'

Magnusson scrambled to his feet. 'Thank you, Sergeant. You certainly seem to know how to move in the dark.'

Atwood grinned. 'I was a poacher once, sir,' he said. 'Not professionally, you might say, but I lived near 'Arewood and 'Er Royal 'Ighness, the Princess Royal, and her husband, Lord 'Arewood, lost more than one of their pheasants to me. Not that I bore 'em any ill will, but it was usually a case of my need being greater than thine, if you see what I mean. The gamekeepers got so unpleasant about it, I decided it was wiser to leave for a bit and joined the army.'

'I'm sure they'd forgive you, Sergeant, if they could see you now.'

They counted noses and found that nobody was even scratched. 'Now for the jetty,' Magnusson said. He glanced at Orjasaeter who nodded.

'I will follow you,' he said none too willingly.

Atwood was fidgeting impatiently. 'Let's get on with it, sir,' he urged. 'Speed's the thing. They'll be expecting the car back and if we don't look slippy, they'll be asting theirselves what's 'appened. While they're watching the car arrive, the rest can nip in and do 'em. P'raps you'll drive again, sir.'

Climbing behind the wheel, Magnusson took off the brake and the car began to coast at once down the hill.

'Let's have the engine, sir,' Atwood said. 'They'll be expecting it, so let 'em 'ave it – large as life and twice as nasty.'

As Magnusson slipped the car into gear, the engine started.

'Right up to the jetty, sir,' Atwood said.

As they stopped, Magnusson heard the squeak of brakes as Orjasaeter's van stopped further up the hill. A moment later the others were round the car.

Atwood seemed pleased. 'Couldn't be better,' he said. 'Will you lead, sir?'

'I'd much prefer you to,' Magnusson said. 'You seem to know a hell of a lot more about it than I do.'

As they climbed out of the car and approached the shed at the end of the jetty, the door opened and a dark figure was framed by a glow of light from a lantern. Atwood jabbed with the bayonet and the German gasped and reeled back. Immediately, the rest of them burst in behind him. When Magnusson fought his way past the crowding men, two of the German sailors inside were already standing with their backs to the wall, reaching for the roof as if they hoped to pull themselves off the ground. A third man groped for his rifle and Atwood promptly kicked him in the face as he bent, while one of the Norwegians brought his rifle round with a reassuring clunk. The German sprawled at their feet and, judging by the blood oozing from his nose and ears, Magnusson guessed that he wouldn't be getting up again.

'Nine rifles, sir,' Atwood reported. 'Two light machine-guns and one pistol. You'd better 'ave the pistol. You're the officer.'

'Much more sense to give it to someone who knows what to do with it,' Magnusson suggested. 'I couldn't hit a pig in a passage.'

Atwood nodded, all brisk military efficiency. 'In that case, sir,' he suggested, 'I'll keep it meself. Now for the 'ead-quarters. Am I still running the show, sir?'

'Not half you aren't, Sergeant. Believe me, when we get back, *if* we get back, I'll make bloody sure somebody knows about this. You might even get a commission.'

'Don't fancy one, sir, thank you. I'm all right as I am.'

There was a faint disdain in Atwood's voice, the eternal British sergeant, contemptuous of inferiors, kindly but firm towards superiors, believing that the British army was run by its colonels and senior NCOs.

Boch, the captain of *Cuxhaven*, was fast asleep when Magnusson touched him on the shoulder. As he woke up and saw Magnusson's face, his jaw dropped. 'Mate Magnusson! What are you doing here?'

'*Lieutenant-Commander* Magnusson.' The reply came briskly and it was full of pleasure at the German's amazement. 'Royal Navy.'

'But you were – !'

'In a sailing ship,' Magnusson ended. 'In disguise. Same as you. Now get up.'

Boch stared at him a moment longer, his blue eyes like chips of ice.

'You wouldn't dare do anything,' he said. 'Like the rest of the English, you are an amateur.'

'Try me and see.'

Boch decided to, and as he reached for the pistol along-side the bed, Magnusson had the pleasure of bringing down his rifle butt on his head. Boch's eyes crossed and he flopped back on the pillow.

'That's the way to do it, sir,' Atwood approved. 'Solid bar gold. You can't bugger about. It's all or nowt.'

'What about the rest?'

'All under control sir. There's enough ammo to sink a ship, a couple of dozen grenades and a torch as big as Blackpool Tower. Two of the Germans is dead. One of the Norwegians did for one. I don't think 'e enjoyed it – the

Norwegian, I mean – and that bloody Pole, Wolszcka, got the other. That bloke's a proper terror, sir. He moves like a bleedin' snake. There's also another with a sore 'ead. *Bloody* sore, I reckon. One of my lads did for 'im with a rifle butt.'

While they were talking, Marques came panting into the room with two of the sailors and two of the Norwegians.

'Glad you made it,' Atwood said. 'We was running short of men to guard the prisoners.'

'The halt, the blind and the lame will be along in a few minutes,' Marques grinned. 'I thought we'd better push along as fast as we could.'

The timberyard seemed as easy as the guard posts and it was only when they started counting noses again, one dead – Wolszcka again – one with a cracked skull and five prisoners, that it dawned on them that one was missing, and one man was quite sufficient to raise the alarm.

As they dashed outside, they saw a blur of white against the dark buildings as a man, minus his jacket, bolted up the road towards where he clearly imagined the men at the machine-gun posts waited to be warned.

Atwood didn't hesitate. Dropping on one knee, he fired and the figure fell.

'Get him, some of you,' he said.

Campbell frowned. 'That's torn it,' he growled.

'Get hold of that torch,' Magnusson said. 'Anybody speak German?'

One of the Norwegian naval officers volunteered.

'Know Morse?'

'Of course.'

'Flash the ship that it was an accident. They'll be wanting to know what's happened.'

A light had appeared aboard *Jakka*. 'Get out of sight, the rest of you,' Magnusson ordered. 'He looks German. Leave it to him.'

A signalling lamp flashed, the beam playing on the sheds. At once the Norwegian began to flash back.

'*Unfall*,' he signalled. '*Kein Alarm*.'

They could hear voices coming across the water but there were no further questions and eventually the light on board *Jakka* went out.

As silence fell again, four of Atwood's men appeared from the darkness carrying the limp figure of a man in his shirtsleeves.

'Is the cook,' Orjasaeter said, and Magnusson was surprised to discover he was still with them.

'You didn't kill him, Sarge,' one of the men observed. 'Only winged him.' He sounded faintly shocked.

4

They decided to give the men in *Jakka* and *Cuxhaven* time to settle down and waited, shivering and nervous, for an hour and a half, until they felt they would all be asleep.

While they waited, Atwood checked the arms they'd captured.

'Two MG42 light machine-guns, sir,' he reported. 'Eighteen rifles. Three Luger pistols. And two boxes of grenades. German types, but I know 'ow to use 'em.' He pointed towards the dark water. 'This is where it gets a bit more difficult. Soldiers ain't so good in boats. Do you 'ave sentries in the Navy?'

Magnusson smiled. Atwood never missed a trick.

'I dare bet they don't out there,' he said. 'They're a hundred yards away from where they can be surprised.' He gestured. 'Only this time, they *will* be. We'll do a cutting out operation. The Navy's supposed to be good at cutting out.'

'What the 'ell's cutting out?' Atwood asked.

'They used to do it a lot in Nelson's day.'

'Bit before my time, sir.'

'The conditions are the same: a sailing ship that can't get away, sailors and soldiers in boats to row alongside after dark and capture it. Haven't you read Hornblower?'

While they waited, Marques's party brought in the prisoners from the guard post on the road up the hill. According to Orjasaeter there was a cellar in the house where they could lock them in.

'Good,' Magnusson said. 'They can stay there till we want 'em. We might even take a selection home with us when we leave. They might be useful to Intelligence.'

While they were talking, they heard the soft sound of muffled oars and the dinghies from Marsjøen with Willie John and several Norwegians bumped softly against the jetty. As they climbed out, Magnusson was surprised to see Annie with them.

'What in God's name are you doing here?' he snapped.

She looked hurt and answered him with a faint hint of reproach in her voice.

'I came to tell you about the families in Marsjøen,' she said. 'They *all* want to go to England.'

The tide was high and the stream was slack as they began to row out into the fjord.

'We takin' Wolszcka, sir?' Atwood asked.

'Can you handle him?'

Atwood grinned. 'I think so, and it's a pity to spoil his fun. 'E's a beaut', proper. 'E's thoroughly enjoyin' 'isself. In fact, I'm bloody glad I'm not a German, because *I* wouldn't like to meet 'im in the dark. Let's give 'im 'is 'ead.'

They had worked out carefully on the table in Boch's room exactly what each boat was to do. One was to handle *Jakka*, the rest *Cuxhaven*, and they had strict instructions to make sure they got every single German.

'Watch those oars,' Magnusson whispered as they reached midstream. 'And make sure she doesn't bump.'

As they slid alongside *Jakka* a door in the wheelhouse opened. They were in the shadow of the fishing boat's hull, and were startled to see one of the Germans, wearing long underwear, appear half-asleep and start to unfasten the front of his underpants as he stood at the side of the ship to relieve himself.

Reaching up quickly, Magnusson grasped his ankle and heaved. Only a faint cry escaped; then the German dropped into the dinghy, cracking his head on the side as he landed.

Someone hit him at once and he was silent.

'Aboard, quick!' Magnusson said.

Hoisting themselves up, they paused to listen.

'Four of you to the forecastle,' Magnusson said. 'I'll look after the cabin aft.'

There were faint scuffling sounds from forward as he opened the door from which the German had appeared.

'*Noch einmal, Hansi*,' a sleepy voice said. '*Seine Blase ist sehr kleine*.'

For a moment, Magnusson wondered whether to lash out, but he found he couldn't hit a half-awake man when he was discussing the size of his friend's bladder. Instead he flashed the torch.

'*Ach, die Lampe –* !'

Magnusson had a glimpse of blankets being pulled over the man's head and of a stout body heaving in the bunk.

'Get up,' he snapped.

There was a second's silence, then the German sat up, his eyes wide. He was fat and unhealthy looking.

'Out!' Magnusson said. '*Raus! Schnell!*'

The German lowered a pair of fat legs to the deck; then Magnusson saw one hand reaching under the blankets. Without compunction he swung the rifle and the German rolled off the bunk, groaning. Wrenching the blankets aside, Magnusson saw that what he had been reaching for was not a weapon but what was clearly a much-loved pipe, burned away at the bowl, the stem bound with sail twine.

Atwood appeared. 'I've left one man forward on guard, sir. No trouble. Let's get aboard the ship. That one looks as though he won't argue.'

No, Magnusson thought, he wouldn't. But the poor bastard had probably only been thinking that if he were going into a prisoner of war cage he might as well take his pipe with him.

As they slipped from *Jakka* to the ship, they saw heads appearing over the taffrail at the opposite side.

'Where do they live, sir?' Atwood breathed.

'Campbell,' Magnusson whispered, 'show 'em the fore-castle. Come on, Atwood, the rest'll be aft.'

By the time they had finished, they had two more dead Germans – both dispatched by the gleeful Wolszcka – two prisoners on *Jakka* and twelve on *Cuxhaven*. One of them was Wolff, Boch's lieutenant, and his reaction as he saw Magnusson was the same as Boch's.

'What are *you* doing here?' he demanded. 'Finland is not at war with Germany.'

'Britain is,' Magnusson said.

Wolff frowned, then he began to smile. 'I think you will regret this, my friend,' he said. 'You do not realize what you have taken on.'

He seemed strangely indifferent, and even cocksure, in a way that puzzled Magnusson. Prisoners shouldn't look as happy as Wolff did. He was still pondering the question when Campbell appeared. He looked excited.

'No wonder this bloody ship could call up the submarines from Narvik to nobble our merchantmen!' he said. 'We've captured a naval vessel.' It seemed to have made his day. 'There are stands for machine-guns,' he went on. 'And that's not all. I think she's a submarine supply ship. The after hold's full of torpedoes, and there are lathes and drills forrard. To do repairs at sea that the submarines can't do themselves. They obviously kept them supplied with food and other things too. There are drums of oil, crates of beer, ammunition, and torpedoes. *With* warheads, but without firing pistols.'

'We'll dump 'em when we've got a chance. Is there a derrick for them?'

'One over the hatch. Obviously put there for that very job. There's also a bloody great receiver-transmitter.'

'Right. We've still got Willie John. Get him aboard and tell him to have a look at it but to make no transmissions until I tell him to. We might be glad to use it when we get clear of this place.'

Bundling the prisoners into the fishing boat's hold and

locking the hatch, they started the engine. Then, using the German signalling lamp to light the edge of the jetty, they brought her alongside the quay at the timberyard. By this time the place seemed full of people, and Magnusson realized that half of the male population from Marsjøen had arrived either by dinghy or on foot and that they had been joined by two or three families from Fjållbrakka.

It was almost daylight when they shoved their prisoners ashore. As they were shepherding them towards the house, the telephone rang, strident in the tense atmosphere. It rang only once; then there was silence and they all stared at each other. After a while, it rang again and there was another silence.

'Party-line,' Orjasaeter explained. 'Everybody has their own code.'

Magnusson's eyes fell on the German-speaking Norwegian. 'Answer it,' he said. 'Carefully.'

They followed the Norwegian into the house and watched as he picked up the telephone, holding it as if it were red hot. They could all hear the telephone clattering and they knew that the voice on the other end of the line was German.

'*So*,' the Norwegian began uncertainly. '*Jawohl, Herr Kapitänleutnant.* I will inform him.'

When he put the telephone down, he turned to Magnusson, his face white. 'That was the captain of the submarine, U49,' he said. 'He was telephoning to inform the people from *Cuxhaven* that they've arrived.'

'Arrived where, for God's sake?'

'At Grude, down the fjord. They were damaged by depth charges at Narvik and they've come in to make repairs. They want as much help as can be given.'

5

Magnusson's heart seemed to have slipped down to his stomach. Their luck had seemed so good for so long he'd been convinced it had changed. But here it was again, the rake handle in the dark, coming up to hit him in the teeth, as he stepped on the head.

No wonder Wolff hadn't been worried. He'd known about the submarine, and that was why *Cuxhaven* was in Marsjøenfjord. Damaged by British action, U49 had radioed and *Cuxhaven* had broken her voyage south to meet her. Wolff didn't expect to be a prisoner of war very long. Damaged or not, a submarine was something they were going to find difficult to get round. Even if she were unable to move, she had a gun on her bow and one shell into *Cuxhaven* would be enough to bring down all her yards.

Submarines also mounted machine-guns – ever since the war had started the British newspapers had been full of stories of how they machine-gunned merchant seamen as they took to their boats when their ships were sunk. Magnusson hadn't believed a word of them and he suspected that, apart from a few old ladies in twin sets and pearls, nobody else did either. But truth was always the first victim of war, and even if the Germans didn't willingly murder torpedoed sailors, they wouldn't hesitate to use their weapons against *Cuxhaven*.

He suddenly felt very tired. The emotions aroused in him by beating up unsuspecting men, bringing rifle butts down on their heads, stabbing and shooting them, was something he hadn't been trained for. Perhaps when the war had been going a little longer, he might have got used to it like Sergeant Atwood and his men, but for the moment it was all a bit new. And to have done so much and then to discover that yet another obstacle was down the fjord across their path was just too much.

The Norwegian was still standing by the telephone.

'Did they say when they expected this help?' Magnusson asked him.

'As soon as possible,' the Norwegian said. 'I told him we were having a little trouble down here. I told him we'd send help as soon as we could.'

Magnusson sighed. 'What do we do now?' he asked.

' 'Ow about 'aving a go at nobbling the submarine?' Atwood suggested.

'You're too enthusiastic by a long way, Sergeant,' Magnusson said.

As the Germans filed past him towards the cellar, Wolff smiled.

'I think you have now decided that you have no chance, have you not, Herr Kapitän?' he said gaily in perfect English. The next second, he was flying down the stairs on his head as Sergeant Atwood hit him between the shoulders with his rifle butt. Magnusson was unmoved. Thank God, he thought, for *someone* who believed in action and didn't worry too much about the consequences.

'Cheeky bastard,' Atwood said. 'Talkin' to a officer like he come to mend the lavatory.' He wiped his nose with the back of his hand. 'Do we send the lorry to Marsjøen, sir, to fetch the women an' kids who want to go on the ship?'

Magnusson drew a deep breath. Things seemed to be happening almost too fast. 'We might be a bloody sight cleverer, Sergeant,' he said, 'if we paused to draw breath. They might be better where they are until we've decided what to do about this bloody submarine.'

Atwood looked faintly resentful, as if he felt everybody had to take their chances.

Magnusson sighed again. 'Those Germans in *Cuxhaven* were clearly expecting her,' he said, half to himself. 'And if we don't do something soon, they'll come to find out what's happening down here. I reckon we'd better go to Grude and have a look at her. Any volunteers?'

'Count me in,' Atwood said at once, and Magnusson decided he was beginning to find the sergeant's enthusiasm just a bit exhausting.

The German-speaking Norwegian stepped forward, and – to Magnusson's surprise – Orjasaeter, who offered to lead them to a spot where they could see without being seen. Magnusson picked two more Norwegians and two more of Atwood's men who, if they didn't know much about ships, were at least murderously enough inclined to be a danger to the enemy. By comparison with Atwood's group, everybody else seemed to be on an infants' school outing.

'We'll take the lorry,' he said, and turned to Campbell. 'Keep a sharp eye on the prisoners, because if the buggers escape, that's it. And send a message by the car to Marsjøen to warn everybody there's a snag and that we'll send for 'em as soon as we've sorted it out. No need to tell 'em what it is.'

When he reached the lorry, Annie Egge was standing alongside the driver's seat.

'I thought I told you to get the hell out of it,' he snapped.

'Don't shout at me,' she snapped back. 'I am here now, so I might as well be of help. I can speak German as well as I can speak English and I can drive the lorry. That will leave the others free.'

'We don't want no women,' Atwood commented and, worried and concerned, Magnusson turned on him at once.

'Dry up, Sergeant,' he said. 'I'll run this show.'

Atwood retreated, his face showing his resentment, and Magnusson found himself hoping he hadn't offended him. Men like Atwood were worth their weight in gold at a time when he needed every bit of loyalty and advice he could get.

They scrambled into the lorry and began to climb out of the village. Magnusson sat next to Annie as she drove, but neither of them spoke, and he could see she was angry, two pink spots of colour in her cheeks.

'I'm sorry,' he said eventually.

She drew a deep breath. 'So am I. Not because I came, but because I have caused you unnecessary worry.'

'Forget it. I'll have a word with the sergeant. He's too good a man to upset.'

The road wound along the edge of the fjord, reminding Magnusson of the roads in Scotland following the curves of the lochs. The countryside was not all that different either, for that matter – rugged, unforgiving and covered with trees. As they drove, he heard Atwood's voice from the rear of the lorry.

'There was me,' he was saying, 'standin' there with a pint in me 'and, and there was this bint with a fag in 'er mouth and not a bloody stitch on – '

Magnusson grinned and touched Annie's arm. 'I don't think we need to worry about Atwood,' he said. 'Somehow, I don't think he's the sort of man to take offence.'

After a while, the road began to rise, and among the trees Magnusson saw a livid scar where timber had been felled. They stopped and began to walk down the slope towards Grude. There was a hint of sunshine that indicated the thaw probably wasn't very far away. Pushing their way through the woods, they came to the area where the timber cutting had been going on. Huge logs lay in the snow, and here and there among the undergrowth severed branches formed a snow-covered cheval-de-frise that made the going very difficult. When at last they found themselves staring down on the U-boat, it came almost as a shock and they retreated hurriedly into the shadow of the trees.

Below them was a house on which they could see a sign with the name, Jensen, painted across it. At the far end of the yard, where it opened to the road, was a large wooden cross and, near the water, several timbered buildings which they assumed were workshops. Across a narrow open space that lay between the buildings and the water was a wide jetty of concrete, timber and steel.

'The water there is deep,' Orjasaeter said. 'Very deep. Big ships can lay alongside.'

The submarine looked black and menacing. Its attack periscope was cocked at an angle as if it had been damaged. The jumping wire hung over the side, as though it had been severed at the same time, and men were working on it, splicing with spikes. There were two machine-guns mounted on the conning tower and a gun on the fore casing. It looked as if it were a 75 mm and that, he knew, was quite big enough to blow *Cuxhaven*'s bow off. If they tried to tackle this fellow, he thought, what had happened to *Oulu* would look like a Sunday School picnic.

For a long time, with Atwood alongside him, he peered downwards.

'They're not carrying arms,' Atwood pointed out.

'Sailors are no' like soldiers,' Willie John said mildly. 'They dinnae make a habit o' loadin' themselves doon wi' weapons. It isnae all that easy ye'll understand, tae haul on a rope wi' a machine-gun slung round y'r neck an' hittin' ye in the balls every time ye bend doon.'

Atwood grinned, unoffended. 'Well, it'll be a help, sir,' he said. 'And we've got two machine-guns now.'

'Not as big as those two they've got down there,' Magnusson pointed out. 'And machine-guns can't do much against a steel casing.'

'Don't make a blind bit o' difference, sir. We could blow the buggers off the deck and prevent any more coming up till the ship's safely past.'

'What happens to the chaps with the machine-guns?'

'They'd get left behind, I reckon.'

'Who do you think would volunteer for that then?'

Atwood considered. 'I expect I would, sir,' he said simply. 'Maybe you could pick me up further down the fjord.'

Magnusson looked at him warmly. 'I appreciate your

offer, Sergeant,' he said. 'But we ought to be able to come up with something better than that.'

He watched the submarine for a while longer. It lay almost a hundred feet below, the waters of the fjord touched with colour where oil had leaked overboard.

'I suppose we couldn't capture the bastard, could we, sir?' Atwood asked.

'And then what?'

'Take her home?'

'I'm not much of a hand with submarines, Sergeant. Are you?'

Atwood grinned. ' 'Ow about on the surface? Wouldn't it be like an ordinary ship?'

'I doubt it. I'd rather put the bastard out of action and sail past her.'

' 'Ow, sir?'

'That, old lad, is the problem. One shell from that gun of hers would be enough to put paid to the lot of us and we've got sixty or seventy people relying on us now to get 'em to England.'

Magnusson turned, staring about him. The woods were silent, gloomy despite the brightness of the morning.

'Even if we disable her,' he said, 'she'll still have a radio to call for help. There could be a destroyer waiting for us as soon as we leave.'

Even Atwood had no answer to that one.

'We'd 'ave to disable 'er, destroy 'er guns and put 'er radio out of action all at the same time,' he said. 'Only one thing would do that – explosives.'

'There *are* explosives,' Orjasaeter said unexpectedly.

Magnusson swung round to him. 'What sort of explosives?'

'Blasting gelignite.'

'We can hardly chuck it at the submarine, and I don't know anything about it.'

'I do,' Orjasaeter said. 'I told you. I handle the explosives for the timberyard. I could blow a fly off your nose without breaking the skin.'

Magnusson's heart thumped for a moment, then it sub-sided again. 'So what are we going to make? It's shells or bombs we need.'

'Perhaps I can think of something.'

'And then we've got to get 'em up against the submarine. I can't see 'em letting us.'

They were still staring down at the submarine, all of them disappointed and frustrated, when Magnusson noticed that Annie had joined them.

'Those logs must weigh hundreds of tons,' she observed, pointing towards a great square stack of timber; thick, thir-ty-foot logs held in place by huge steel girders driven into the ground by a pile driver to stop them rolling down the slope.

'The cranes take them to the saw mill,' Orjasaeter said. 'If they are going by sea as deck cargo, they are taken by lorry and lifted aboard by the ship's winches. Sometimes if the tide's right, they're rolled down the hill further along, towed alongside and lifted up by the ship's derricks. When the tide's making, they float into the bay there – ' his hand jerked to where a small spit of land jutted into the fjord hiding Fjållbrakka and *Cuxhaven*. 'If it's ebbing, they float up against the barrier there.'

Following his pointing finger, they saw that a barrier had been built in the fjord. Several logs looped with rope lay against it.

Magnusson stared at the logs, feeling sure they ought to suggest something, but his mind seemed blank and it was Annie who hit on the solution.

'If we could remove the girders,' she said, 'the logs would then roll away. Some might perhaps reach the submarine.'

Orjasaeter shook his head. 'Once, twenty years ago, after the thaw, the girders came loose and five hundred tons of logs went down the slope. In those days the timberyard was directly below. Seventeen men lost their lives. They swept away every single building and smashed into a ship at the jetty. After that, Jensen moved the sawmills to Marsjøen and built the stands further back. The logs wouldn't reach the water from there. They're too far back, the bank's been sloped upwards at the lip and it runs to the water behind the jetty.'

'Suppose,' Magnusson said slowly, 'that the edge of the bank was removed and sloped *downwards* instead, and that the slope was changed *towards* the jetty.' He paused. 'And *then* we shifted the girders.'

Orjasaeter shrugged. 'That is different! But it would take a lot of men with a lot of strength a long time to do all that.'

Magnusson frowned. 'Or,' he said, 'one man with a lot of explosives only a short time.'

6

They stared at him, their mouths open. Annie's eyes had grown bright and a smile was beginning to curl Atwood's mouth.

'It would destroy the jetty,' Orjasaeter said.

'It'd destroy the bloody submarine, too, I reckon,' Atwood said cheerfully. 'All them logs coming down on it brisk as a bleedin' kipper. One or two bouncing about on top of the guns'd be enough to put a bend in 'em enough to shoot round corners. It'd probably bung up that deck thing, too, where the periscopes come out – '

'Conning tower,' Magnusson said.

'What you said. It would fetch down the aerials, bend that periscope a bit more, bust that there direction finder, mebbe jam the controls, and give anybody who 'appened to be on deck a severe 'eadache.'

Magnusson grinned at Atwood's enthusiasm. 'You've put it in a nutshell, Sergeant,' he said. 'That's exactly what I was thinking.' He turned to Orjasaeter. 'Could you do this?'

'Of course.' Orjasaeter looked faintly shocked. 'I'm an expert. I've been using explosives all my life.'

'This isn't a tree stump.'

Orjasaeter smiled. 'Sometimes, the government employs me when they're building roads – to remove things just like that – change slopes and alter banks of earth on the sides of hills so they can run their road through. That's what I'd be doing here.'

'It raises another point, though,' Magnusson said. '*Would*

you do it? You wouldn't be able to stay here afterwards.'

Orjasaeter frowned. 'The wireless says they are shooting anybody who resists them or causes them trouble. They would know at once where the explosives came from and who placed them. I'm the only man round here who can do it.'

Magnusson shrugged. 'It's up to you. We'll take you with us, of course. *If* it works. If it doesn't and they manage to stop us getting away, then I'm afraid I can't do anything to help you.'

The Norwegian considered for a moment. 'Will my wife and children be allowed to go?'

'Of course.'

'I think others, too, will wish to come. Now. My wife has told me.'

'*Cuxhaven* can carry as many as wish to leave.'

'Then I'll do it.' Orjasaeter smiled suddenly. 'Perhaps in England I can show the English how to do it too, and they will then perhaps return and blow up the Germans.'

'God willing.'

'When must this be done?'

Magnusson considered. 'It'll have to be tomorrow. We now have *Jakka* and *Støregutt*, and *Cuxhaven*'s got an auxiliary which will take us down the fjord to find the wind. We could get everybody aboard and be ready by this evening.'

Orjasaeter seemed eager to get to work. 'We shall need picks and shovels,' he advised. 'And as many men as we can get. We shall have to dig out part of the bank and the slope to plant the explosive. That will entail deep holes in three places. I can also plant charges below the girders that hold the logs. If we do as I say there'll be no mistake.'

The thought seemed to please Atwood. 'Five 'undred tons of softwood comin' down on their 'eads ought to keep 'em busy.' He grinned. 'I think I'm going to enjoy this. At least it makes a change – as the parrot said wot laid square eggs.'

Back at Fjållbrakka, Orjasaeter unlocked the explosives

store, a small shed behind the house with a skull and cross-bones stencilled on the doorway.

'Jensen was always a bit worried about it being close to his house,' he said. 'But it's quite safe. Without detonators it can't go up.'

As he opened the door, he stopped and frowned. 'We shall have to warn the watchman,' he added. 'He lives at the loading quay.'

'Will he give up his home?'

Orjasaeter shrugged. 'He admires the Germans. I've heard him talking. We'd better go and see him after dark. He'll have time to collect what he wants. If he doesn't agree, he and his wife will have to be brought away by force.'

'There'll be a look-out on the submarine,' Magnusson pointed out. 'What about him?'

'He'll not see us in the dark,' Orjasaeter said. 'And in the morning, he'll have no chance. The logs will be on him before he can do more than shout a warning.'

'Can't we make up some charges to shove down the gun barrels?' Atwood asked. 'Or against the conning tower thing, and the rudder or whatever it is they use. Make a bloody good job of it.'

Marques had served in submarines and they decided that if they put a heavy enough charge against the conning tower, it ought to blow a hole large enough to cripple her.

''Ow about making up a really big charge, sir,' Atwood said enthusiastically. 'To drop down the 'atch of that bridge thing – '

'Conning tower?'

'Yes, that. Drop a couple of grenades down first to sort out everybody below.'

'Then a bluidy big charge tae smash the controls, boy, an' blow the ladder away so they cannae get oot,' Willie John added.

'Why not a charge down *all* the hatches?' Atwood said briskly. 'To blow *all* the ladders away.'

'When do we do it?' Campbell asked, his eyes shining

with enthusiasm. 'Exactly.'

'Tomorrow morning,' Magnusson said. 'First thing, when the hatches are opened. We can spend the night getting ready.'

'Suppose the bastards come down here to Fjållbrakka to see us? They might walk it.'

'Over nine miles? I've never met a sailor yet who's prepared to walk that far.'

They spent the day preparing the charges.

'Not too big to handle,' Orjasaeter said. 'But big enough to do the job. In the confined space below deck, the blast will do all we wish.' Now that he had committed himself he had thrown off his earlier reluctance and even seemed excited.

They decided on 2lb charges, but, with most of them amateurs at the game, these took a long time to prepare. Most of the explosive was dynamite, which was contained in ten-pound tins, and it was decided that if they dropped one of these through the hatch attached to a grenade the explosion of the grenade would be sufficient to detonate the dynamite. To be safe, they made two for each hatch, in the hope that if the first one didn't explode, the second would.

'It also works under water,' Orjasaeter said.

'Then why the hell,' Campbell asked, 'don't we get a rope and sling a couple over the stern where the propeller is?'

Orjasaeter smiled. 'It could be done. I have time pencils. They are new things from America. The acid eats away a wire to fire a detonator.'

The cans produced no problem; the other charges were made from a type of explosive known as 808 which had a powerful sickly smell that made their heads ache. They made ten bombs, two each for the five hatches, bigger charges to place against the periscopes and anywhere else they felt they might be useful, and small charges to stuff into any hole that looked vulnerable.

Meanwhile Atwood was collecting tools and detailing men

to do the digging. Among them were four Norwegians who normally worked with Orjasaeter and three former miners from among Atwood's men who, if nothing else, knew how to dig.

Meanwhile, Haldursen, the captain of *Støregutt*, had rounded up every Norwegian who wished to go with them, and Annie Egge told them exactly what they would be allowed to take and when to be ready.

As she was reporting to Magnusson the telephone rang. The chatter stopped at once and they all looked at each other.

'Answer it,' Magnusson said.

Orjasaeter lifted the telephone gingerly. It crackled and he answered warily. 'The German captain is aboard *Cuxhaven*, sir,' he said.

The telephone crackled again. Orjasaeter clapped a hand over the mouthpiece and looked imploringly at Magnusson. 'He wishes to speak to the petty officer in charge.'

Magnusson sighed to the German-speaking Norwegian. 'Tell him you're the petty officer. Tell him we're having trouble with the locals. The captain will be over tomorrow in person.'

The Norwegian took the telephone and spoke cautiously. 'This is Maat Hammenkep, Herr Kapitänleutnant. There was a disturbance during the night and an attempt to take over the fishing boat, *Jakka*.'

The telephone crackled again and he shook his head. 'No, Herr Kapitänleutnant, we don't need help. It's under control now but I think the captain wishes to deal with the matter at once. He has orders to consolidate our hold here and there will have to be an execution, I think.'

The voice on the telephone went on and the Norwegian spoke again.

'You have no transport, of course, Herr Kapitänleutnant. I will inform the captain. Perhaps he will place the car at your disposal. He will come and see you tomorrow morning. It will all be over by then.'

The Norwegian replaced the receiver and turned. 'By which time,' he added, 'it will be too late.' He managed an uncertain smile. 'I think we are safe. All they have is a rubber dinghy and I don't think they'll attempt to paddle fifteen kilometres in that.'

Cuxhaven's auxiliary engine was of German manufacture and it didn't take long to work out how to start it. Letting go the buoy, as the tide carried them astern, they went ahead in a wide circle and, putting *Cuxhaven*'s bow to the jetty, put a rope ashore. With the tide carrying the stern round, they soon had her alongside facing down the fjord.

'What time's high tide?' Magnusson asked.

'Nine o'clock.'

'Let's have the sails set and furled.'

There were so many men aboard now with a knowledge of sailing ships the job was quickly done. They spent the evening completing their plans. Once the submarine was immobilized, they were to send the vehicles to Marsjøen to ferry everybody who wished to leave to Fjållbrakka.

The office and sheds of the timberyard were full of people now. Nearly the whole hamlet of thirty-three people wished to come with them; only the old people had decided to stay behind to look after their children's properties. As they began to gather in the yard, Magnusson found himself standing next to Annie Egge.

She was studying him quietly. He was tall and strong, with a good nose, eyes as blue as her own and the fair complexion that tradition ascribed to Norse pirates. There seemed to be the anticipation of a joke in his eyes and his mouth always looked ready to break into a smile, even at his own expense.

'You have Norwegian eyes,' she said, almost before she realized she had spoken.

He looked at her, startled. 'Shetland was Norse once,' he said.

'And Norwegian culture is Viking.' She spoke as though

242

all the others weren't worth considering. 'What is it like in your northern isles?'

Magnusson stared at the high sides of Marsjøenfjord and glanced upwards at the sky, suddenly feeling an overpowering urge to see the low hills of his own islands.

'What are they like?' he said. 'Remote. Desolate. Empty. You could say all that. But there's something else. The sky's clear – brilliant when the cloud lifts. And the wind blows as often as there are days and nights.'

'Will you live there when you are old?'

He smiled. Beyond her, he could see Atwood getting his men into a group, nagging at them quietly. Not for him a casual movement to the next battle. They were going to do it properly – by numbers and dressed by the right. Somehow, he even seemed to have got them to smarten themselves up.

'God willing,' he said. 'Islanders always return. People get the wrong impression about them. They don't dress smartly and they live in small houses. But they sometimes have big bank balances and they're not as simple as outside people think. Most of them are sailors and many have visited the great ports of the world – New York, San Francisco, Hong Kong, Singapore, Cape Town, Vladivostok.'

'They sound like Lofoten men,' she said.

Atwood was peering at his men now as if looking for dirty buttons and indifferent haircuts. What a pleasure it must be, Magnusson thought, to be so absorbed by your job that the idea of danger didn't enter your head. Campbell had gathered the sailors together as well and they were stamping their feet in the slushy mud, a very different brand from Atwood's soldiers, more easy-going, technicians and seafaring men all of them. He saw Annie looking at him anxiously. Willie John watched them quietly, shabby and stooped in the hideous checked windcheater.

'You will go to sea again?' she asked.

He stared at her. This was no Wren Dowsonby-Smith wanting a glib answer. She knew the sea and she knew seafaring men.

'Yes.'

'Why?'

He remembered what Ek Yervy had said. 'You just do,' he said. 'You come back and you go off again. The tide comes in and goes out. It's like that.'

She moved her shoulders. There was a suggestion of tiredness in the gesture. 'My brother went to sea,' she said. 'His wife waited. She was never angry because she knew the sea was in him. I would never be angry if my man went to sea. I would like to see your islands some day.'

Willie John, four of the Norwegians and two of Atwood's men had been left to guard the prisoners, and Magnusson heard Atwood whisper to the infantrymen. 'Don't trust nobody,' he said, with a glance at Willie John. 'Remember Rora. We 'ad it cut off the crusty part there. Any nonsense, let 'em 'ave it.'

He faced his men and, just to make sure they were on their toes, gave them a rapid five minutes rifle drill. There was no question – despite their red noses, hungry looks and stained uniforms – but that they knew what they were about, and it was clear that Atwood had them well under control.

They packed the first party into the lorry, along with the picks and shovels and weapons. Orjasaeter patted his pockets gently.

'Detonators,' he said.

While they waited for the lorry to return, Magnusson noticed Annie Egge standing alone.

'Aren't you cold out here?' he asked.

'No. I am coming with you.'

'We don't want women on this job.'

'Nevertheless, I am coming. I am a skilled nurse and you might get yourself hurt.'

He looked quickly at her. 'And would that matter?'

She stared him straight in the face, her eyes honest. 'Yes,' she said. 'Now.'

Orjasaeter had already got his party digging when they arrived at Grude, burrowing away by the light of dimmed torches into the bank under the girders that held the logs. There was only the faintest click and scrape of shovels and spades as they worked and a radio was blaring through the hatch of the submarine to drown the sound. The last men arrived soon afterwards in the car and the van, all well briefed, tense and excited, and they had just parked out of sight when the look-out whistled and called out softly.

'Two men! They're coming up!'

Hurriedly collecting their tools, they vanished into the trees. When the two Germans, both of them officers wearing submarine sweaters, appeared, there was no sign of what had been happening beyond the holes dug in the snow. The Germans walked straight past the turned earth, however, with no idea what it meant. They were deep in conversation and Magnusson watched them head slowly up the hill. As they crouched, not daring to move, the cold began to eat into his limbs.

'Christ, why don't they hurry?' he heard Campbell mutter.

The silence seemed so vast it was almost painful and the air was like frozen nectar, so cold it hurt the lungs when he breathed. His feet were icy; he couldn't remember ever feeling the cold as much as he did at that moment. Below them the country lay still, harsh yet beautiful with its lakes and fjords, a fairy-tale world of snow, the setting for a Norse legend.

The Germans returned a quarter of an hour later and headed down the hill. They watched the lights from inside the submarine vanish as the hatches were closed, only the one in the conning tower remaining open. By the fact that it was momentarily obscured from time to time, they guessed there was a man moving about on watch there. The radio still blared out the music.

They started work again, whispering and muttering, pushing and thrusting at the hard earth, their breath heavy on the frozen air. Eventually, Orjasaeter decided they had sufficiently undermined the bank to do what he was after and began to stuff in his charges and lay his wire to the battery from the lorry.

He gestured at the plunger. 'When that goes down – ' he cocked a thumb at the banks and the logs ' – those will go up.'

Atwood and his men were crouching over the parcels of plastic explosive, counting them again and again like misers with their money, muttering Orjasaeter's instructions over and over so that they knew exactly what to do. Assisted by the Norwegian sailors, they were to slither down the bank to the submarine when the logs had come to rest, and drop their charges through the hatches. It was going to be tricky, because some of the logs might well be lying in dangerous positions, and they'd been warned to take no risks.

'It's about time the watchman was brought away,' Magnusson said to Marques. 'Let's go and get him.'

They crept quietly down towards the loading quay. The watchman's house was an ugly wooden structure only fifty yards from where they could see the loom of the submarine lying against the jetty. The door was locked when Marques tried it gently. It presented a problem until Marques discovered a sloping hatch at the side of the house leading to a cellar. Opening it softly, they crept inside, wondering at their luck. The cellar was small and contained a boiler and several old items of furniture, and when they climbed the half-dozen steps that led into the main part of the house they found the inner door was locked.

'Can you break it down, Chief?' Magnusson asked.

'Yes, sir.'

As Marques's big shoulders hit the panels, they heard the jamb splinter and they were through in a second. The Norwegian watchman was just leaping out of bed as they appeared, and his wife's terrified face peered over the top of the bedclothes. Guns were thrust in their faces, with orders to keep silent, and Orjasaeter began to talk to them swiftly in their own language.

Immediately, the woman shook her head. Orjasaeter spoke again and the two exchanged glances. Eventually, he made them realize they hadn't much choice and they scrambled from the bed. The woman thrust her legs into a pair of ski trousers and stuffed her voluminous nightgown in with them. Grabbing heavy clothing, she began to push a few belongings into a small canvas bag.

'Tell them to hurry.'

The watchman hesitated and said something in Norwegian.

'He wishes to get something from the living room.'

As the Norwegian vanished, Marques glanced after him and they hardly noticed him leave the room until they heard a soft thump and a cry. They found Marques standing over the watchman who was sprawled on his face by the open front door.

'The bastard decided to bolt,' Marques said. 'I bet he was going to tell the Jerries.'

They got the watchman on his feet and bound his hands. Gagging him, they pushed him and his wife out into the frosty night air and prodded them up the road to where the others waited. Pushing them into the back of the lorry, they placed one of the sailors on guard, left another to watch the submarine and settled down to wait for the night to end.

Daylight came sheepishly, edging over the mountains to the east. The sky was clear and it looked like being a bright morning. One by one they stood up in the snow-covered undergrowth, stamping their feet and thrusting icy fingers deep into pockets. Rubbing frozen limbs, they passed cigarettes round, lighting them and taking quick puffs before handing them on to the next man. Orjasaeter had brought a flask of akvavit with him and he handed it quietly to Magnusson. As he swallowed from it, Magnusson felt the glow of the liquor moving through his body, pushing out small tendrils of warmth from his stomach into his frozen limbs.

As the light grew stronger, they could see the look-out on the bridge of the submarine, leaning against the coaming with his hands in his pockets, half-dozing in the cold. The Germans had partly unshipped the attack periscope and ropes and wires lay along the deck; and they could hear the clink of tools from the open engine-room hatch.

'They start work early,' Atwood observed brightly. 'Right little worriers, aren't they? What's the signal to go?'

Magnusson smiled. 'I shouldn't think you'll need a signal, Sergeant. When the logs stop bouncing, that's the moment. And, for Christ's sake, go steady with those charges. Don't blow yourself up.'

Atwood sniffed at the suggestion of inefficiency. 'All attached to grenades,' he pointed out. 'Nothing can go off until the grenade goes off, and the grenades can't go off until the pins is pulled.'

As they spoke, they saw the forward hatch open, and a man climbed out and began to relieve himself into the fjord. Other hatches were thrown open one by one until there were several men on the casing smoking cigarettes.

'Didn't expect that, sir,' Atwood admitted. 'Makes it more difficult.'

After a while they smelled coffee, and a man put his head out of the forward hatch and called something; the German sailors tossed their cigarettes into the water and began to climb back through the hatches, with the exception of the solitary man on the conning tower. For a moment, he stared round him; then he climbed down the ladder to the casing and went to the forward hatch. A head appeared and he was handed a mug that steamed in the cold morning air.

'Anybody ashore?' Magnusson asked.

Campbell gestured. 'One. A petty officer. He's got what looks like part of a periscope and a handful of tools. He's in the workshop.'

'I don't think we can wait any longer. Can you detail

someone, Atwood, to attend to him?'

'No sooner asked than done, sir,' Atwood said. 'We've got just the bloke for it – Taddy the Pole.'

He jabbed Wolszcka with his elbow and pointed to where the German had disappeared into the hut. 'See 'im off, kid,' he said. He jerked the flat of his hand across his throat and Wolszcka grinned.

'And make it bloody quick,' Atwood added. 'We can't wait.'

If Wolszcka could understand no one else, he seemed to understand Atwood. As he vanished, Atwood turned to Magnusson.

''E'll see to it, sir,' he said approvingly. 'You'll curl up laughin'. He's a good boy, Pole or no bloody Pole. I wonder if 'e'd like to join the Koylis when we get 'ome.'

After a while Wolszcka returned and spoke softly to Atwood. The sergeant turned to Magnusson.

'Right, sir. Done. We're all ready now. You've just got to give the word.'

As he spoke, a man climbed out of the engine-room hatch, walked along the casing, crossed the little gangway to the quay, and headed towards the workshop. The man on the conning tower called to him and he turned and waved.

'He'll find the other one,' Atwood whispered.

'Where is he?' Magnusson said.

'Wolszcka said he left him on the floor.'

'Dead?'

''E wouldn't be daft enough to leave 'im any other way, sir.'

Magnusson glanced about him. If the man now walking across the quay towards the workshop found the corpse, the alarm would be given at once.

The Norwegians were watching, ready with Marques and the sailors to hurry after Atwood's men. Orjasaeter crouched in the snow with the plunger. His face was pale and his nose was red. Just behind him, Annie Egge waited.

She lifted her hand nervously as she saw Magnusson turn, and gave him a shy wave.

The German sailor was just entering the workshop. Magnusson could see the light burning there and he knew it had to be now.

He glanced at Orjasaeter and stuck his thumb up. Orjasaeter answered him with a wave and Magnusson made the motion of thrusting home a plunger. Orjasaeter nodded and waved again. Then Magnusson saw him throw his weight downwards.

7

The explosion came surprisingly loud in the silent fjord, echoing across the water and bouncing back from the cliffs at the far side.

The flash came in a curious flicker of light that dazzled Magnusson for a moment, then he realized that what he'd seen was not one explosion but several. Trees on the edge of the clearing quivered in the blast, shaking veils of white to the ground and two separate clouds of brown smoke billowed up from the bank. Out of the smoke rocks and stones flew high above the fjord with a cloud of pulverized earth, before bouncing and rolling down the hillside.

The German sailor standing on the casing had swung round, staring upwards, still holding the steaming mug of coffee, and they heard him shout and point; then Magnusson saw that the slope above the submarine was shifting.

Orjasaeter had done his job well and a whole section of the slope had vanished. With it went the bank in front of the logs, sliding away, slowly at first, then faster and faster down the hill towards the water, taking with it shrubs and small trees. A window in the watchman's house shattered as a rock hurtled through it. Behind them the stand of logs was already on the move.

The girders wrenched out by the explosions, the logs were falling and they saw the first of them bounce over the ledge of the slope where the lip of the bank had been torn away. The water all round the submarine was already pitted with ripples and splashes as debris bounced into it off the casing, and they saw the look-out drop his mug of coffee and bolt behind the conning tower for shelter. By now the whole mass of logs was rolling, and after another explosion that echoed like thunder against the slopes of the fjord they seemed to leap out from the bank and start bounding towards the water, pushing earth and small trees ahead of them.

The man behind the conning tower stuck out his head, then withdrew it like a tortoise beneath its shell. The logs were going down now in a solid wall, flinging snow high as they began to turn end over end, digging in their tips and then leaping again to fling up the earth, like some enormous animal having a dust-bath. The man behind the conning tower was screaming now and, as he tried to run to safety along the deck, the first log caught him, striking him between the shoulders and flinging him into the water twenty yards away. He surfaced once, but made no attempt to save himself, and vanished again as if his back were broken.

Another man had thrust his head and shoulders out of the engine-room hatch but he dropped out of sight again at once. As he reached up to close the hatch cover a log smashed down across it and even above the din they heard him shriek as his arm was crushed. More young trees went down, followed by more boulders plucked from the face of the slope, and the sailor who had gone into the workshop reappeared at a run. He was clutching the petty officer's cap and it was obvious he had just found the dead man. For a moment he stood still, his jaw dropped open, his eyes dilated with horror. He stared upwards at the avalanche of logs, and Magnusson saw Atwood lift his rifle to shoot him. There was no need. One of the logs struck the bank, turned in its course and twisted like a living thing to strike the German as he bolted for safety. It lifted him thirty feet into the air, and, as he dropped to the ground, another great wave of logs roared down and he was lost to sight beneath them.

The logs were now half-hidden in a cloud of whirling

snow, and Magnusson saw a whole pile of them, going down like ninepins, hit the watchman's house which immediately disintegrated in a shower of separate planks and tiles. A hut was swept aside like chaff and a row of poles carrying a telephone wire snapped off like pipe stems. An electricity cable went down with flashes of blue light where it snapped and shorted.

There was no sign of life on the submarine. The gun on the foredeck reared up crookedly, and the aerials and jumping wire running from stem to stern had been swept away. Huge lengths of timber were still bouncing off the casing, hammering at the periscopes, tearing away the rail round the guns, the antennae, every single thing that protruded from the outer skin, valves, pieces of casing, even a winch, all smashed by the tumbling logs as if by a great brown monster.

As the last log catapulted into the fjord, the din stopped. They could hardly see the submarine beneath the criss-crossed pile of timber. Beyond it the water had been stirred to foam and the trees were floating now, some on top of others, moving slowly upstream on the tide under a fine spray and a cobwebby cloud of drifting snow.

For a moment, nobody moved or spoke. Then Wolszcka came abruptly to life, and they saw he was working frantically with a crowbar to lever a last log over the lip of the slope. As it went, rolling and bouncing, he began to laugh and cheer, jabbering away in Polish and shaking his fist at the wreckage below.

At the sound, Magnusson and Atwood began to slither down the torn, scarred slope to the quay, now almost collapsing after the pounding of the logs. Magnusson was the first to reach the tangle and for a while he stood wondering what in God's name to do. Not in a thousand years could he have imagined the destruction they had caused and he hadn't the slightest idea how to mount the pile of intertwined logs to reach the submarine.

The forward hatch was free of wreckage and, as he watched, he saw two men scramble out of it. Without hesitation, Atwood brought up his rifle and the two men were lifted over the side to drop into the fjord and drift away on the tide, one of them passing Magnusson just below the surface of the water, a hand sticking out, the fingers clawing in agony. Immediately, Wolszcka, who had hurried after them down the slope, scrambled across the logs and on to the casing, and Magnusson saw him running towards the forward hatch.

He crouched above it to drop his charge and slam the hutch shut. Almost at once, it lifted and fell back with a clang, and Magnusson heard the thump of the explosion and saw the puff of blue smoke. As the smoke disappeared, Atwood ran like a monkey up a log that was resting with one end on the shore and the other alongside the conning tower, where it was held in place by the wreckage of the periscopes. Reaching the hatch, he fished in his pocket for a grenade and Magnusson saw him pull out the pin and throw it in. The flat slap of the explosion stirred Magnusson into action. The log he chose was not securely wedged and it moved, almost throwing him off. He reached the after deck, found the engine-room hatch and tossed a grenade down. It bounced off the ladder inside and vanished. As he drew back, the metallic clang of the explosion sent out a puff of blue smoke.

Atwood seemed to have the balance and dexterity of an acrobat, performing a tight-rope act down a log to the after escape hatch. As he reached it a man pushed his head through and Atwood kicked at it on the run with his heavy boot as if he were a footballer aiming for goal. As the German's head snicked back and he disappeared without a sound, Atwood wrenched the pin from another grenade, dropped it through the hole after him, slammed the hatch shut and stood on it until the muffled thump proclaimed that the grenade had gone off.

Other bombs had been dropped through the forward

hatch, and at this point Magnusson realized there was another hatch in front of the conning tower and behind the forward gun that was used by the gun's crew to reach their weapon quickly. Even as he headed for it, he saw it open and jam against a log. Scrambling up, he slipped a grenade through the gap. There was a yell of fright as the hatch dropped back, and he ducked against the conning tower. There was a flat crack below him, then no further sound.

By this time, the men with the home-made charges were scrambling aboard, moving more cautiously with their heavy loads. One of them climbed up to the conning tower and, wriggling between the logs, wrenched the pin from the grenade that was to act as a detonator and dropped his charge down the hatch. As he scrambled clear the deep, muffled explosion flung up smoke and fragments of what could have been clothing or fittings or even human flesh. Campbell and Marques were uncoiling a rope over the stern to lower a charge over the side; then they ran along a tree towards the shore. As they reached the far end, they jumped, landing up to their waists in water, and as they struggled ashore, there were two muffled thumps and two huge columns of water rose up alongside the submarine's stern.

As the explosions died away, they all stopped to draw breath. Outwardly, there was little to show for their efforts, all the devastation had been wrought inside the submarine. If there were men left alive, they would be so shocked and terrified it would be a long time before they would dare move. When they did, and scrambled clear, they would find they were manning only wreckage moored to the jetty by the splintered pile of logs.

Atwood, who had been stuffing charges into every hole he could find, was standing now near the watchman's wrecked house, staring round him, panting, as if overwhelmed by the destruction they had caused.

'Christ,' he said quietly.

For once he seemed satisfied.

8

For a long time they stood still, only Wolszcka grinning and chattering to himself as he touched the others on the arm or shoulder and gestured at the wreckage. Then Magnusson pulled himself together and, fishing under his jacket, he unrolled the white ensign he had rescued from *Oulu*.

Watched by Atwood, he took his bayonet and stabbed it through the corner of the flag into the bulk of one of the logs that stood upright among the tangle. Breaking down a loop of telephone wire, he attached the lower corner of the flag. Rather to his surprise, Atwood solemnly saluted it. In one as murderous as the sergeant, it seemed a surprisingly sentimental thing to do.

'Just to let 'em know, sir?' Atwood asked.

'Yes. And so the bastards don't take it out on the Norwegians when we've gone. They'll decide the Royal Navy did it.'

This was too much for Atwood and, dragging out a clasp knife, he busied himself carving KOYLI on the tree trunk beneath the flag.

'Not all of it, sir,' he said. 'Not by a bloody long chalk. The Koylis 'ad a share.'

He stood back, admiring his handiwork. Then he grinned at Magnusson, turned to the men watching him, and began to shout in his high-pitched angry yelp. 'Okay, back to the vehicles! Everybody aboard! We're goin' 'ome!'

The words seemed to bring them all back to life and they started to scramble up the slope. Magnusson's mind was numb and he worked his way up as if in a daze. Annie was at the top, staring down, relief on her face.

They climbed into the vehicles, packing people in like sardines, but there was still not room for everybody. Atwood was undeterred. He formed his men up in threes – no nonsense about any panic retreat for him – and as the vehicles began to move, Magnusson heard him addressing them calmly.

'We are The King's Own Yorkshire Light Infantry,' he was saying. 'Remember that. No 'urry. No running. Only gets you out of puff. Just a good light infantry pace. One 'undred and forty to the minute. We might even thunderfoot it there afore 'em.'

As the lorry ground up the hill, the infantrymen set off at their quick step and Magnusson began to think Atwood might even be right.

The entire population of Marsjøen had gathered at Fjållbrakka to see them arrive. As the vehicles swept down the winding road, and the men started to cheer and grin, they began to dance in the roadway, grabbing their hands as they jumped down.

As the lorry shot off again to pick up Atwood and his men, Marques appeared.

'Prisoners, sir,' he asked. 'What do we do about 'em?'

Magnusson grinned. 'Why not take 'em with us?'

'Why not indeed, sir?'

The Germans were coming out, their hands above their heads, in a long line, blinking against the light, as the lorry returned, coasting down the slope.

Boch's face was dark with rage. 'You cannot do this,' he said. 'We are German sailors.'

'And we're British sailors,' Magnusson said. 'And I think you'll find we can.'

Atwood immediately took over and marched the Germans aboard *Cuxhaven* to where Marques was waiting with the hatch of the hold open.

'Down you go, mate,' Atwood said to Wolff. 'They're going to be bloody pleased to see you lot when we get back to England. It'll be one up to the Koylis that we've brought prisoners back, and no mistake. I bet nobody else has. An' it ain't often light infantry put a naval vessel out of action, so that'll be a feather in our hats too.'

The watchman and his wife were waiting apprehensively in the timberyard.

'I think we'd better take them as well,' Magnusson said. 'Then they won't be able to incriminate anybody who's decided to stay behind.'

As the villagers began to come aboard, Magnusson sent Annie ashore.

'Tell 'em it's the last chance,' he said.

One old man, frightened of being alone, changed his mind. The rest stood in mute silence, unable to leave their homes and prepared to endure the Germans rather than give up the possessions of a lifetime.

Campbell appeared. He seemed elated with what had happened. 'Willie John reports he can handle the transmitter,' he said. He grinned unexpectedly. 'He's in the radio shack now with a bottle of akvavit.'

'Where the hell did he get it this time?'

'Off one of the old boys at Marsjøen.'

Willie John, Magnusson decided, didn't have much future in the Navy. 'He's quicker than a rat up a drain,' he said. 'What's he doing?'

'He's trying to call up on an open frequency. He says somebody in England's bound to pick it up.'

'Tell him to get cracking then. Tell him to get a signal to Cockayne to say we're coming home – with *Cuxhaven* instead of *Oulu*.'

'What about the torpedoes? We were going to dump 'em.'

'Better leave 'em,' Magnusson decided. 'Perhaps they're a new kind our lot don't know about and they might like to examine 'em.'

'Let's hope that other fishing boat, *Iversen*, doesn't appear from Trondheim with her new pop-gun,' Campbell said. 'Even a seventy-five millimetre shell among 'em would make a big bang.'

'Pity we can't pack the German prisoners round 'em,' Magnusson suggested. 'That would damp it down a bit.'

Campbell's eyes gleamed suddenly. 'Look,' he said, 'that submarine. When the Germans arrive they'll clear her and repair her and sink ships with her. Why don't we do her for good and all, with a torpedo each side of her to blow her in half.'

'I don't know a damn thing about torpedoes.'

'I do. A bit, anyway. And Marques did his time in subs. They're fitted with warheads but you couldn't detonate 'em with a hammer at the moment. Why don't we do it with explosive and a time pencil. That ought to be enough to send up the warhead.'

'Can you do it?'

'Let's ask Marques.'

Marques seemed to think they could. For safety they checked with Orjasaeter. The Norwegian's eyes lit up and he nodded. 'Of course,' he said. 'I can do it.'

'Right,' Magnusson said. 'Then we will.'

They were already preparing to hoist up two of the torpedoes on the specially fitted crane when the last of the Norwegians came on board. Captain Haldursen watched them but made no attempt to follow.

'I am not coming with you,' he said. 'I am taking *Støregutt. Jakka* is coming too. We've refuelled her from the diesel the Germans took. Perhaps your country will have need of such boats. With Norway defeated, she will perhaps use them to fetch other Norwegians who are eager to leave, or perhaps to land Norwegians who wish to carry on the fight. Perhaps they'll bring arms or radios or messages.' His face was alight with hope. 'I cannot believe now that the war is over for Norway.'

The two little vessels, each of them only sixty feet long,

cast off as they hauled *Cuxhaven*'s gangway aboard. The auxiliary engine was chunking away below and, as the last ropes left the land, *Cuxhaven* began to edge slowly from the quayside. The few people left ashore gave shy waves and there were a few thin cries of farewell. Gathering speed, the great ship began to move down the fjord against the tide, the anchor trailing a tiny bow wave in the water.

By this time, Campbell and Marques had the two torpedoes hoisted up from the hold on to the deck. Their warheads were swathed with rags and Campbell gave Magnusson a quick grin.

'All ready. Every bit of the know-how of Lars Orjasaeter, CPO Marques and yours truly.'

As they drew near Grude, they were brushing past logs moving slowly on the tide. U49 was still swamped below its load of criss-crossed timber, and there was a slow curl of smoke rising up near the engine-room hatch. As they drew closer they saw flames and realized that some of the timber had caught fire.

'Let go the anchor.'

As *Cuxhaven* came to a stop, swinging on her anchor chain, a shot rang out from the shore and they heard the swift crack of a bullet passing overhead.

'Somebody's survived.' Magnusson turned to Campbell. 'Right. It's up to you. We'll cover you. Get everybody below.'

As the women and children disappeared into the saloon, Sergeant Atwood, Wolszcka and a few more poked machine-guns over the taffrail and sent bursts ashore. A single shot came back in reply, but nothing more.

'Get cracking and make it fast,' Magnusson said. 'We don't want to be caught here by that bloody *Iversen* with her gun.'

The ship's boat already hung just over the water. As she touched, Marques began to swing out the first of the torpedoes.

'Lay on that rope,' he was saying. 'And quick about it!'

With the two torpedoes floating at the stern of the dinghy, Orjasaeter, Marques and Campbell climbed over the side. They were just about to set off across the fjord when Wolszcka started to climb after them. Atwood pulled him back.

'C'm' 'ere, you daft bugger,' he said. 'You'll blow the bloody lot up if you get in there! Leave it to them what knows 'ow.'

Wolszcka didn't argue and as the dinghy began to move slowly across the fjord, Campbell looked up.

'Come and watch the *real* Navy at work,' he called.

As they approached the submarine, another shot rang out from the shore.

'From the cross,' Magnusson snapped. 'There are a couple of men there.'

Sergeant Atwood nodded. 'Seven hundred,' he snapped. 'Half left. Bloke on cross. Five rounds, concentrate, fire!'

There was a rapid clatter and, through his binoculars, Magnusson saw chips flying from the wooden cross. There was no more firing from the shore.

The dinghy was alongside the stern of the submarine now, the only part clear of the logs, and they could see Marques leaning over the side. Magnusson glanced at his watch. They seemed to be taking a long time, and he was terrified that *Iversen* would appear in the fjord with her gun.

'For Christ's sake,' he muttered. 'Look slippy!'

As he raised his binoculars again, he saw the three working by the submarine scramble back into the dinghy and begin to pull on the oars like men demented. Magnusson found himself tensing as he waited for the crash of the explosion. It seemed to take all day for the dinghy to cross the fjord and bump alongside *Cuxhaven*.

'Let's go,' Campbell panted as he scrambled to the deck. 'We've got a quarter of an hour, I reckon.'

Even before the boat was properly clear of the water, the anchor was hauled up and *Cuxhaven* started to move forward.

'Anchor a-cockbill,' Marques yelled.

'Leave her there for the time being. We can hoist her inboard when we're clear.'

'Boat secured.' Campbell arrived, panting, at Magnusson's side.

'Let's have some canvas on her. Topsails and foresail.'

The two fishing boats had gone ahead of them and were waiting a mile down the fjord, the tonk-tonk-tonk of their engine filling the gash in the land with its deep thump.

They were all staring towards the submarine as it slid astern. The white ensign was still fluttering from the end of the log where Magnusson had placed it. It was whipping in the breeze now, standing out straight, clear and sharp against the dark background of the scarred earth and the drift of grey-blue smoke coming from the burning timber.

Campbell looked up from his watch. 'Now,' he said.

But nothing happened and he looked quickly at Magnusson, then at Marques and Orjasaeter.

'I make it *now*, sir,' Marques corrected politely.

'Wait,' the Norwegian said. 'The time pencils are not exact to the second.'

The submarine was disappearing well astern now.

'The buggers have misfired,' Campbell said, his face full of disappointment.

'Wait! Wait!'

They had almost reached the bend in the fjord and Magnusson had just given up hope when they saw a huge column of water lift from the stern of the submarine. The logs appeared to heave together and the whole vessel seemed to rise out of the water. Almost immediately they heard the roar of the explosion, and a moment later another as a second column of water went up alongside the collapsing remains of the first.

Everybody was on deck now, staring back – men, women and children together – and as they stared they saw the submarine's stern begin to settle. Wolszcka, looking wilder than ever, began to caper about the deck as the submarine vanished slowly beneath the water and the logs which had been weighting it down floated free. Only the fore end of the vessel, presumably sealed off by watertight doors, remained above the surface.

'Wow!' Campbell said.

'I think we must have blown the stern off,' Marques said. 'They won't salvage much from her.'

As the thin sun appeared, Magnusson could still see the white ensign, a mere speck now, against the land. Then they reached the turn where the fjord opened out to the sea, and as Otno Island appeared the submarine slowly vanished from sight behind the trees.

Annie Egge was standing near Magnusson on the poop, her face bleak.

'It might be a long time before you come back, Annie,' he said.

She turned, the frown on her face giving way to a smile. It was tremulous and uncertain for a moment; then her head lifted.

'But we *shall* come back, Magnusson,' she said. 'We shall all come back. Norway will hold up her head again.'

'It won't be long.'

Her smile faded. 'I think it will,' she said. 'Perhaps many years. But we shall come.'

Campbell appeared. He seemed transformed, all his stiffness gone in the joy of success. 'Willie John says he's in touch with some operator in the Shetlands,' he announced. 'He's passed a message to be sent on to Cockayne via the Admiralty.'

Magnusson grinned. 'That'll make the old bugger sit up.'

The fjord widened. To the south lay Otno Island, topped with a clump of trees. The wind was on the quarter, fresh enough to lift the tops off the waves and bringing with it the smell of pines and damp earth and land. The ship, heeling steadily with the wind, was running at nine knots, the speed increasing all the time. The sky was grey with a layer of broken cloud.

Magnusson glanced upwards. 'Covered enough to keep aeroplanes away,' he observed cheerfully. 'We're going to make it home.'

Willie John appeared. 'We've had a signal, boy,' he grinned. 'From Cockayne himself, via the Admiralty, via the Shetlands. We're tae make for Rosyth. We'll be met an' escorted.'

Magnusson looked up at the sky again.

'Shove up the topgallants,' he said.

It was surprising how different it was in the entrance to the fjord, with the land slipping away on either side. The wind was gusting strongly now and big seas, coming round the island, were beginning to charge at them, bearing the ship up, filling the air with lashing spray.

'Rosyth for tea, boy,' Willie John said.

The sea was bubbling into the lee scuppers and the air was filled with the squeak and clang of freeing ports as the deck cleared. The ship was making twelve knots as they coiled the falls down on the belaying pins. The huge course sails looked like the bellies of giant sows, and round the ship the sea was surging and hurling itself into the air, leaping the rail by the mizzen braces and filling the deck again with a whirl of frothing white water.

Going below, Magnusson found Annie in the chartroom. 'Another hour,' he said, 'and we'll be safe.'

The glance she gave him was warm, trusting and affectionate.

As he went back on deck, the look-out called and, hurrying forward, he followed the pointing hand to see the square box-like structure of a fishing boat ahead of them. It lifted on a wave so that its red lead showed. Then it sank out of sight in the next trough, almost as though it were going down on its last dive into the vast darkness of the sea-bottom.

As it lifted again, he realized it was flying the swastika of Nazi Germany and that a small gun was mounted on the bow.

Campbell was studying it, his eyes narrowed. He turned and looked at Magnusson.

'*Iversen*,' he said in a flat voice.

9

It was Willie John who broke the long silence as he appeared at Magnusson's side with a signal pad in his fist.

'Yon bastard iss callin' us up by radio,' he announced.

'What's he saying?'

'I cannae tell. It's in German.'

The Norwegian naval officer translated it quickly.

'It is from Kapitän-zur-See Langfels, Senior Naval Officer, Sjambad–Marsjøen–Kurigsdal. To *Cuxhaven*. He says "Where are you heading?" '

Magnusson hesitated then he shook his head. 'Ignore it,' he said.

Two minutes later, Willie John was back. 'He's repeatin' it, boy, and sayin' "Answer at once." '

'Continue to ignore it.'

Two minutes later it was Marques who spoke. 'She's flashing now, sir.'

'Can you read it?'

'Yes, sir. But it's in German.'

The German-speaking Norwegian appeared at a rush with a signal pad in his hand. After a minute or two's scribbling, he looked up. 'He is saying "Return to port at once. British Navy at – " then he gives a position. Does it make sense?'

'Have you got that position written down?'

'Yes.'

'Then it makes splendid sense. I feel like replying "Thanks for the information." Anything else?'

'Yes. "Reply by radio if possible." '

266

'Make "Radio unserviceable. Must proceed. Orders from Berlin." '

The lamp clicked and the fishing boat swung, flashing again.

'He makes "Ignore all orders prior to today's date. I have orders for you." He repeats his name, rank and title.'

As they argued, Marques spoke. 'He's gone over to international code, sir. He's flying "U". "You are standing into danger." '

'Must have decided we're a bit thick. Acknowledge it, Chief. Then give 'em "E". We'll alter to starboard away from 'em.'

The flags clattered and flapped as they ran up.

'He replies with "X", sir. He wants us to watch his signals. Hello, now he's got "L" up. He's got something to tell us.'

'We don't want to know. Give him "E" again.'

'Right, sir.' There was a pause. ' "T" now, sir. "Do not pass ahead of me." '

'The bugger's becoming incoherent.'

'I think he wants to come aboard.'

'He's got a hope. Keep giving him "E".'

'He's still sending "L", sir.'

'Oh, Christ – ' Magnusson was growing irritated ' – just answer him with anything. Baffle him. Blind him with science.'

He could see a German officer standing by *Iversen*'s wheelhouse, staring at them through binoculars.

'That chap's got scrambled egg on his cap,' Campbell said. 'He must be the SNO, Sjambad–Marsjøen–Kurigsdal–Victoria–St Pancras and all stations west.'

'He'll find his command's shrunk a bit.' Magnusson glanced at the log. They were still travelling at twelve knots with the wind roaring in the foresail. 'Break out all sail,' he said.

As Campbell shouted, men swarmed up the rigging and the canvas unfurled, snapping and cracking as it shook out its creases and filled with wind. Hauled taut by the men on deck, it billowed into curves.

'Log?'

'Twelve knots. Coming up to thirteen.'

'Good. Good.' Magnusson smiled. 'Stand by, helmsman.'

With every one of her sails set and drawing hard to the thrust of the wind, *Cuxhaven* was tearing along like a mail-steamer, the splash of white at her forefoot creaming away to a broad foaming stream of wake behind her. The fishing vessel was moving towards them on a converging course and a light began to flash again.

'What's it say?'

The Norwegian frowned. 'He's saying "Where is U49"?'

'He might well ask.'

The fishing vessel was still heading across their course, clearly expecting her signals to bring the barque to a halt, with all her sails aback.

'He's flying "K" now, sir,' Marques said. ' "Stop instantly." '

'Bit less friendly. I think he's decided we're not quite what we seem.'

Marques hauled down *Cuxhaven*'s hoist and sent up another.

'What are you saying to her?' Magnusson asked.

'B-A-L-L-S, sir.' Marques grinned over his shoulder. 'I don't know what they'll make of it.'

Magnusson smiled and gestured to Myers. 'Starboard a point.'

Campbell was peering ahead. 'At this rate,' he growled, 'we'll hit her.'

'So what?' Magnusson asked.

'Christ!' Campbell's head jerked round. 'You're not going to try it, are you?'

'We have a steel hull. *She*'s made of wood. Soft wood at that.'

'She's got a gun and we've got a lot of torpedoes on board.'

'They couldn't hit a pig in a passage. Not the way the

sea's moving them.'

'They can radio our position.'

'They'll have to be quick.'

As Magnusson spoke, the fishing boat fired a warning shot. They saw the splash of the shell a thousand yards off the port bow.

'Across the bows,' Campbell said. 'The next one'll hit us.'

'Right, let's panic them. Steer directly towards her, helmsman.'

'Steer towards, sir.'

'Look to the yards.'

As *Cuxhaven* swung, the men at the ropes hauled. The sails moved and the ship changed course, coming up towards *Iversen*.

Immediately, the fishing vessel began to put on speed, as though believing *Cuxhaven* was trying to pass across her stern, and she began to head towards the bigger ship's starboard hand.

'Leave her there, helmsman! Prepare to come about!'

The two vessels were drawing closer now, *Cuxhaven*'s broad bank of sails clawing at the sky. *Iversen* was working her way round, making heavy weather of it in the lumpy sea. They could see two or three men crowding round the little gun on the foredeck. There was another puff of smoke, and over the roaring of the wind and the crash of the waves, they heard the whine of the shell. A hole appeared in the foresail, then the shell dropped like a stone into the sea astern of them, throwing up a spout of water.

The men on *Iversen* had seen their danger now. The big ship was heading directly towards them and a machine-gun began to fire. Small holes appeared in the sails.

'Yards! Starboard, helmsman!'

Cuxhaven was bowling along at a tremendous speed, every sail drawing, creaming through the water so that their ears were full of the hiss and crash of the sea. *Iversen* was still trying to cross their bows to reach safety and Magnusson saw the men on her struggling to hoist a sail to give her more speed.

'Tell 'em to give the auxiliary all it's got,' he said. 'Touch more wheel, helmsman.'

Cuxhaven's head moved again, and suddenly it seemed they were looking straight down on *Iversen*. They could see the Germans' faces as the great spike of the jib boom rushed towards them. The officer in the gold-laced cap was yelling frantically and a few of the Norwegians from Marsjøen were on deck, pointing and shouting back at him.

'Tell those bloody idiots to get down!'

The machine-gunner on *Iversen* started firing again and everybody fell flat on the deck as the bullets whistled through the air. But they were already too close. *Cuxhaven* was towering over the fishing vessel, and the bullets struck the steel bows and whined off to port and starboard.

'Let's hope they don't remember the gun,' Campbell said.

But by this time the crew of *Iversen* were concerned only with getting out of *Cuxhaven*'s way. The little boat turned, presenting her stern to the barque as she tried desperately to scuttle back to safety the way she had come. But she was already too late and the thump as *Cuxhaven* hit her was hardly felt. The barque, over three thousand tons and three hundred feet long, smashed into the smaller vessel, rolling her over. The mast scraped along *Cuxhaven*'s side with a scream of tortured metal, then it broke off and fell across the fishing boat, trailing wires and rope as *Cuxhaven* swept on.

They saw *Iversen*'s red bottom as she rolled over, and the Germans jumping into the sea. The crash had cut her in two, and a wreckage of splintered planks swept astern as *Cuxhaven* roared by. The German sailors, flung about in the boiling wake, came up gasping and yelling for help.

Wolszcka was hanging so far over the side, shaking his fist and yelling insults, Magnusson thought he was going to fall into the sea. Campbell was staring over the stern.

'Haldursen's picked up the bloke with the scrambled egg on his cap,' he announced. 'I think he's got others too.'

Magnusson grinned. 'A few more for the bag,' he said. 'When we're clear we'll stop and bring 'em on board. Get Willie John to make a signal to Cockayne to the effect that we have a complete German crew as prisoners and that he'd better make sure that something's around to escort us home. I'll enjoy seeing his face when we arrive.'

Cuxhaven had hardly faltered in her stride but horrible clanking noises had started to come from aft.

'Tell the engine-room we've finished with the auxiliary,' Magnusson said. 'You'd better check the damage, too, while you're at it.'

As Campbell vanished below, Magnusson looked back. The last obstacle had gone. *Støregutt* and *Jakka* had slowed and were circling to pick up the rest of the German sailors. Then they saw the puffs of smoke start again from their tall funnels and heard the tonk-tonk of their engines as they followed in *Cuxhaven*'s wake.

Magnusson looked about him. Apart from *Altmark* they'd failed with their task in *Oulu*, but they could chalk up an armed fishing boat and a submarine whose crew, Magnusson was sure, had been almost totally wiped out. In the hold they already had a handsome batch of prisoners, and on board were Atwood's survivors and every man, woman and child from Marsjøen who had no wish to live under the German yoke.

Finally – Magnusson glanced across the deck – there was Annie Egge.

The Germans seemed to have wiped the floor with the British in Norway. There were still Allied troops in Narvik but, with all the other pockets of resistance wiped out, Magnusson couldn't imagine they'd be there long. When they'd finished, the Germans would have a thousand miles of coastline full of little inlets from which their submarines and warships could prey on British shipping. It was a daunting prospect and he had a strong suspicion that the Germans would take advantage of their success to strike somewhere else.

He glanced again at the girl. God knew what she was going to do or what he was going to do with her. It was clear she was expecting him to suggest something. He somehow thought he'd manage it.

Campbell appeared with Willie John. 'No damage to the hull,' he reported cheerfully. 'Everybody all right.'

'An' yon torpedoes didnae explode either,' Willie John said.

Magnusson grinned. 'They didn't?'

Campbell laughed. 'But the auxiliary's useless. The shaft's gone.'

'An' the screw iss buggered, boy.'

Magnusson stared upwards. 'Oh well,' he said. 'We've always got the wind.'

It was a crisp wind and full and fair for the Northern Isles. The barometer was high and around him there were only the great arches of canvas leaping outwards above his head. The ship was beautiful and sails were the loveliest things ever made.